Cassidy Blake, alias Cassandra Leblanc, had been primed to bring Derek down.

She knew his kind too well. Only one thing mattered, and that was getting what they wanted, all else be damned.

But last night he'd held her in his arms while she sobbed against his chest. He'd refused to take advantage of her vulnerability.

The rules had changed. How could she view the man with the edgy eyes but tender hands as the enemy, when he, and he alone, had helped exorcise her grief? How could she crusade against him, when she craved the touch of his body, the mindless escape of his passion?

She knew better than to get involved. Especially with a suspect. But all the training in the world hadn't been enough to prevent her two worlds from colliding.

Dear Reader,

Once again, Intimate Moments invites you to experience the thrills and excitement of six wonderful romances, starting with Justine Davis's *Just Another Day in Paradise*. This is the first in her new miniseries, REDSTONE, INCORPORATED, and you'll be hooked from the first page to the last by this suspenseful tale of two meant-to-be lovers who have a few issues to work out on the way to a happy ending—like being taken hostage on what ought to be an island paradise.

ROMANCING THE CROWN continues with *Secret-Agent Sheik*, by Linda Winstead Jones. Hassan Kamal is one of those heroes no woman can resist—except for spirited Elena Rahman, and even she can't hold out for long. Our introduction to the LONE STAR COUNTRY CLUB winds up with Maggie Price's *Moment of Truth*. Lovers are reunited and mysteries are solved—but not all of them, so be sure to look for our upcoming anthology, *Lone Star Country Club: The Debutantes*, next month. RaeAnne Thayne completes her OUTLAW HARTES trilogy with *Cassidy Harte and the Comeback Kid*, featuring the return of the prodigal groom. Linda Castillo is back with *Just a Little Bit Dangerous*, about a romantic Rocky Mountain rescue. Finally, welcome new author Jenna Mills, whose *Smoke and Mirrors* will have you eagerly looking forward to her next book.

And, as always, be sure to come back next month for more of the best romantic reading around, right here in Intimate Moments.

Enjoy!

Leslie J. Wainger
Executive Senior Editor

Please address questions and book requests to:
Silhouette Reader Service
U.S.: 3010 Walden Ave., P.O. Box 1325, Buffalo, NY 14269
Canadian: P.O. Box 609, Fort Erie, Ont. L2A 5X3

Smoke and Mirrors

JENNA MILLS

Silhouette®

INTIMATE MOMENTS™

Published by Silhouette Books

America's Publisher of Contemporary Romance

SILHOUETTE BOOKS

ISBN 0-373-27216-2

SMOKE AND MIRRORS

Visit Silhouette at www.eHarlequin.com

Printed in U.S.A.

JENNA MILLS

grew up in south Louisiana, amid romantic plantation ruins, haunting swamps and timeless legends. It's not surprising, then, that she wrote her first romance at the ripe old age of six! Three years later, this librarian's daughter turned to romantic suspense with *Jacquie and the Swamp*, a harrowing tale of a young woman on the run in the swamp and the dashing hero who helps her find her way home. Since then her stories have grown in complexity, but her affinity for adventurous women and dangerous men has remained constant. She loves writing about strong characters torn between duty and desire, conscious choice and destiny.

When not writing award-winning stories brimming with deep emotion, steamy passion and page-turning suspense, Jenna spends her time with her husband, two cats, two dogs and a menagerie of plants in their Dallas, Texas, home. Jenna loves to hear from her readers. She can be reached via e-mail at writejennamills@aol.com, or via snail mail at P.O. Box 768, Coppell, Texas 75019.

This book would not be possible without the love and support of so many people, only a few of whom I have the space to name. My grandparents, the Allisons and the Aucoins, for showing me the beauty of dreams and the magic of love that lasts a lifetime. The best friends a girl can have, Cathy, Diane, Linda and Vickie, for sharing and caring. My agent, Roberta Brown, for believing. And always, my husband, Chuck, for loving and supporting me every step of the way. Quite simply, you're all the best.

Prologue

Frigid waves pounded the jagged rocks lining the shore of Chicago's Lake Michigan. Icy pinpricks of water sprayed up toward the pale blue sky, then rained down like a hail of bullets. The shards stung Derek Mansfield's face, splattered his long trench coat.

He didn't give a damn.

He stared out over the choppy water, watching a single sailboat fight the wind. It was barely a stain on the horizon from this distance, a blur of red and blue and yellow.

"Are you even listening to me?" his friend Lucas Treese barked. "Have you heard a word I'm saying?"

Derek tensed. Inevitability loomed closer. Everything he'd been working toward now threatened to crumble between his fingers.

"Don't you get it?" Luc persisted. "Personal agendas don't matter now. The timing's wrong. You could wind up at the bottom of this damn lake if you're not careful, with nothing but concrete shoes to keep you company."

Derek released a jagged breath, then turned toward Luc, the man he trusted with his life. "The hell you say."

"The hell I *do* say," Luc retorted. "The hotel is crawling with Feds. You may not give a damn about what happens to you, but I'm not interested in signing your death certificate."

Derek slipped his hands into his pockets. "It's mine to sign, not yours."

"The hell *you* say." Luc's sharp response earned the questioning, frightened glance of a nearby woman strolling along the lakeshore with an infant. She hurried away.

"Time," Luc counseled for the hundredth time. "Let the smoke clear. Then, if this fool plan is still what you want, I won't stand in your way."

"Like you could."

"You're damn straight I could."

Derek turned back toward the lake. "Vilas won't be happy about a delay."

"You're the one he wants," Luc reminded. "He knows what you can do for him. He'll wait. You should, too."

The need to move forward burned through Derek, but he wouldn't get far without help. In fact, he might just find his butt in prison. Or at the bottom of the lake. Luc had backed him into a corner from which he couldn't escape.

His friend was right. Vilas would wait. The bastard wasn't a man to walk away from a quick fortune, just as Derek wasn't a man to walk away from the chance to make his mark.

He looked out over the lake. "Six months, no longer."

"A year," Luc countered.

Derek considered. In twelve months time sailboats would again dot the azure backdrop of Lake Michigan. Illusions, they were, seductive images of an innocent world that didn't exist.

"Six months," he insisted. October. Everything would be cold then, gray and dead. Perfect. "That's all. Nobody will stop me then. God help the fool who tries."

Chapter 1

Detective Cassidy Blake stepped from the elevator and took the long hall at a brisk pace. Farther down the hall, a party raged out of control. She had to settle the rowdy punks before they upstaged the main event.

Derek Mansfield was back.

After all the research and profiling, the preparing, she figured she knew the man as intimately as a woman could without having crawled into his bed. Now she looked forward to meeting her prime suspect in the flesh.

She wanted to bring him down.

He'd been gone for six months. Some thought the heir to the Stirling Manor hotel empire at the bottom of Lake Michigan, but Cass believed him too smart to become fish bait. Clever, dashing and relentless were only a few of the adjectives commonly attributed to Mansfield.

She'd researched the man enough to know they were all true.

The mere image of his insolent smile was enough to heat her blood with anticipation. She looked forward to getting inside the reprobate's head, discovering what made him tick. Then she looked forward to locking him away for a long, long time.

Excitement hummed through her, joining forces with the rock and roll blaring from the room down the hall. Cass slid her hand into the front pocket of her black suit jacket, her fingers caressing the cool metal she found there. Undercover as an assistant hotel manager, she could only use the Smith & Wesson as her last resort, but she was too well trained to walk into a hornet's nest unarmed. Security had promised to meet her at the room.

The corridor stretched before her, a Persian rug running down a never-ending sea of hardwood. The attention Mansfield's grandfather had lavished upon the stately hotel never ceased to amaze her. Even this passageway resembled the hallway of a manor house. Richly paneled walls. Ornate molding. And, what Cass considered the crowning touch, portraits.

Hundreds of them lined the walls of every corridor of the hotel's eighteen floors. God only knew who all those dour-looking people were. Sir Maximillian certainly didn't. His staff had scoured European estate sales, laying down top dollar for collections of family portraits. They were proudly displayed, side by side, ornate frame after ornate frame, one family after another.

Cass thought it bizarre, a desecration of someone's family tree. The painted eyes seemed to track her progress down the hallway.

The music grew louder as she approached the door. Mentally preparing herself, Cass recalled the group of young men who'd checked in earlier that evening. Ivy League college had been written all over them, money and prestige, insolence. They'd made a commotion at the registration desk, the one named Chet requesting a personal escort to their room.

Now, adrenaline pumping, she rapped her hand against

the door and waited. The noise didn't lessen, the door didn't open.

She sighed. Damn, but she didn't need this. Not tonight. She knocked again, this time harder, louder, the sound of it sharper than before. "Open up! It's hotel management."

Just like that the door swung open, and a beefy arm snaked out, grabbed her wrist, yanked her inside. The smell of beer and cigar smoke hit her like a punch to the lungs. She quickly untangled herself from the offensive grip, but a semicircle of leering drunks pushed her back against the wall.

"Well, now," the one named Chet drawled. Clearly the ringleader. "When we called room service and asked for a babe, I didn't really expect them to come through for us. But now that you're here—"

"Now that I'm here, you're going to quiet down this party, or we'll have to ask you to leave. We have other guests—"

"Oh, we'll quiet down, all right." This from the tallest. He swiped off his T-shirt and stepped closer. "All the noise will come from you, honey bun."

Irritation sparked. Cass itched to teach these boys a lesson, but couldn't risk blowing her cover. She searched for what a frightened woman might say, rather than what she wanted to say. "Get your mind out of the gutter."

"Why, it's not in the gutter, sugar. It's somewhere a whole lot more fun." To the encouraging cheers of the other men, the shirtless one lunged at her.

Years of training and experience had Cass spinning out of reach. She ducked through the semicircle of men and scooted around a table. The adjoining room offered another exit, but as she dashed across the carpet, yet another man stumbled out from the bathroom. "My, my. What have we here?"

Cass slammed to a halt.

Chet swaggered over and snaked an arm around her shoulders, jerking her to his side.

Cass went completely still. No one touched her. *No one.*

"Room service just served her up," Chet bragged. "All we need now is some whipped cream."

Cass rammed her elbow back into his gut, taking satisfaction from his surprised grunt of pain. She ducked quickly out of his reach, but the four other men blocked her escape.

"Going somewhere?" one of them asked. "So soon?"

Instinct took over. She reached for her gun, but found her arms yanked from behind her back before her fingers could curl around the cool metal. Chet jerked her toward him, the unnatural position of her arms causing her chest to jut out.

"Take your hands off me," she snarled.

But they ignored her. "LeBlanc?" the one who'd just emerged from the bathroom inquired, eyeing her name badge. His trousers hung open. "Hell, Chet, I've always wondered if it's true what they say about French women."

"Well, Animal, looks like we're going to find out." While he held her wrists in one beefy hand, Chet yanked off the band securing her French braid and began unweaving her hair. "You want to know why we call him Animal?"

Not especially, but Cass wanted to keep them talking. That way she could engineer the right moment. Between her head and her feet, she still had effective weapons.

"Because his brain's so small?" she answered glibly.

Laughter filled the room. Animal swaggered forward, his eyes somewhere between glowing and stoned. "I'll show you small, Frenchie, so small you'll never be satisfied with anything less."

Repulsed, she bit back the sharp retort that rolled to her tongue. She needed them to keep thinking of her as the weak, frightened female they clearly already did.

"You *really* don't want to do this," she tried one last time.

Animal lumbered closer. "Don't tell me what I want, Frenchie. I'm going to show you instead."

He rambled on, but she paid no heed to his words. He and his friends had stolen enough of her precious time. She drew a breath and prepared to teach these clowns a lesson they'd never forget.

"Lay one hand on her, and you're a dead man."

The words rushed through Cass like a gale-force wind, but she had no idea who spoke them. The menacing voice resonated from behind her, but Chet's hold prevented her from turning toward it.

Animal stopped dead in his tracks.

"Take your hands off the lady, son, and back away."

"Mind your own business," Chet snarled. His grip tightened.

A low rumble filled the room, a perverse, distorted laugh. "The lady *is* my business."

"Yeah?" Chet swung around and pressed Cass to his body, giving himself a look at the unseen cavalry, but preventing Cass from doing so. "I don't see no ownership tags."

"Are you fond of your front teeth?"

If the threat hadn't been uttered in such a deadly tone, Cass would have laughed. Adrenaline, she knew. The thrill of danger, the rush of anticipation.

She couldn't remember the last time she'd felt so alive.

The inebriated frat boys stood mute, mouths agape, eyes fixed on the source of that low, commanding voice. Even Animal made no move to prove his name. He just swayed from side to side, looking like the Jolly Green Giant ready to topple to the ground.

Chet pulled her tighter against his sweaty body. "She your lady?"

"More mine than yours."

Everything inside of Cass went very still. The blatant,

take-no-prisoner's tone reminded her of a cop, but she'd never heard this particular voice, nor had she ever felt the charge this voice sent racing through her. Anticipation warred with her better judgment, curiosity with sanity. She struggled against Chet's grip, wanting a glimpse of the voice's owner.

"You have five seconds."

Cass wasn't willing to give Chet that long. She slammed her foot down on top of Chet's and rammed her knee into his groin. He yowled in pain and doubled over, releasing her. Cass whirled toward the voice and froze.

A man stood there, eyes fierce and challenging, long coal-black hair against his hardened face. He tossed a switchblade from hand to hand, blatantly daring someone to take him on.

Cass barely managed to catch her breath, but she knew. Without a doubt, unequivocally she knew.

Derek Mansfield.

She'd never seen the man in the flesh, only heard the stories, read the reports, seen the grainy videos. But she had no doubt of his identity.

"Honey," the longtime desk clerk had quipped less than an hour before, "if Derek Mansfield were here, you wouldn't have to ask. You would know."

Seeing him up close and personal for the first time brought the thrill of adventure, an unexpected surge of inevitability. She'd been anticipating this moment for a long, long time.

But this was hardly the meeting she'd had in mind.

Silence filled the room. Cass inched away from Chet, toward Mansfield. Out of the frying pan and into the fire, she thought wryly, but couldn't have stopped had a gun been pointed at her heart. Mansfield's presence drew her like a rookie to his first big crime scene.

She'd heard that about Mansfield, had just never believed what had seemed to be an exaggerated claim. Until now.

Mansfield took her by the wrist and pulled her toward him, putting himself between her and the rest of the room. Chet was still howling in pain, but Animal and the others stood frozen. Their eyes were wide and glassy, focused on the switchblade.

"The lady and I will be going now," Mansfield said in a low voice. He held Cass pressed to the hard muscles of his back and buttocks. "If you know what's good for you, you'll wait for security, then quietly let them escort you off the property."

"We're paying custom—"

"Your rights ceased the moment you laid hands on this woman." Mansfield backed her toward the door. "It's called assault, son, and if she's so inclined, she could throw the book at you."

He would know, Cass thought grimly. He would know.

Mansfield's movements were slow and deliberate, the back of his powerful legs brushing the front of her hips. She followed his lead, finding the whole situation ironic as hell, but potentially useful.

Vincent Fettici, head of security rushed in. "Ms. LeBlanc, we got here—"

"Too late," Mansfield finished for him. "Now take care of these lowlifes before I have to do that for you, too."

Vincent stiffened. "Yes, sir."

Mansfield led Cass into the hallway. Adrenaline pumped through her. Anticipation. Here was her chance to lay that last layer of groundwork and begin building. "I'd like to thank—"

"Are you okay?" he demanded harshly.

She swallowed her surprise. "I'm fine."

His expression darkened. "Then you must be out of your mind. What the hell were you thinking, going in there alone?"

The harsh tone, more than the actual words, stung.

"You pay me to do a job, sir. It's my responsibility to keep this hotel running smoothly."

Those killer eyes focused on her, so narrow and concentrated they made her long to look away. But she didn't. Couldn't.

Nothing had prepared her for the reality of this man. To say he had an arresting presence would be a gross understatement. *Commanding* came closer. The videotapes had not conveyed his blatant masculinity, his magnetism. They'd only shared his classic male physique, the broad shoulders and narrow hips, his long legs. And his face. The intensity of it, the savagery. Sharp and angular planes. High slashes of cheekbones. Deep-set, go-to-hell eyes.

A man who had seen too much, done too much.

"Ever heard of security?" he demanded.

"They were supposed to meet me here."

"Ever heard of waiting?"

She reached behind her head and began rebraiding her long, tangled hair. "Not my style."

"This isn't about style, honey. It's about good common sense."

Her hands abandoned her hair and clenched into tight, combative fists. "I resent your tone."

"And I resent having my first night home disrupted by your risk taking. Do you have any idea what those punks could have done to you?"

Like he really cared. "Mr. Mansfield, I'll have you know I'm trained—"

His eyes narrowed. "Ah, so you know who I am."

Again his tone, this time the suspicion in it, made the statement sound like an accusation.

"We've been expecting you for a long time," she said.

"Well, here I am," he said wickedly, "the prodigal son home at last." He leaned so close his whiskey breath feathered her cheekbone. "Tell me, doll. Was it worth it?"

Oh, yeah...

Cass blinked, the only way to combat those electric-blue eyes. "Was what worth what?"

A smile curved his lips, an uncivilized one that had the power to stop a woman's heart cold.

The reports hadn't warned her about that, either.

"The wait." A gold earring winked at her through his long hair. "Was it worth it?"

Not giving her time to answer, much less breathe, he chucked her chin and strode away. Cass was left standing there, alone, save for the wall of orphaned ancestors. They watched her from their gilded frames, and now they seemed to be laughing.

Derek threw open the door to his half brother's office. "You've got a strange idea of a welcoming committee, baby bro."

Kicked back in an oversize leather chair, Brent Ashford looked up from the magazine in his lap. He had his legs stretched out, his crossed ankles resting on his Louis XIV desk.

"Derek. I didn't realize you were here already."

Derek strode farther into the cushy room. "You mind explaining what I walked in on? Just what the hell's been going on here since I left? Have you ever heard the word lawsuit?"

"Well, hell, it's good to see you, too, Dare, but I'm afraid the fatted calf isn't quite ready yet."

Derek ignored the sarcasm and halted in front of Brent's desk. He leaned forward, splaying his hands across the highly polished surface. "Thanks all the same, but I'd rather know why we've got assistant managers risking personal safety to do security's job."

Brent's nonchalance slipped. "What are you talking about?" he asked, sitting up and lowering his feet to the floor.

"If I'd been five minutes later, that little lady would

have been..." The sight of those animals pawing at the brunette, of the way that punk had held her against his sweaty body, still had Derek's blood boiling. He didn't want to imagine what could have happened to her. He may have turned his back on society, but that didn't mean he condoned taking advantage of a woman.

Nor did he need the extra attention. Cops. The media. You name it, they'd shine a spotlight on the Stirling Manor so bright he'd be forced into another delay.

He didn't have time to clean up another one of his brother's messes.

His grandfather said he made life too easy for Brent, always bailing him out, never letting his brother suffer the consequences of his actions, but Derek took his role as older sibling seriously, even if he did sometimes want to strangle his brother.

"There were five of them, drunk and out of their mind. What in the world was that brunette doing up there with them?" he wanted to know. "Where were *you?*"

Brent stood, and his already fair skin went a few shades lighter. "Cass?"

"I didn't catch her name."

"What'd she look like?"

The image fired to life in his mind like a shot of fine whiskey. The woman's dark hair had been wild and tangled around her face, her cheeks flushed, her chest thrust out, but she'd still looked defiant. Courageous. Evocative as hell.

Derek banished the image before it could distract any further. "Long, dark hair, amber eyes, a body that could tempt a monk."

Brent swore under his breath. "Cass. My God, is she all right?"

Satisfied he had his brother's attention, Derek eased back off the desk. He walked over to a crystal vase containing darts and picked one up. Turning it over in his

hand, he made a production of studying the finely sharpened instrument.

"Damn it, Derek! Is she all right?"

"She is now," he growled. "No thanks to you."

Brent crossed to Derek's side. "What happened?" The
question was strained, almost personal.

"Who wants to know?" Derek asked. He knew his
brother well enough to know when he was holding something back. "Her manager, or someone else?"

"I don't see how that's any of your concern," Brent
answered a little too quickly.

Derek studied the shiny dart clenched between his
thumb and forefinger, then hurled it toward the waiting
target. It sailed across the room, slammed into the bull's-
eye.

"It's a simple question, baby brother. Are you involved
with the daredevil who damn near got herself mauled by
a bunch of drunken idiots, or not?"

Derek didn't know why the question mattered so much,
but it burned through him, demanding an answer.

Outrage blasted into Brent's eyes. "Mauled? Is she still
here?" he asked, heading for the door. "I want to make
sure she's okay."

"It's after midnight. Her shift is over."

Brent stopped dead in his tracks.

"And since she didn't come running to you, I'm as-
suming the answer to my question is no." Derek zinged
another dart; this one landed a fraction of a millimeter
from the first.

Brent stormed across the room and grabbed a dart of
his own. "We have an understanding," he snarled, then
hurled his dart toward the board.

It bounced off Derek's and crashed to the floor.

Derek resisted the urge to laugh. "What kind of understanding?"

Brent shrugged. With his golden hair, golden tan and
golden eyes, he looked as if he belonged on a California

beach, not in a Chicago hotel penthouse. His pressed trousers and starched button-down were the only hints of his UCLA M.B.A.

"You know how it goes," he muttered. "Don't want to move too fast. Things are better when you draw them out."

Now Derek did laugh. "In other words, you struck out."

Humiliation shuttered Brent's gaze. "Not exactly."

"Exactly." Derek fired another dart straight into the bull's-eye. He could still picture the fire sparking in the woman's eyes, her long dark hair, the set of those proud shoulders. She reminded him of a woman about to be burned at the stake but refusing to back down and recant the accusation of witchcraft.

Witchcraft. Maybe that was the reason he could still smell her soft musky scent, hear her honeyed voice. A man would have to be deaf, dumb and blind not to respond to the woman his brother called Cass.

Derek was neither deaf nor dumb nor blind.

But there was no room in his life for the distraction a woman like her inspired. They'd all be better off if he forgot the jolt of awareness he'd felt upon seeing her.

"I know that look in your eyes," Brent said. "I know how your mind works. You think you can waltz in here and sweep Cass off her feet, then toss her aside when you're done playing with her, don't you?"

The protective clip to Brent's voice fascinated Derek. His brother didn't typically put his neck on the line for others.

He had never had to.

"Relax, baby brother. I don't plan to be here long, and I've got far more important things to do than wine and dine our assistant manager."

"Wining and dining has never been your style."

"It's never had to be."

Brent's scowl deepened. He crossed to the minibar,

fixed himself a stiff drink, tossed it back. "So how was Edinburgh?" he asked, blatantly changing the subject. "I'm surprised the old man let you come back."

"It wasn't his choice." And he hadn't been happy about it, either. The old codger wanted Derek to stay in Scotland, where he could keep an eye on his grandson, make sure he didn't stir up the hornet's nest once again.

Derek had hated leaving him, hated even more the worry on his grandfather's face, the awareness they might never see each other again. But he hadn't had a choice. Brent had seen to that.

"What's the matter?" he asked his brother. "Afraid I'm checking up on you?"

Brent shrugged. "Just curious."

Like hell. "Trying to give me a run for my money again?"

"You forget. I've tried on your shoes, Dare. Didn't like the way they fit."

Derek joined him at the wet bar. "That's because they're too big, baby brother. Too much room for you to slip around and hurt yourself. You're better off leaving the danger to me."

Brent frowned. "Dream on. You're the one who ran out of here, leaving the whole damn city wondering where you went, if you were even alive. And poor Marla…"

Derek slammed his tumbler against the bar. "Don't say her name to me."

"She was going to be your wife."

Memories slithered forward, the lies and betrayal, the aftermath. "She's dead to me now. I suggest you remember that."

Brent studied him long and hard, traces of genuine concern and curiosity flickering through his gaze. "I'm sorry, man. I didn't mean to drag up a bad memory."

Derek headed for the door. "We'll talk more tomorrow. I'm beat." Physically, mentally and in every other way imaginable. He was stepping into the hall when Brent's voice stopped him.

"Derek?"

He turned back toward his brother. "Yeah?"

Brent raised his glass and grinned. "Welcome home, bro."

The stately grandfather clock chimed the hour. One in the morning. The last of the guests had shuffled out of the lobby thirty minutes before, their bleary eyes indicative of the late hour and the chess table they'd stared at too long.

Cass stoked the glowing embers of the fire. Her insides felt much the same: simmering remains of the night's excitement. At last. Derek Mansfield was home.

His arrival flicked the lead domino into motion; the rest would topple in no time. She thrilled to the prospect of chipping away at his fortress, contributing to his fall. It would be methodical and gradual, undeniable.

"There you are!" Ruth Sun's sensible heels clicked across the marble floor, then the hardwood, then over the plush Persian rug. "If you keep me waiting one second longer I'll just die." Excitement sparkled in the older woman's dark eyes. The veteran desk clerk was as much a fixture at the hotel as the antique furniture. Nothing escaped her notice. "Start talking, missy—now! I want details."

Cass flashed a curious smile. "About what?"

"Like you don't know. The boss. I want to know what happened between you two."

"What makes you think something happened?"

"Oh, I don't know, maybe the look on his face when he took off running toward the elevator, or maybe—"

"What look?"

"Let's just say no one was going to get in his way."

A rush surged through Cass. She knew the look Ruth described, had seen it herself. Furious and fierce, lethal.

"You should've seen him, Cass. He'd only been here a few minutes. Everyone was staring, falling all over themselves to make him feel welcome. Then Cloyd came running down the hall."

Cloyd. The elevator attendant. Cass should've known.

"He was frantic about trouble on the twelfth floor. And you. I told Derek about the drunks, and he just took off." Awe gleamed in Ruth's eyes, laced her voice. "My God, to have that man charge to my rescue…"

She prattled on, but Cass hardly heard a word. It was more than a little amusing, to see the older woman so flustered. But then, Cass couldn't blame her. Mansfield had an aura about him, a magnetism that stirred a woman's blood despite her best intentions. Cass's partner, Gray, had it, too, and Cass had watched its impact on other women. A happily married woman, she'd been immune to it. Then, after her husband Randy's death—

After didn't matter. The woman in her had shut down, leaving no room for anyone but the cop.

"So what happened?" Ruth asked again, this time more insistently. "It's not fair to keep me in the dark."

"I'll tell you what happened."

The low voice surged through Cass. She pivoted toward it, found Mansfield lounging against the mantel, black T-shirt, black jeans, black boots. She hadn't heard him approach—unusual for her—had no idea how long he'd been standing behind her.

Nor did she know why the mere sight of him, the sardonic curl of his lips, sent her pulse sprinting.

But it did.

Chapter 2

Derek watched her eyes widen, the color rush to her cheeks. All flushed like that, with tangled wisps of hair loose around her face, she looked like a woman who'd just rolled from her lover's arms.

Dangerous thoughts, he realized, and detoured quickly. "Fearless, here, decided she could handle a roomful of drunks all by her sweet little self."

Ruth's eyes widened. "I told her not to go up there," she replied. "I warned her, but she wouldn't listen."

"It wasn't *that* dramatic," Cass said, pushing the hair back from her face. "I had everything under control."

Thinking back on the scene he'd walked in on, Derek felt a boiling rage begin to build. He knew what could have happened if he hadn't arrived in time, and it sickened him. "Under control, huh? I suppose that's why one of them was feeling you up, while the others moved in for the kill?"

She shot him a sharp look. "They were harmless, just a bunch of college boys playing cool."

"Honey, if you thought that was playing, I'd love to see your version of the real thing."

Ruth gasped, but Cass smiled. It was a wide, slow smile, one only a confident woman could offer. "I'll just bet you would."

Slowly he let his gaze slide down her lithe body in the scarlet-and-black suit that served as her uniform. "You can be sure of that."

His affirmation seemed to startle her—he almost thought she winced. Those eyes of hers, he realized. They spoke volumes. Sure, she kept a sturdy shield of bravado in place, but he'd played too many games of chance in his life not to see the secrets lurking beneath.

"It's late," he said, surprised by the tender note in his voice. "You've had a rough evening. Why don't you get on home?"

She cocked a brow. "Trying to get rid of me?"

If he was smart. "Nope, just trying to get you home in bed."

She pulled her battered braid over her shoulder. "What if I'm not tired?"

"Who said you had to be?"

Her eyes flared, but other than that, her composure remained rock solid. "You're pretty sure of yourself, aren't you?"

Derek's blood heated, not just at her words, but at the provocative sight she made standing there, all rumpled and flushed. "Sorry, honey," he said, detouring from the dangerous path, "this has nothing to do with my confidence level." He didn't have time for distractions right now, no matter how intriguing a distraction she made. "This has to do with making sure my employees are safe and sound." He moved closer, his six-foot-plus frame crowding her against the wall. "Tonight you were neither."

She lifted her chin. "But I'm both now."

She would be, Derek amended, if he left her alone. "So

you are, but you can't blame a man for being concerned."
He abruptly stepped back and hooked an arm around the
small of her waist, steering her toward the front door.
"Now get on home before I have to take you there myself."

She stiffened, as though he'd just taken his switchblade
to her heart, rather than his hand to her back. Odd, Derek
mused. The woman could take on a roomful of drunks,
but she shut down when he touched her.

Smart, he amended, and the danger she posed ratcheted
up another notch.

She stepped away from his touch. "I can take care of
myself, thank you very much."

"I just bet you can."

She flashed him a tight smile, then headed for the door.
He let her go, physically, but couldn't resist one parting
shot. "What's the matter? Not afraid, are you?"

She stopped, pivoted toward him. "Not on your life,"
she said, the light sparking back into her eyes. A defiant
smile touched her lips. "It's late. I'm simply calling it a
night."

And the Cubs were going to win back to back World
Series, Derek thought as he watched the door close behind
her. The woman had more secrets than he did, and something deep inside him wanted to know what they were,
why she kept them.

Too bad discovering them could get them both killed.

Cass set down one of countless pictures from her file
on Mansfield and frowned. He'd seemed so charming and
gallant the night before, it was hard to believe he'd in-
volve himself with an international criminal like Santiago
Vilas, as the picture of the two smiling men suggested.
But the photos taken only six months earlier spoke for
themselves.

The walls of her small home office closed in on her,

prompting her to stand. She needed fresh air. She needed to work off this restlessness before reporting for duty.

Seven miles would do the trick, she decided. Deliberate, not fast. Steady, not rushed. Whereas some people drank wine to unwind, Cass ran.

She never stopped to ask herself why.

Anticipation burned through her, as much for the endorphins of the run as for the endorphins of the chase.

Mansfield. Over the past six months she'd collected a library of news clips, sound bytes, and exposés about her current target. She was nothing if not methodical, and in his absence she'd contented herself with information rather than the man.

A weak substitute, she now realized.

Several magazines had run features on the Stirling Manor and its founder Sir Maximillian. They always tried to include Mansfield, but he had never consented to an interview, forcing reporters to resort to images of him from his merchant marine days, when he'd been wild and uncivilized. Not that he was civilized now, but at least he'd rejoined the family fold. He could be labeled a businessman now, even though Cass thought that was stretching things.

Semantics, she corrected. Whether or not Mansfield was a businessman depended upon how one defined business and how one defined a man.

She preferred to focus on the business.

Cass pulled her hair behind her head and began braiding.

Six months. Twenty-six weeks. One hundred eighty-two days. That's how long had passed since the chief had outlined the case to her.

Shadowy linkages to crime had tarnished the Stirling Manor's pristine image. At first it had seemed an unfortunate coincidence; an out-of-hand party here, an ill-fated meeting there, an occasional guest with a questionable reputation. But the coincidences gave way to pattern, pattern to rumors and suspicions. The trails led straight to the top, precisely where the motivation became muddy. Sir Maximillian's heirs had more money than they could spend in one—much less two—lifetimes, leaving only two reasons for spreading corruption through Chicago's streets.

Power and greed.

Enough circumstantial evidence existed to warrant an investigation. Once the authorities zeroed in on the manor, identifying a target hadn't been hard. Mansfield and Vilas were seen together in dark alleys and on the pier. Mansfield had even made a trip to Vilas's home country. And if that wasn't enough to incriminate him, the fact all activity had dried up when Mansfield left the country six months before left little doubt.

Cass sat on the floor and began stretching. Her big St. Bernard, Barney, rushed over with such force he toppled her to the carpet, straddling her as he assaulted her with his tongue. The overly-eager dog interpreted Cass sitting on the floor as an invitation to wrestle. Laughing, she obliged him.

Hours later, invigorated by her lengthy run, she strolled through the Stirling Manor's mahogany doors. A crystal vase of bloodred gladiolas greeted her, as did her scowling partner. He was clearly still angry about the chance she'd taken the night before. "You're late."

"Five minutes, Gray. Don't hassle me." A glance around the elegant lobby revealed little activity. "Seems pretty quiet. Anything unusual?"

"There you are!" Ruth hurried across the hard wood floor of the lobby. "Derek's looking for you."

"Derek...? Oh." Cass thought of him as Mansfield. Use of his first name seemed alien to her, too intimate for a suspect. "What's he want?"

"Wouldn't say." Ruth's smile erased ten years from her face. "He's been calling down to the front desk every ten minutes. He wants you in the penthouse. Immediately.''

The words *want* and *her* in the same sentence, a sentence uttered by Mansfield, sent an uneasy rush of excitement through Cass. Disconcerted, she turned to leave, but Gray grabbed her arm. He didn't say anything, didn't need to.

The glitter in his green eyes communicated his warning.

"Quit being such a brute—" she laughed for Ruth's benefit "—he's the boss." Some thought Cass and Gray involved in a torrid affair, a rumor far safer than the truth. "We can finish later."

She shrugged free of his hand, gave Ruth an exasperated smile, then hurried toward the elevator.

The twenty-fifth floor arrived quickly. Cass could feel the adrenaline stream through her. Questions. Caution. But no time existed to indulge any of it, she had to be a dutiful employee, obeying her boss's summons.

The thought nearly made her laugh out loud.

She'd been on the penthouse floor before, at least the wing Brent occupied. Cloyd directed her to the wing she'd been chomping at the bit to gain access to for months now. Here, too, gilded frames of ancestors watched her progress, and yet there was something different about these portraits.

Dark, restless eyes. Insolent smiles. The "been there, done that" expressions. These weren't just random ancestors, she realized with a start.

They were Mansfields.

A shiver ran through her. She paused a moment before she forced her legs to move. The uneasiness didn't abate, nor did her excitement.

The hall seemed to stretch forever, but finally she arrived at the entryway Cloyd had described. No door, only a panel in the wall, marking what looked to be a secret entrance. The panel slid open, revealing an immense chamber. Quite certain she was supposed to, and unable to do anything else, Cass stepped inside. The panel slid shut behind her.

It took every ounce of willpower she had not to gasp.

The vast chamber conjured images of another world, another time. Further back in time than manor houses, this room reminded her of the great hall in a once impregnable castle. The vaulted ceiling sported huge wooden beams spanning its width. Toward one side sat a massive table, obviously used at one time for eating, now for meetings.

On the other side of the room resided a desk. Not a dainty Chippendale, nor an elegant Louis XIV like Brent used. It was simple, classical. With its claw-foot legs, the desk suggested the man who occupied it didn't need frivolities to make a point.

Because he didn't.

The enormous burgundy chair swiveled to face her. Mansfield reclined there, the size of the chair doing nothing to dwarf the size of the man. Actually, chair and man looked tailor-made for each other.

"It was my grandfather's," he said by way of greeting.

The intensity of his voice, his eyes, sent her heart racing. "It's breathtaking."

"So are you."

The words hit hard. She'd heard he was lethal when he zapped up the charm, she just hadn't realized how overpowering his energy would feel.

Feel. She mentally batted the offensive word aside, knowing it had no place in her interactions with Mansfield.

"Why, thank you," she drawled, as she always did when ducking behind a shield. "Ruth said you wanted to see me?"

"What man wouldn't?" A predatory gleam moved into his cobalt eyes. "Come closer. Have a seat."

Despite his silky voice, his orders emerged crisp and clear. She moved forward, acutely conscious of how snugly her scarlet-and-black uniform clung to her body.

In that moment she wished she still wore clothes a size too big, that Gray's wife hadn't convinced her to buy the eight instead of the ten.

If only the office didn't feel so hot, her body so damp.

Only one chair faced his desk, a straight-back with a leather burgundy seat—no armrests. The structure didn't invite occupants to hunker down, but to sit at attention. She did just that, demurely crossing one leg over the other.

"What can I do for you?" she asked.

His smile turned insolent. "That's what I'd like to find out."

"Oh? How's that?"

He lounged back in his chair, swiveled it a degree to the right, then a degree to the left. Those intense eyes never left her face. He looked supremely male sitting there, confident, bordering on arrogant. Sexy. No, make that dangerous.

"Mr. Mansfield?"

From the corner of his desk he retrieved a leather portfolio, opened it, laughed. "New Orleans—I should have known."

Suspicion jackknifed through her. "Known what?"

"Only daughter in a family of five kids. Four older brothers. Father's a French Quarter cop. Mother stayed at home with her brood. Catholic girls school, followed by Loyola. Graduated with honors."

The made-up litany of her life echoed in her ears. The extra details she'd created for her alias had categorically *not* been on her résumé. The department had manufactured a past for her, yet she'd requested one to mirror her own. The fewer lies, the better. There could be no linkages to the Thibodauxs of New Orleans, she reminded herself, nor to Cassidy Blake, the name on her marriage license. The department made sure of that. But still, that Mansfield had discovered details of her fictional life made it clear she'd caught his attention. The man had done more than a little homework.

"Sure are a long way from home," he mused.

Situations like this were nothing new to her; she'd been trained how to interrogate, and be interrogated, time and again. "Sometimes a girl needs a change of venue."

"Change of venue from what?"

"From the South to the North," she answered simply, knowing that was no answer at all. "Kind of like joining the merchant marines, wouldn't you say?"

His lips curled into an uncivilized smile. "So that's how it's to be," he drawled. Not one drop of anger or suspicion marred his low, rumbly voice. Only intrigue. "Not many people would say that to me, but I think you know that. Care to tell me how you learned to be so brave?"

Ah-h-h-h, the chase. There was nothing like it. "And if I do care?"

He cut her a sharp look that told her what she thought didn't matter.

"You said it yourself, Mr. Mansfield. I grew up in the French Quarter." She served up an extra thick drawl, with just the right New Orleans clipped tone. "There a girl learns to do what a girl has to do to survive."

"Mr. Mansfield," he mocked. Oh, he was enjoying this all right. "Now there's a nice Southern touch. Doll, you can't be more than five years younger than me. I'd prefer you use my given name."

Doll. The endearment was crude, insulting and one hell of a call to arms. "But *Mr. Mansfield,"* she said through gritted teeth. "That wouldn't be proper—you're *the boss.*"

"Precisely, doll. That means you do as I say."

She licked her lips, fighting the urge to sink her teeth into him. Figuratively, of course. "So it does."

"And right now that means I want to hear you say my name—*my first name.*"

Cass shifted in the uncomfortable chair, milking the moment for all it was worth. She uncrossed her legs, then recrossed them, again leaving her calves exposed. A long time had passed since she'd felt this exhilarated, this heady, so she went with it, deciding there was no law against enjoying her job.

Mansfield watched her with an expectant gleam in his cobalt eyes. He had that edgy look some women found irresistible, the kind they naively thought masked vulnerability. An intriguing theory, Cass noted, but not one she could afford to explore.

Her gaze met his, her smile widened, and when she spoke, her voice held an extra dose of Southern honey. "Dare-ek."

The two syllables whooshed out more like a caress than an address.

He leaned back and linked his hands behind his head. "Again."

"*Dare*-ek."

"Again."

She shifted in the chair. Never before had merely saying a man's name felt like foreplay. "Derek."

This time her voice betrayed her, delivering the word softer than before, huskier, like a satisfied lover might coo as she rolled into a pair of strong arms.

A smile curved his lips. "A man could get used to that."

"So I've been told."

"Have you, now?"

The role of sultry New Orleans beauty, fish out of water in cold, brutal Chicago, was one she looked forward to exploring. "Just curious. Did you call me up here for a reason, or did you just want to hear me say your name?"

"Is that a crime?"

She conjured an innocent smile. "Would you care if it was?"

He leaned back farther, bringing his crossed feet to rest on his desk. "What do you think?"

That you are one dangerous man. She pushed the truth aside, refused to linger on his blatantly sexual position. "I don't think you give a damn."

He laughed. "Not only beautiful, but smart, too."

She knew better than to let him bait her, but couldn't let his sexist comment pass. "Not only insolent," she tossed right back, "but a real charmer, too." She slid up the sleeve of her jacket and made a show of checking her watch. "Now, if we're done, I should head back downstairs."

"What's the hurry? You don't like playing truth or dare?"

She stilled. At least ten feet separated them, including his desk, but the way he looked at her made her feel like they were pressed body to body. "Is that what we're doing?"

"It's a great way to get acquainted, wouldn't you say?" He punctuated the question with a razor-sharp smile she hadn't found in any picture, any video.

"Is this how you welcome all new employees?" she asked.

"This has nothing to do with you being my employee, Cass." The glitter faded from his gaze, leaving only challenge. "This has to do with the way you took on a roomful of drunks last night with no fear in your eyes, but acted like a butterfly on a spring day the second I put my arm around your waist. Not many people are bold as sunshine one minute, mysterious as midnight the next. I was just curious why."

The observation knocked the breath from her lungs. "I didn't realize you were into pop psychology, Mr. Mansfield."

"It's Derek," he corrected, "and I'm not."

"Sure sounds like it to me."

He laughed. "Relax. I'm not trying to steal all your

secrets, I just make sure I know who I'm dealing with.''
He lowered his feet to the floor and leaned across his desk.
''You can go on downstairs now. We've covered enough
for one day.''

He was toying with her, she realized, dismissing her
just when their conversation was going somewhere. His
instincts were clearly as lethal as hers.

''How gallant of you,'' she murmured, drawing her
braid over her shoulder. ''But what if I'm enjoying our
conversation? What if I'd rather continue our little game
of truth or dare?''

Surprise sizzled in his eyes. He recovered quickly, that
supremely male expression easing back into place. ''Hate
to shatter your illusions, honey, but I learned a long time
ago you can't always get what you want. Sometimes
wanting only makes it more impossible.''

''Ohh, I don't know about that.'' She absolutely refused
to consider that she might not bag her man. ''Guess I'll
have to wait and see.''

She stood, pivoted, sauntered from his office. Her pace
was slow and steady, remarkable considering how wildly
her heart thrummed.

A long time had passed since anything, anyone, had
burrowed beneath the mechanics of the job and tapped
into her core of femininity. She could play the role of
sultry hotel worker, and she would if that's what the job
demanded, but as she recalled the seductive invitation in
Mansfield's eyes, she realized how careful she needed to
be.

The line between woman and cop had blurred once before, and the consequences had been deadly. In the five
ensuing years she'd carved the line as deeply as she could,
made it as dark and uncrossable as possible.

She stayed on the side of the cop exclusively. It was
smarter that way, safer for everyone.

Even though there was no one.

Mansfield's arrival changed nothing. Heightened every-

thing. She couldn't let the line blur now, couldn't afford
to pay attention to the side of her that was the woman.

Not with Mansfield primed to pounce.

The sun dipped beneath the horizon, leaving a cloudless
black sky in its wake. Far above, a canopy of stars flirted
with the earth, a brisk wind stirring to their fierce command. Many a night had been spent like this, lying on
deck of a ship and watching the sky. Out in the middle
of the ocean, thousands of miles from land, everything
seemed more vivid. No towering skyscrapers to taint the
view, no airplanes to interfere with the deafening silence,
no lies to obscure the truth.

But Derek was no longer a merchant marine, no longer
a rebellious youth getting back at his family and searching
for his identity. He was a man who knew the score.

The stay in Edinburgh had been good for him. Some
had accused him of retreating, yet he and Luc knew the
truth. His furlough in Scotland had nothing to do with
admitting defeat and everything to do with preparation.

I don't think you give a damn.

The sting of Cassandra's words lingered. He couldn't
help but wonder what she would think when everything
was said and done, when his score was settled.

Derek bit back the ridiculous notion before it seduced
his imagination any further. A woman of sunshine and
mystery had no place in his thoughts. A woman like her
clouded a man's judgment, made him forget lessons he'd
learned the hard way.

A woman like her was a dangerous distraction he could
neither afford nor risk. He had only to resist.

Piece of cake.

Chapter 3

You can't always get what you want.

Mansfield's prediction stayed with Cass. The words crawled into bed with her, tossed and turned with her, stood under the shower spray with her. They now accompanied her down one of the long corridors of the Stirling Manor. All those dour-looking ancestors tracked her every step, but she refused to acknowledge them. Too much anticipation hummed through her.

Mansfield was wrong. She would get what she wanted. Him. Behind bars.

As she passed, a door opened. That was the only warning she got. Before she could glance back, arms closed around her waist and dragged her into a dark room. Adrenaline spurted. Her heart rate surged. The cop in her took over, and a quick maneuver had her breaking free and spinning toward her captor.

Mansfield had a lot of nerve—

Gray laughed. "Easy there, partner."

She froze midattack. "You fool! Are you out of your mind?"

The man known to the hotel staff as John Dickens, but whom Cass knew as Detective Mitch Grayson, closed the door behind him and leaned against it. "Expecting someone else, dear heart?"

"You mean someone other than the big bad wolf?"

"Sorry to disappoint you."

She narrowed her eyes, refusing to label the quick drain of adrenaline as disappointment. Of course Mansfield wouldn't make a move on her like this, right out in the open. Cat and mouse was more his style. Truth or dare.

He'd made that abundantly clear last night.

"Sorry to surprise you like that," Gray said, "but we need to talk, and I didn't want an audience."

Her nerves still jangled, but she squelched them. "What's up?"

"He's been spotted."

She almost rolled her eyes. "Of course he's been spotted, big guy, he's been back several days now."

"Not Mansfield—Vilas."

That grabbed her attention and snapped her to alertness faster than the three mugs of black coffee she'd already guzzled.

"Santiago Vilas," she said, recalling the photo of the Latin man shaking hands with Mansfield.? "Well, well, well. So he surfaces again. Will miracles never cease?"

"Some coincidence, huh?"

Like hell. The man had vanished when Mansfield did, and now he'd surfaced concurrently, as well. Another domino. "What's the lowdown?"

"Last night. Navy Pier. Seven o'clock."

"Practically broad daylight," she mused. "Mansfield with him?"

"He was alone when he was spotted, then he gave us the slip."

Cass let out a jagged breath. "Damn."

Gray swiped off his gold-tassled hat and crossed to her. He was all cop now, despite the benign image of his bell-man uniform. "Can you account for Mansfield's where-abouts last night?"

I want to hear you say my name—my first name. But after that, there'd been nothing. "AWOL, I'm afraid."

Gray shoved a hand through his dark hair and began to pace the length of the elegant room. Behind him the an-tique cherry poster bed sat unmade, the damask sheets tangled, waiting for housekeeping to come and put every-thing to right.

"There's no such thing as a coincidence," Gray growled.

"No there's not." A lesson she'd learned the hard way, one snowy Christmas Eve. "But there's usually an expla-nation."

"You know something I don't? You holding out on me, Cammy?"

She smiled at the nickname, let it soothe her edgy nerves. Cammy. Short for chameleon. A reminder of all the aliases tucked away in her repertoire, that she could be anyone, anything.

"Meet me at the front desk in five." She turned to leave, then pivoted back toward him. And grinned. "Put your hat back on—boss's orders."

His frustrated growl followed her as she closed the door. Seeing her ruggedly handsome partner in his staid bellhop uniform never failed to make her smile, especially the scarlet hat with its little gold tassel. Gray did every-thing he could to get out of wearing it, but as assistant manager, Cass had the authority to make bellman John Dickens put it back on. No one else understood the heated glare he sent her way; maybe they didn't even notice, but Cass found it priceless.

Midmorning was typically leisurely at the Stirling Manor, and this morning proved no different. The busi-ness crowd had long since charged forward with their days, leaving a few guests, mostly there for vacation, milling about.

The lobby, the front desk, they looked the same as they had mere days before, but Cass knew appearances were often deceptive. That's where other senses came in, most notably a sixth sense Cass couldn't explain. With Mansfield back, the Stirling Manor felt different, more charged, explosive. Electricity sizzled through the air, an undercurrent zinged around the halls.

"Hey, kiddo," Ruth called. "Where have you been hiding?"

"Just checking a few rooms." Cass went to the computer and looked up reservations. "Well, I'll be damned."

"What—" Ruth's words stopped when Gray strolled over.

"Mornin'." His voice rumbled, as deceptively lazy as his eyes. "Anything special happening today?"

Cass glanced at the dubious look on Ruth's face. The clerk had no doubt heard the rumors about her and the bellman, and was looking to validate them. "Not much, just a small, international conference of financiers checking in today."

"Oh, great." Gray sounded every bit the overworked, underrespected bellman. "Just what I need, a bunch of suits strutting around like they own the joint. Anyone famous?"

She scanned the list of names on the computer. "Bjorn. Duvall. Heffinger. Novachek. Sclafani. Vilas."

Gray's eyes sparked at the familiar name. "Sounds like a real bore—when does the fun begin?"

"Usual time," she said, pleased Vilas and Mansfield were arrogant enough to bring their business right here to the hotel. "After lunch."

"Well, guess I'll just—"

The front doors swung open, and a woman with long, blond hair sashayed into the receiving area.

As soon as her feet hit the hardwood floor of the foyer,

she whipped off her cat's eye sunglasses, revealing cat's eyes of her own. Her dress was short, form fitting, black.

As far as entrances went, hers ranked right up there among the grandest, rather the kind of entrance Cass had been expecting from Mansfield.

"Where is he, darling?" The woman floated to a halt in front of Cass. Her blue eyes sparkled. "Just point me in his direction. I shan't wait any longer."

"I'm afraid you'll have to, ma'am," Cass bristled. Another puzzle piece, her gut told her, but she wasn't sure which one. "I have no idea who you're talking about."

The woman laughed. "Oh, darling, you *are* new here, aren't you?"

Condescension, maybe amusement, shimmied between them. Cass had not seen this striking woman in any of her research on Mansfield but clearly she felt she had some kind of claim to him. Cass didn't stop to consider why that fact unsettled her so much.

"Be that as it may, if you're looking for somebody—"

"Don't get your back up against the wall, luv," the woman said in a rich, animated voice. "I merely find it amusing anyone in the Manor organization could be so naive."

Gray's hand slipped onto the desk and covered Cass's. Normally he wasn't one to make intimate contact in public, but this was clearly a warning.

Cass manufactured a smile. "Yes, well—"

"Sorry, Brooke," Ruth interjected with a warm smile. "He's not around right now—haven't seen him in—"

"Derek, darling!" The woman called Brooke abandoned them, seemingly gliding across the foyer, her high heels making virtually no sound against the hardwood.

Mansfield stood beside the curving staircase. His dark hair was secured behind his neck, a shadow clung to his jaw. His smile was of the variety from which a woman never recovered. "Brooke."

His low voice resonated across the lobby. He opened

his arms and pulled the woman to him, swung her into the air.

Their laughter splashed around Cass like a cold shower.

She stood frozen, an unwelcome pit stretching and deepening in her stomach. Brooke? There'd been no mention of another woman in Mansfield's life.

His gaze met hers for the briefest of seconds. Awareness glittered in his eyes, a wicked intensity. The man held another woman in his arms, yet his gaze was making intimate promises Cass knew better than to acknowledge.

"Cass?"

She ignored Gray and held Mansfield's gaze, refusing to be the first to look away. He was good, all right.

But she was better.

"Cass?" Gray's tone was sharper this time, more insistent.

She heard the question he didn't ask, remembered too late Gray could read her like a book. Through years of partnership, an intimacy had formed, a relationship rather like a marriage, but without the sex. She usually found it comforting, but now the familiarity made her squirm like a burglar caught in a spotlight.

"Put on your hat," she snapped, then turned and vanished into the office.

Santiago Vilas. Derek Mansfield. And now Brooke. Three arrivals in three days. Cass stared at the vase of gladiolus on the granite counter. Red burgeoned up from the centers, a sharp contrast to the deep yellow of the petals. The flowers looked as if they'd been cut open and were bleeding from the core.

Cass stilled.

The analogy cut painfully close.

For someone who'd been high as a kite for two days, this plummet to rock bottom didn't sit well with her. Confidence and optimism were more her style. Like magic tonics, they'd pulled her through the dark times, helped her out of tough jams and were fundamental to bringing down Mansfield. Moping would not do.

But that didn't change the way she felt.

Felt. The word cropped up out of nowhere and had her frowning. Feeling had nothing to do with her job. Thinking did.

Three arrivals in three days—there had to be a connection.

Rumor had it Santiago Vilas fronted a major cartel. He made the connections and built the network, smuggled illegal goods into the United States and the greedy hands of his distributors.

A year ago action had been hopping, but when the boys from the DEA and FBI moved in to put Mansfield out of business, he had vanished. After a few weeks of coming up empty-handed, the Feds backed off, and the chief considered pulling the plug, as well, but he'd decided to give it a little more time. Time for Mansfield to return, time to embed Cass and Gray more deeply into the fabric of the Stirling Manor.

And now all the players were on stage and poised for the final act.

"If that's how you look at my baby brother, no wonder he's sunk."

The deeply amused voice jarred her out of her musings. Cass glanced up to find the object of her thoughts standing there, eyes glittering, lips curled into a wicked grin.

"Why, Mr. Mans—" She broke off and smiled sweetly. "*De*rek." She injected enough honey in her voice for it to roll off her tongue nice and thick. "I didn't hear you come over."

"You weren't supposed to." Dressed in black from head to toe, hair pulled back and leaving the gold stud earring for all to see, he looked more like a dangerous pirate than heir to a posh resort. "However, I must tell you that when my employees are on duty, I prefer for them to be here."

She picked up a gold pen and nonchalantly studied it. "Far be it from me to fail to meet your expectations, boss."

"Where were you just now, then? You were at least a million miles away, and from the look on your face, wherever you were is somewhere I'd like to go."

She looked him dead in the eye. "Why, I was thinking about you."

Surprise registered in the blue of his gaze, followed by amusement. Then challenge. "Thinking, or fantasizing?"

A blast of heat rushed through her. "Wouldn't you like to know?" she fired right back, ignoring the mental warning bells clamoring wildly.

Mansfield arched a brow. "Only if you'd like to tell me."

"Dare!" Brent Ashford strolled down the hall, his neatly tailored, gray business suit a sharp contrast to the black double-breasted suit his brother sported. "Where did you hide Brooke? I heard she's back."

Mansfield's smile became so warm and endearing it made Cass's heart turn over. "She was tired," he told his brother. "She's upstairs resting."

"Tired, huh?" The glib remark slipped out before Cass could stop it.

Both men swung toward her.

Swift move, she scolded herself, then, because she had no other choice, widened her eyes in innocence. "Tired just seems like such an understatement. Something tells me after a few hours with you, exhausted is more likely the case."

Brent merely smiled and glanced around the lobby, obviously ignoring Cass's insinuation. But Mansfield's eyes narrowed. He knew what she meant, and he wasn't denying it, either. "Maybe you'd like to find out someday."

"Maybe I would." She reached over her shoulder and retrieved her long, dark braid, noting a few strands had worked themselves free. "Then again, maybe I wouldn't."

Part dare, part rebuff, her words hung between them. He didn't look away. Neither did she. Slowly Derek's hand journeyed over the counter and snatched the braid from her fingers. He drew it toward him, pulling her closer to him in the process, so close she could feel the heat radiating from his body.

He ran her twined hair along his lips. "You give as good as you get, don't you?"

"You got a problem with that?"

"No, but perhaps you should."

"Meaning?"

"Meaning a smart woman usually steers clear of a man like me."

Her lungs closed in on her. Ruth had not exaggerated. The man *was* lethal. Right here in broad daylight, in the middle of the lobby while his lover napped upstairs, he was coming on to her so strong, her legs threatened to turn to lava. Her insides already had.

"Steers clear?" she repeated a little more breathlessly than she liked. "Or perhaps you mean she's run off by a man who knows when he's met his match?"

The shocked expression on his face felt good, real good, until it faded, leaving only ashes of amusement, the promise of wicked challenge.

He laughed. "Ah, Cass. A man could go his whole life and never find a woman like you. Too bad I'm leaving in just a few weeks."

Leaving? That little tidbit of information resonated through her. In just a few weeks? The cop side of her went on red alert.

"Hey, Cass?" Brent asked, turning toward them.

Mansfield instantly released her braid, freeing it to swing back behind her head. She found a smile, or some semblance thereof, and glanced at Mansfield's brother.

She still couldn't get over the fact these two men were related.

One represented day while the other personified night.

"I'm still holding that rain check," daylight commented. A hopeful light gleamed in his eyes. "How about dinner?"

The temptation surfaced, to use one brother to spite the other, but the cop in Cass kept the naughty woman in check.

"Oh, Brent, thanks, but we've talked about this before. I don't think it's a good idea."

A mischievous light fired up in Mansfield's eyes. "Not a good idea to disobey the boss, either, is it, doll?"

"And just what do you deem disobedient?"

"Brothers have to look out for each other. I see no reason for you to turn Brent down." He grinned. "Unless, of course, you're holding out for me."

She laughed. "Now who's fantasizing?" She recognized a challenge when she heard one. She would go out with Mansfield's brother, more to get even with him than anything. Just to prove she could. She turned toward Brent.

"Vincent's. Meet you there at nine."

That said, she didn't stick around for postcoital banter. Instead she strode into the office.

Mansfield's amused laughter shattered her perfect exit.

Brent eyed his brother. "What was that for?"

Because he was a fool, Derek grimly acknowledged. "Fair is fair, little brother. Encouraging Cassandra to go out with you is no different than a thousand other things I've done for you. Don't get your hopes up, though. We both know she's too much for a man like you."

Brent bristled. "Setting me up with a woman you obviously want is hardly the same as taking the blame for breaking the antique chandelier."

"Or the weed growing at the back of the estate?" Derek inquired. He'd been furious with Brent for his little experiment with marijuana, had threatened him within an inch of his life.

Then Brent's father had beaten Derek within an inch of his.

"Dad would have killed me," Brent groaned.

"No, he wouldn't have," Derek muttered. "He would have sainted you, thinking you were protecting me." After all, once a bad seed, always a bad seed. They'd fallen into their roles easily, Derek the protector, Brent the baby, and no matter how many years passed, how many arguments, nothing changed the fundamentals.

"I saw the way you were looking at her," Brent said. "I know you want her. Why are you pushing her toward me?"

Because Derek didn't want to see anyone hurt. He glanced toward the door behind which Cass had vanished. "She's a beautiful, smart woman who deserves to be treated as such."

"And you've finally looked deep enough into the mirror to realize you can't treat her that way?" Brent quipped.

Derek skewered his brother with a pointed glare. "This has nothing to do with how I can, or can't, treat a woman. Your reflection is no more pristine than mine."

Brent narrowed his eyes. "That's all in the past, and you know it."

Derek's patience snapped. He loved his brother, but the innocent act was wearing thin. "Do I really? Last time I was in Chicago—"

"Leave it alone, Dare." Brent stepped closer. "Leave her alone, too. She's too good for you."

Derek could only laugh. "After all I've done to bail your ungrateful butt out of trouble, you've got a hell of a way of saying thank you."

Brent's face reddened. "Back off, Dare."

"What's the matter?" he teased. "Hit a nerve?"

"I mean it. Back off." With one last glare he turned and stormed away.

Derek watched him vanish up the staircase, then glanced back at the door to the office. Cass was in there, alone and furious. He could stroll through the door, and they'd pick up right where they left off.

Maybe even go further.

Derek stilled, jarred by the direction of his thoughts. Brent was right. He needed to leave Cass alone. It would be simpler that way, safer for everyone. But he was having a damn hard time staying away. She was like a smooth, fine wine. One sip and a man wanted more.

Derek curled his hand around the doorknob. A woman like Cassandra LeBlanc didn't come along everyday, and he'd been alone for too long. She was the kind who could make a man like Derek forget the hard lessons the world had drilled into him since the day he was born. She could chase away the dark clouds that followed him everywhere.

She could erase the scars on his soul.

Derek swore under his breath and released the cool brass as though it had burned him. Any thought of the sultry New Orleans beauty and erasing scars on his soul was reason enough to steer clear. He knew that wasn't possible. He knew better than to let himself hope, dream. He'd returned to Chicago to settle a score, fry a bigger fish.

There was no room, no time, for a woman in his plans.

"I thought we'd never get everyone settled," Cass commented to Ruth later that afternoon. "I ask you, where's the cavalry when you need them?"

"Cavalry, hon? What century are you living in?"

"Not this one, that's for darn sure." Dumb analogy, but after the way Derek had swaggered to her rescue, that's how she'd come to think of him. "I was referring to our illustrious owners, Sir Max's dashing grandsons."

Ruth let out an unladylike snort. "You must be out of

your mind if you think Brent Ashford is going to lift a finger to—wait a minute. Now that I think about it, Brenty-boy *has* been much more solicitous since you came on board.''

Cass picked up a pencil and gnawed on its end. She smelled something, and leaped at the opportunity to gain more insight. "I would have thought Brent eager to follow in his grandfather's footsteps."

"The high life, yes. The responsibility, no. That was always Derek." Ruth's expression grew faraway as though she could once again see the boy Derek had been when she had begun her employment twenty-five years ago. "When he was a kid, Derek followed his grandfather around every spare minute he could find. I used to think it was so sweet, that the kid's birthright really meant something to him." Her eyes focused. "Heck, maybe it did, but then I found out why he spent so much time here, and it darn near broke my heart.''

Pencil in mouth, Cass stilled. "Oh, yeah? Why's that?"

"Dare and Brent aren't full brothers. And Dare didn't have the greatest relationship with Brent's dad. Sir Max tried to compensate by making him welcome here. Dare, well, he ate up the attention like a kid does an ice cream cone."

"Then how did he end up straying so far off course?"

"Max traveled a lot, too much to take a little boy along with him. He was only in Chicago a few months a year, and those months weren't enough for a kid like Dare.''

Cass looked away. Unwanted images flashed before her, of an eager little boy following his grandfather around like a devoted puppy. Research had taught her much about Mansfield's life, but Ruth humanized the facts in a way Cass found unsettling. "Freud could have a field day with that, couldn't he?"

"It doesn't take Freud, Cass. A moron could see what Ted Ashford did to that poor kid."

"He isn't a kid anymore," she pointed out, too aware

of the fact herself. "He's a full-grown man with a track record for making trouble."

Ruth waved her hand through the air. "Ah, posh. You can't take everything at face value, sweetie. You're way too literal."

Cass almost choked. Literal? Not even close. She knew better than anyone the importance of digging beneath the masks people presented to the world.

"Something tells me Mansfield gets by just fine. Where is he? I haven't seen him in a while."

"And you won't. When he and Brooke get together, you can just tuck away all your secret hopes of seeing him lounging around the hotel. She'll occupy every second she can steal."

"I just bet." Occupy was such a plain, clinical word for what a woman would do with a man like Derek. Feast came much closer. Indulge. Savor. Sin.

"Have they come up for air yet? Or are they still upstairs?"

Ruth's blue eyes sparked with amusement. "Oh, Cass. You do have a way with words. But no, they're not upstairs. They cut out of here a while back. We won't see Dare again until Brooke decides she's had enough."

Enough. Somehow Cass didn't think there could be such a thing with a man like Derek Mansfield.

Thirty minutes later Cass stood on the diving board of the Manor's Olympic-size swimming pool. Ashford and Mansfield weren't expected back for hours, Gray was on his way to the penthouse, and she had an hour or so to unwind. Nothing like a good swim followed by a deep-muscle massage. Just the thought of it had her body humming in anticipation.

Her racing suit clung to her body as she dove into the water. She broke the surface and began a freestyle stroke. One lap, two laps, three laps, four. That was considered her warm-up, then the fun started. Back-to-back individual medleys. Fifty meters of butterfly, followed by fifty of backstroke, then breaststroke, concluding with free-style.

Only a moment was allowed for catching her breath before the whole routine started again.

When it came to physical exertion, Cass knew no limits. Not only was it imperative to her job, but crucial to her sanity. On more than one occasion she had lost herself there, snapping up the endorphins of physical release and using them as a natural narcotic. She supposed it only normal to consider her exercise the way she thought of illegal substances. The drug subculture consumed her life, and it had for a long time. Too easily she related to the junkies and the escape they sought.

She only differed when it came to method.

She was stunning, no other word for it.

Derek couldn't tear his gaze away from the sight of Cass's lithe body slicing through the water. A strange sensation for him, for despite rumors to the contrary, his whole life had been a study in discipline and denial. Hell, he'd even left Chicago when every instinct had screamed to stay. But he knew the danger of charging headfirst after something he wanted, the value of keeping a clear head and not acting on impulse.

Luc had taught him that.

But he was only a man, and she was one hell of a woman. With that gorgeous dark hair and her sultry eyes, she conjured images of sin and salvation. Her full breasts and sharply indented waist, her long legs and curvy hips could tempt even a saint. As bold as sunshine, he thought again, as mercurial as moonlight.

A rare and priceless gift.

A dangerous distraction he couldn't even begin to afford.

Or risk.

He knew what he had to do, the attraction he had to crush.

He glanced over at Maurice, who stood waiting by the sauna. The masseur smiled nervously. Any minute now. Any minute. A creature of habit, his Cassandra was.

Soon she would learn just what that folly invited.

He would show her.

She always took a massage just after her swim, and Maurice was not a man to say no to the boss. Already Derek could feel her skin beneath his hands, hear the sighs of satisfaction tearing from her throat. Just the thought of it had him adjusting his slacks, which had become uncomfortably tight.

Anticipation heated his blood. Self-preservation cooled it.

In less than thirty minutes the tempting Cassandra LeBlanc would hate him. Derek tried to savor the thought, the implication, the fact he'd be free to concentrate on the business that had brought him home in the first place.

Instead he couldn't quite suppress the hollow taste of disappointment.

Chapter 4

Cass pushed herself to the brink. When she stepped from the pool, dripping and breathing heavily, exhilaration rushed through her. She grabbed a scarlet hotel towel, wrapped it around her chilled body, then padded toward the spa.

Maurice stood waiting. He smiled and gave a jaunty little wave when he saw her. The man may have been diminutive in size, but those hands of his...they were the closest Cass had come to heaven in far too long.

"*Bonjour*, Cassan*dra*," he greeted. She never knew if he used her formal name out of respect, charm, or simply because he liked the way it sounded. The "dra" always rolled off his tongue with some vague attempt at a French accent. "You are ready for your massage, *oui?*"

"Oh, yes. More than you could know."

A flattered smile lifted his lips toward his thin mustache. "Very good, then." He led her to his private massage room. "You get ready, I shall return when you flip the switch."

"Thank you, Maurice." She moved toward the table and the black sheet awaiting her, but pivoted toward the door at the last minute. "Just a fair warning, Mo." She grinned when he frowned at her butchery of his name. "I'm wound pretty tight. Think I'll need an extra dose of your magic tonight."

Something peculiar flickered through his eyes. "Of course," he said after a moment's hesitation. "When you walk back out this door, you shall be a new woman."

He closed the door behind him.

Damp braid draped over her shoulder, Cass stood a moment, taking in the ambiance. Maurice took great pride in creating the right atmosphere for relaxation. Dim lighting, the enticing scent of incense, soft New-Age music.

She peeled off her damp swimsuit, ran a towel over her body, then climbed onto the massage table and lay on her stomach. Seconds later, black sheet strategically placed over her body, an eye mask blocking out all light, she flipped the switch and signaled Maurice to return.

Soft music overtook her senses, the sound of roaring waves crashing against a beach. Seconds rolled into minutes. She wasn't sure how long she lay there breathing in incense before she heard Maurice's reassuring voice.

"Sorry to keep you waiting, Cassandra. Let us begin."

The door closed, and the sound of footsteps moved toward her. "Ah, Maurice, you know how I feel about waiting. It only makes the prize better."

"Like fine wine." His heavy accent muffled the words.

"Yes," she agreed, smiling to herself. "Like fine wine."

And like fine wine, his hands went to work on her body. He moved aside the sheet and exposed her right leg, then took her foot in his hands. His fingers fondled each toe before taking her arch between his palms and squeezing gently. With the tips of his fingers he gave it extra attention, gently pushing upward, seducing every nerve ending in her body.

Cass had once heard any physical ailment, whether it be headache, toothache or muscle ache, could be relieved through a good foot massage. She'd never really believed it, but as Maurice caressed her foot, alternating between light strokes and deep, probing pressure, she began to believe. The stress and tension literally drained from her body.

"Oh-h-h, Maurice. That's wonderful."

He said nothing, not with words, but indulged her by continuing to play with her foot. Five minutes must have passed before the exquisite torture ended and he moved on to her calf. His fingers were nimble but sure as he kneaded the firm muscles. Her addiction to physical release had given her a lean body, but her muscles still ached, particularly after a workout like she'd indulged in tonight.

Yet now Maurice was making her forget. With both hands he skillfully eased the tension from her calves then slid up her thighs, working his magic all the way. Had she known how much extra attention her little warning would have warranted, she would have taken that approach long ago. His clever fingers shimmied along the backside of her thigh, carefully, squeezing and caressing.

Two thumbs pressed against a pressure point, creating a sensation so intense, she gasped. And jerked. His powerful hands slipped against her skin, his left coming to rest against the juncture of her buttocks and thigh, exactly where her panties would've been, if she'd been wearing any. She was acutely aware of his hands mere inches from her most private parts. The flesh there was sensitive, untouched by another for five years.

"Forgive me," he mumbled, the sheet immediately yanked over her exposed leg.

Then nothing. No more touching. No more words. Only the sound of his breathing, more labored than usual.

Cass lay there, her breathing strained as well. Confusion riddled her formerly relaxed muscles. Maurice had been giving her massages for six months. Never had there been a misstep. Her fault, she realized. She'd been the one who jerked when he invoked a pressure point, forcing his hand to slip into its precarious position. He hadn't moved it a stitch.

Remorse spread through her. Maurice was obviously ashamed, so much so he didn't dare touch her.

"Maurice," she said tentatively. "You're not done yet, are you?"

Several beats of silence passed before he answered. *"Non."* His hands returned to her left leg, where he delivered the same pleasure he'd bestowed upon the right. Except something was different this time, more tentative.

Guilt gnawed at Cass, ruining all Maurice's work. She willed herself to let go, yet not until he completed her legs and moved up to her side did the tension again slip from her body.

Maurice took her right hand in his and began to work his magic. Fingers first. Each finger, one at a time, from the tip of her index finger, down its length to where it joined her palm. Then came her middle finger. Then the fingers on which she'd once worn Randy's ring. Then her pinky. Her thumb. Her palm. The feel of his fingers pressing into the sensitive flesh there sent awe streaming through her blood.

"Oh-h-h, Maurice," she said on a moan. "You're killing me here."

In truth, rebirth seemed more like it. His massages had never seemed this sensual before. She lost herself beneath his masterful hands, and purposefully held thoughts of the case at bay. Minutes drifted away as Maurice worked his way up her wrist, along her forearm, over her elbow, and onto her upper arm. The sheet scooted back further, baring her back. She was so content she would never have noticed, if not for the slight chill of air against her skin.

A shiver ran through her.

His hands went to work against her back, easily spanning its width. Thumbs skimmed her spinal cord, fingers wrapped around her ribcage. He began massaging, gently at first, deeper as she moaned. She couldn't help herself, the pleasure just tore from her throat, mixing with the thunder rumbling in the music.

"Ah, God," she sighed. She hadn't realized how tense she was until his fingers found the Mansfield-created knots and coaxed them away.

Mansfield. The name gave her pause. Somehow, just thinking about him as she lay naked being massaged by another man seemed far too intimate. And yet, some wicked corner of her mind instantly envisioned his hands on her body, the way he would rub and relieve, the way he would turn a woman liquid and wanting.

Cass destroyed the image before it destroyed her. She couldn't let herself think about Mansfield's hands on her skin, wringing pleasure from her body. Too long had elapsed since her last massage, she realized. Much longer since she'd known a man in the intimate sense. Now the two were blurring, her body humming to life.

Humming to life. She tensed, realizing Maurice's hands curved around her rib cage, his long fingers precariously near her breasts.

Desire tingled through her.

"No..." Shocked, she rolled to her side in one swift move and jerked to a seated position. At the same time she grabbed the eye mask from her face, realizing the intimate atmosphere was playing tricks on her. Then she froze.

Shock burned away the haze.

The incense and sensuous music weren't playing tricks on her. Mansfield was. He stood before her, dark hair loose around his perfectly chiseled face, blue eyes blazing down at her.

"You bastard!" she shrieked.

She reared back to slap him, but he grabbed her hand as it made contact with his cheek. With his free hand, he draped the sheet back over her body, but his eyes never left hers.

"What's the matter, fearless? From the way you were coming unglued there, I thought you were on the brink of something powerful and unforgettable."

Heat suffused her cheeks, and other parts she didn't want to acknowledge. "You arrogant—"

"Bastard. We've already covered that. Keep up."

The game stretched before her, inviting her to join. What game, she wasn't sure, but knew she had to play.

Her fingers relaxed against his stubbled cheek. "Mansfield, what a surprise. Who would have thought a man like you had such...talents." No wonder her massage had been different tonight, deeper, more demanding.

"I'm a man of *many* talents."

She let the invitation slide. "What happened to Maurice?"

"Now look what you've gone and done." He trailed a finger down her now stiff back. "I had you all nice and relaxed, putty in my hands."

"Don't you wish."

He arched a brow. "You want me to answer that?"

She gritted her teeth. "What—are—you—doing—here?"

"Like I told you, I take care of what's mine."

"Like Brooke?" she fired back.

"Like Brooke," he agreed calmly. "And you."

"I'm not yours." Despite her retort, she moved her fingertips against his cheek.

"You work for *my* hotel. Ergo, you're my responsibility."

"Typical male," she mocked. "Give 'em an inch, and they claim the whole damn mile."

His eyes took on a purely masculine gleam. "Oh, it's a lot more than an inch, doll. You can count on that."

Her mouth almost dropped open. She'd been around a

lot of crude people, but never had such a blatantly suggestive statement caught her so off guard.

Of its own will, her gaze flicked to the area of his body in question. A pair of tight jeans clung to his lean hips, proudly championing a bulge definitely more than an inch in size.

Again Cass's eyes widened, this time at the realization he was as aroused as she.

The heat zinging through her body should have been rage. But it wasn't. "What are you doing in here? One woman isn't enough for you?"

He shrugged innocently. "You looked like you could use a massage, and I've been told I'm good. I couldn't have you all tense and uptight for dinner with Brenty-boy, now could I?"

What kind of game was he playing?

Part of her wanted to fire off a clever retort, but the other part wanted to laugh. Here she was, naked as the day she was born, save for the sheet she hugged to her breasts, sitting across from her prime suspect. His hands had been all over her body, doing deliciously intoxicating things.

And now he had the gall to insinuate this whole scene was designed to make her enjoy her date with his brother?

"Well, well," she drawled. "I appreciate your concern, but what happens between me and Brent is none of your business."

"Now that's where you're wrong. Like I keep telling you, I watch out for people in my care."

She gritted her teeth. "So full body massages are just another part of my compensation package?"

"Not if we're smart." He backed away from her. "Enjoy your dinner with my little ladies' man of a brother. I'm sure he'll be much more civilized than I am."

A surprising flash of disappointment cut through her, followed by repulsion. The thought of Brent touching her turned her stomach. "One can hope."

That killer smile of his touched Mansfield's lips, and before Cass could pull back, he'd taken her still-damp braid into his hand. With it, he tugged her toward him. She obliged, because he left her no choice, but she had no idea of his intent until it was too late.

If she had, she would have put up more of a fight.

At least that's what she told herself.

Derek's mouth swooped down on hers. "A little something to think about," he murmured against her lips, "while you're with baby brother." Then a bit of pressure, followed by a flick of his tongue against her lower lip.

Sensations assailed her. "And for you to think about while with Brooke?" she tossed back a tad too breathlessly.

He eased away from her, eyes simmering. "She's a beautiful woman, isn't she?"

Cass bit back the sting of jealousy. "Yes, very."

"Smart, too."

"How nice for you."

"Looks and intelligence," he summarized, his grin widening. "Family traits, you know."

The need to scratch his eyes out surfaced again, blurring the impact of his words. "Family traits?"

"At least on the Mansfield side that is."

"Mansfield side?"

Derek laughed. "Brooke's my cousin, Cass."

"Cousin?"

"And despite the lurid tales you've chosen to believe, even I wouldn't carry on with family."

Then he was gone. And Cass was left alone, sitting naked atop the massage table, clutching the black sheet to her body, every nerve ending exposed and raw.

Feeling. Dear God, he'd done it to her again.

Derek rubbed his temples and leaned back in his chair. He'd spent the majority of the day in meetings, an annoyance he hadn't missed for one second while in Scotland with his grandfather.

"Vilas is here," he said into the phone cradled between his ear and shoulder. The line was secure. "And you were right. The waiting only made him more eager."

Luc laughed. "Of course I was right. What about the smoke? Has it cleared?"

"Looks that way. From what I can tell—" His words died when he caught sight of Cass in one of the security monitors. She eased behind the reception desk, then looked around furtively, as though she expected to find someone watching her.

If only she knew how right she was.

He'd caught himself several times during the day, studying her from across the lobby, seeking her out on the video screens. Her hair was back in its trademark braid, her form-fitting suit revealing her generous curves and distractingly long legs. But she looked robotic, maybe even tired, like she hadn't slept much the night before.

The fact she'd been with Brent seared a hole in his gut.

He knew he should let her be. But he couldn't ignore her, not when she watched him with those searching eyes of hers. That's why he'd challenged her to go out with Brent, why he'd crossed the line with the massage. Damn, but he could still see her sitting on that table, naked except for the black sheet clutched to her chest.

He could still taste the temptation on her lips.

His plan had backfired.

"I've got to go," he growled into the phone and stood abruptly. "We'll talk more later."

For ten hours he'd contented himself with watching from a distance, but now he strode across his office and to the elevator. Just a few more nudges, he told himself. Push a little harder, for a little longer, and he'd sever this dangerous attraction before someone got hurt.

She strode from behind the counter with a large leather

satchel slung over her shoulder. Her walk was hurried, determined.

"Got another hot date?" he asked by way of greeting.

Cass stopped dead in her tracks. He saw her shoulders go rigid, her body stiffen. It was a moment before she turned to face him, revealing the first real spark he'd seen in her eyes all day.

Derek tried not to stare, but he was never prepared for the impact she had on him, like a free fall from a high cliff. "You weren't going to leave without saying goodnight, were you, honey?"

A slow smile curved her generous lips. "How can I say good-night if you're nowhere in sight?"

He looked beyond her to where Ruth stood, watching with interest. "Correct me if I'm wrong, Ruth, honey, but you can see me, can't you?"

"Absolutely," she answered. "Just as I've seen you off and on all day."

The news seemed to startle Cass, forcing Derek to realize just how distracted she'd been.

"Spying on me?" she asked.

"Just admiring," he replied with a wicked smile.

Her eyes flared wide. "Then I hope you enjoyed the show," she said curtly, then turned back toward the front doors.

Derek wasn't ready to let her go, not when she made him feel so damn alive. In three strides he was by her side, his hand on her arm. "Why the rush?"

Slowly she met his gaze. "Maybe I do have another hot date. Is that so hard to believe?"

Just like that, his good mood crumbled into dust. "Baby brother again?" he asked coldly. The thought of Brent and Cass together in an intimate way sent a low roar thundering through him. His pulse pounded. "Was last night that good?"

She blinked up at him. "Why, Derek, I'm not a kiss-and-tell kind of girl. How do you *think* he was?"

He went very still. "Don't play games with me."

"Games?" she asked innocently, obviously enjoying the upper hand. "Whatever are you talking about?"

He pulled her closer. "I'm talking about you and me and the fireworks that go off whenever we're within ten feet of each other." Like right now, damn it. Just standing close to her made him hard. And that made him mad. "Did baby brother have any idea you were remembering the way I made you feel when you gazed into his eyes, laughed at his jokes...tasted his lips?"

Her eyes flared. "Don't flatter yourself."

"Don't lie," he countered. "We're playing a dangerous game here, doll. You realize that, don't you?"

She twisted free of his grip and stepped back from him. Fire flashed in her defiant gaze. "I'm not the one who insisted I go to dinner with your brother. What do you want from me, *Dare-ek?* What kind of game are *you* playing?"

Damn but she was a sight to behold when she rallied like that. He tried to remain stern, but in truth he wanted to grin. The woman gave as good as she got. "You have to ask?"

"What I have to do is leave, before—"

"Cass, love, there you are!" Brent hurried across the hardwood floor, like a man eager to fall into his lover's arms.

Cass stepped back, clearly using space to erect a barrier between her and Brent.

And Derek had his answer.

The satisfaction he felt was damning, at best; deadly, at worst.

Brent took Cass's hands and ridiculously kissed the back of her knuckles. "I've been trying to break away all day, but—" the angelic-little-boy smile that kept him out of trouble as a kid appeared, and he shrugged "—running a hotel leaves little room for anything else."

Derek bit back a snort of laughter, earning Cass's startled glance. A smile played in her eyes, as well. They both knew Brent barely lifted a finger to run the hotel. His brother was all charm and good intentions, but very little follow-through.

"No problem," Cass said. "I was just on my way out...."

"But—"

"Excuse me, Brent," Ruth interrupted. "You have a call on line three."

Frowning, Brent reached for the phone. "Don't go anywhere," he told Cass, then pivoted and began talking in hushed tones.

Cass turned to leave, but Derek snagged her wrist before she could take a step. "You heard baby brother," he teased. "If you walk out on him like that, he'll be crushed."

"Like you would care."

"Of course I care. He's my brother."

She glared up at him. "I don't know what kind of game you're playing, and frankly I don't care. But—"

"Daddy!"

The exuberant cry stopped Cass's tirade cold. She spun toward the direction of the voice, where a dark-haired boy raced through the lobby.

Derek's mood instantly lightened. He dropped to his knees and opened his arms. "Whoa there, little man," he said, intercepting Ryan and wrapping him in a big bear hug. He hadn't seen him in months, had fought like hell to make sure Brent didn't lose partial custody of him during the divorce hearing.

He didn't want his nephew to grow up without a father, the way he had. "Daddy's busy right now, but I've got a surprise for you waiting upstairs."

The boy pulled back and grinned. "Is it a puppy?"

Derek took in the hope in the boy's eyes and made a mental note. "A puppy? Now what would you do with a puppy?"

"Teach him to play fetch," Ryan answered, as though it was the most obvious thing in the world.

Derek laughed, then pushed to his feet. "Cass, I'd like you to meet—"

But she wasn't there. She was hurrying across the marble floor of the lobby, her strides incredibly long, considering her straight black skirt. She almost looked to be running.

A bad feeling settled low in his gut. His woman of sunlight and shadows wasn't one to run from a damn thing, not even when she should. "Cass?"

She didn't stop, didn't hesitate, just pulled open the door and vanished into the gray of twilight.

Daddy?

The word circled Cass like a vulture moving in for the kill. She stood on the periphery of the bustling park, trying to block the image of that adorable little boy launching himself into Mansfield's arms. The implications shredded her.

Her research hadn't uncovered one word about Derek having a son. She'd had no idea she was about to throw a young boy's father behind bars.

How could she have missed this, too?

Around her signs of happiness and vitality raced on, children laughing and playing, young adults, the elderly, but Cass just stood there, watching. Remembering.

Dear God, a child...

The thought brought a deep ache to her chest, and reality came slicing in. Once, the thought of children had lit up her world. Now she could hardly look at a little boy or girl without falling apart. She'd had a child once, a son. He'd been her heart and her soul and everything in between.

A part of her had died with him, as well.

In the ensuing five years she'd thrown herself into her job, leaving no room, no time, for anything, anyone, else.

But when she lay alone in her bed at night, in her quiet house, with her son's dog at her feet, she couldn't escape the truth.

Work was a sorry substitute for love. Work couldn't throw arms around her after a long, grueling day, couldn't smile and melt away her troubles, couldn't laugh, sure as hell couldn't love her back. Couldn't grow up, go to school, get married.

Couldn't replace her son.

Shaking now, Cass wrapped her arms around her midsection. She felt the tears streaming down her face, but didn't bother swatting them away.

They were all she had left of her son.

She'd had her chance, and she'd blown it. Nothing could change that cold reality, just as nothing could bring back her family. Sometimes she fooled herself into thinking the grief had receded, but the darkness always seeped back, reminding her that the past could not be erased.

That's why she'd quit trying.

If only she could quit remembering.

The sight of her standing there hacked through Derek like a serrated knife. She looked beautifully serene, still as a statue, staring at the madness surrounding her. Then he noticed the tears. Two silvery tracks down her pale cheeks, a silent testimony to inner pain.

Her sadness created a palpable shield around her, a barrier so intense Derek could feel it from where he stood. Go to her, instinct demanded. Wrap her in your arms and hold her tight.

But preservation held him back. For himself, but most of all for her. Sex was one thing, but this pull he felt for Cass was something altogether different. And dangerous as hell. It ran too deep. He wanted Cass in his bed, but he didn't need her anywhere else. Especially not the place that kept demanding he chase away the ghosts making those tears slide down her face.

Around them life marched on. Women pushed strollers. Kids ran and played chase. Dogs raced after Frisbees. Joggers trotted by. And somewhere across the park a soccer game was in high gear. Life, with all its accoutrements, in full display.

Yet Cass was crying.

The dichotomy of the two scenes struck him; her utter despair rocked him. Both reactions shocked him to the bone. A long time had passed since he'd experienced either. He'd forgotten how uncomfortable they were, how controlling, how demanding.

But he knew better than to listen to them.

So in the end he did the only thing he could.

He turned and walked away.

Chapter 5

"Anything?"

The voice startled Cass, but it didn't surprise her. Gray frequently sneaked up on her, snatching precious time to compare notes. She made a quick survey of the front office before responding. "Nothing."

"Tapes are clean, too. If he's up to something, he's damn covert about it."

So it would seem. But just because Mansfield hadn't given them something concrete to go on yet, didn't mean they had the wrong man. "Vilas is still here, but I haven't seen them together."

"Have you been looking?"

The cutting question, so out of character for Gray, snagged her roaming attention. "What's with you?"

"Just—" His words broke off as Ruth returned to the desk. She busied herself rearranging the gladiolus, yet to the trained eye her interest in their conversation was obvious.

"I'll be back in a sec," Cass called to Ruth, then eased out from behind the sanctity of the counter.

Gray led her to the bell captain's station. "Just calling it like I see it," he continued as though Ruth had never interrupted. "You're not yourself, Cammy. You seem distracted."

His assessment hit too close to home. Between her dinner with Brent and the appearance of Derek's son the night before, she was having a hard time focusing. She'd hoped Brent would reveal some clues she could use against Derek, but he'd practically sung his brother's praises.

Despite the fact they ribbed each other constantly, there really seemed to be a bond between Derek and Brent. "I'm fine."

"The hell you are. We've been together too long for me to miss the signs—what gives?"

For a fleeting moment Cass was glad they were ensconced within the confines of the hotel lobby. Gray had to restrain his questions here, and therefore, could not drag up the truth.

He was right. She wasn't herself. Little cracks were springing up all over the place, giving way to a steady stream of doubt.

"Gray," she began, her voice carefully controlled. "You should focus that energy on the case, not my welfare. I'm fine."

"Damn it, Cass." The curse was so heartfelt it soothed her like an embrace. "You can't keep it all bottled up like that."

She averted her eyes. "I don't know what you're talking about."

"Right. That's why you can't stop staring at the kid."

Cass stilled. Once again Gray had pegged her with uncanny accuracy. She was doing it now, she realized, staring at the boy. Ryan sat across the lobby on the Oriental rug in front of the fire, where he held court with a magic kit. Around him guests loitered, businessmen and women, vacationers, middle-aged honeymooners. The continuous parade of magic tricks wasn't what captivated them, though, that honor belonged to the boy himself. His wide smile—those trusting eyes.

Even from a distance the innocence of it drilled a hole through Cass's heart.

"Cass." Gray laid a hand on her arm. "Quit torturing yourself."

"We need to toss Vilas's room again. I'll—"

"Cass." His fingers tightened around her wrist. "Your shift is over. Go home. Go for a run. Do anything, just get out of here before you drive yourself crazy."

As always, his prescription was right on target. She needed to get out of there, but home was the last place she wanted to be. Nothing awaited her there but her dog Barney, God bless his loyal soul. "We've got work to do, Gray. Mansfield's been back for a week now, yet we're no closer—"

Warning flashed in his eyes. "Don't look now, but we're about to have a visitor."

"What—"

"Ah, fearless, there you are."

His voice came out smooth as whiskey. "Hello, Derek," she greeted, turning toward him. He stood decked out in his trademark black, his olive skin appearing darker than usual. "I was just leaving."

"We need to talk."

"Not tonight."

"Tonight." He shot Gray a look of dismissal. "You've been less than truthful with me, doll, and I want to know why."

A rush of adrenaline spurted through Cass, and she sensed Gray tense as well. "Oh?"

Another sharp look, this one also at Gray. Then Mansfield took her hand and led her away. In some distant corner of her mind she laughed at that, first Gray, now Mansfield, both dragging her around like a rag doll.

But it was all part of the guise, so she stumbled after him. She didn't think her cover had been blown—there'd been too much amusement in the deep blue of his eyes.

A leafy ficus tree stood sentinel by one of the private offices under the curving staircase. Mansfield swung open the door, ushered her inside, then sealed the room off from prying eyes and ears. He turned to face her, his hand still curled around her fingers.

"Why the questions, doll?"

"Questions?" she asked nonchalantly. "What questions?"

"Did the other night leave you curious? Didn't you understand what I was trying to tell you? I would have thought you'd be steering clear by now."

"Like a smart woman?" she asked, recalling one of their initial conversations. "Is that what you were trying to do by putting your hands all over me? Prove a point? Show me why a smart woman stays away?"

"You really think I'm that noble?" he asked darkly. "Maybe I just can't stay away from you. Maybe you intrigue me, make me wonder what makes you tick."

"Ah, that sunshine and moonlight bit? How romantic."

His expression darkened. "Trust me, there's nothing romantic about it." Everything about him looked sharper, more fierce. His eyes. His cheekbones. His mouth. "Brent tells me dinner with you was like facing the Pardon Board, only I was the derelict in question."

"Oh?" Anxiety tightened her body. She'd thought her questions innocent enough that Brent would have no reason to replay them to Derek.

"You've got questions about me, you ask me."

She had questions, all right. Starting with his son. "I—"

"Better yet," he murmured, leaning closer, "we can cut the foreplay and get down to business." His mouth came down on hers, wholly and completely. He pulled her body against his, laid siege to her soul.

For a stunned moment, Cass was too surprised to react. The shock receded seconds later, replaced by a burning hunger that drowned out all sanity. His assault on her senses happened so fast, so thoroughly, without warning or thought, she was left with nothing but instinct.

A dark need tore through her, prompting her to push up and grant Derek better access to her seeking mouth. All that restless heat and energy she'd sensed about him combusted into a passion like she'd never known. His lips ground against hers, thoroughly, almost desperately, like he could never get enough.

God knew she couldn't.

All she could do was plaster herself against him, reveling in the hardness of his body. Easy to lose herself there, in his arms, his heat, his kiss, and simply feel.

Feel. Oh, she was feeling, all right. Every male inch of him. And he was right. It was definitely more than an inch. Far more. His erection pressed against her belly made that abundantly clear.

Desire. It was a heady drug, one she had no idea how to combat, one Derek Mansfield knew how to use. His talented hands were everywhere. Against her back. Sliding under her scarlet suit jacket. Squeezing between their bodies. Cupping her aching breast. Teasing. Taunting—

A knock sounded on the door. "Uncle Dare? You in there?"

She stilled in his arms. She heard Mansfield's labored breathing, followed by a frustrated rumble. "Ryan, that you?"

Cass's heart gave a betraying little lurch.

Uncle—not father. The scene in the lobby came back to her, and she realized Brent had been standing there, too. Mansfield had only intercepted the child, occupying him until Brent got off the phone. She'd heard about

Brent's messy divorce, the custody battle, but she hadn't realized Ryan was his child.

"Sorry, Uncle Dare," the boy said. He opened the door and peered in. "Just wanted to show you my new trick."

Cass sucked in a jagged breath, but it did nothing to stop the burning inside.

"I'll be out in a second, son, you can show me then." Derek held her tightly against him, hiding the fact that his hand rested against her breast. "You'll have to make it quick, though," he told the boy, "I've got a meeting."

"But it's after dark," Ryan protested. "Meetings only happen during the day."

Above-the-board meetings, Cass silently amended. Other meetings, the kind Cass was trying to uncover, were best conducted under the cloak of darkness.

Mansfield mumbled something to the boy, then waited until Ryan scampered away and closed the door behind him. He returned his attention to her, eyes dark and intoxicating.

"Now, where were we?"

On the way to heaven, Cass thought grimly. Via hell. What in God's name had she just let happen? "I was just leaving."

To prove her point, she attempted to pull away.

"Not so fast, honey." With his hips still pressed against her abdomen, he tilted her chin toward his face. "You know what happens when things keep simmering, don't you?"

She did. "They lose their flavor?" she offered glibly.

Delight danced into his eyes. "Only if you aren't careful." He pulled her braid toward his mouth and pressed it against his lips. "And believe me, fearless, I'm a very careful man."

How well she knew that. "Oh?"

He dropped her braid, letting it fall between them. Then he leaned closer. "We can play your game a while longer, but remember, the more we simmer, the more we burn."

* * *

Somehow Cass kept herself together as she left the coat closet. She tried not to stare at Mansfield's tall, dark form as he went in search of Ryan, but her eyes had a mind of their own. So did her traitorous body.

Gray came up beside her. "Everything okay?"

"Just rosy." She was a cop, damn it. A cop. But she was also a woman. Only once before had the two collided so violently. The consequences had been deadly.

She couldn't let that happen again.

"I'm going home, just like you suggested."

Gray opened his mouth, but he clamped it back shut and watched her stride away.

Thirty minutes later she eased a nondescript gray sedan onto the street and blended in with traffic. Mansfield's Ferrari was two cars ahead of her; her red sports coupe sat alone in the garage.

You'll have to make it quick, though. I've got a meeting.

Tonight, Cass thought. With any luck, Mansfield would hang himself tonight, and this mess would be over, before a dangerous attraction brought her down, too.

Traffic crept through the one-way downtown streets, giving her time to glance in the mirror and check her cover. White Sox baseball cap, hair tucked out of sight. Dark sunglasses. Wide shoulder pads. Well-worn Bears T-shirt.

Perfect. Anyone looking at the tinted windows of the sedan would never see the woman inside the drab male clothing.

But Mansfield wasn't looking behind him. Arrogantly he wove his car in and out of the snarled traffic. Cass kept pace with him, unable to forget the way he'd kissed her so thoroughly, the shameful fact she'd done nothing to resist.

Because of the charade, she told herself, but recognized the lie. She'd never used sex to crack a case and had no intention of starting now. Yet without that nasty scapegoat, she was left with the grim truth.

She'd responded to him as a woman, not as a cop. And that woman in her, the one who'd gone without for so long, had reacted to the burning hunger. Like a sinkhole, it grew larger and larger, increasingly dangerous, sucking her down into its depths.

It was a hell of a note. After all this time, that Derek Mansfield was so easily tapping into her dormant sexuality dismayed her. Purely physical, she told herself, and therefore understandable. He was a devastatingly attractive man. A woman would have to be dead to be immune to those smoldering blue eyes, that insolent grin, that big, graceful body.

Cass was certainly not dead.

She swore under her breath, then flicked on the stereo and cranked up the volume. Rock and roll blasted her, instantly soothing away the restlessness, just as she knew it would.

Off to the west, the sun dipped below a swell of angry dark clouds. In all likelihood, the ball of fire would not be seen again until tomorrow. The stunning streaks of gold and magenta were likely the last light of day.

The car separating her from Mansfield turned into an exclusive neighborhood, forcing Cass to hang back. She'd been expecting a covert meeting, on the pier perhaps, not a jaunty drive up the shore of Lake Michigan. Wherever he was leading her, the terrain grew more remote by the minute.

Turn around. Call Gray. Arrange a backup. The thoughts swirled, yet Cass held them at bay. Now was not the time for opting out. Now was the time to topple one more domino—once she found it.

Darkness descended, making the narrow winding road harder to navigate. The angry clouds that swallowed the sun hovered overhead, unleashing the first fat drops of rain.

And Cass thought of home.

Thunderstorms always did that to her, reminded her of New Orleans, with all those humid afternoons leading to spectacular displays of Mother Nature's fury.

The Ferrari made a sudden turn to the left. Had she not been following so diligently, Cass would have thought he'd vanished into thin air. But, flicking off her lights, she followed him into the secluded lane.

That's what it was. A winding, country lane. Despite its quaintness, Cass knew it could lead anywhere. A deserted cabin. A crumbling barn. A trailer. An out-of-the-way meeting spot.

A place to hide merchandise, dispose of evidence. Or witnesses. Or cops.

Her blood quickened, yet she refused to define the source of her excitement.

Navigating the dark road demanded all her concentration. She couldn't follow too closely, so she hung back and eased her way down the path.

A clearing opened before her. The lights of Derek's car went out, casting the lane into darkness. Had there been stars or moon, they might have lit her way, but the clouds muted all light. Cass instinctively stopped the car to avoid smashing into one of the towering trees that lined the road.

The fiercely cold wind whipped at her the second she opened the door. A cold front racing out of Canada, Cass realized, her Southern blood making her instinctively shiver. But she crept forward, one cautious step at a time, until she reached the mouth of the clearing. Then she froze.

The house was spectacular, no other word would do. The grand structure rose up from a neatly manicured lawn like a palatial country estate.

Yellow pools of light glowed from the windows, beacons in a storm. A wide veranda offered a warm greeting. Supported by huge white columns, the porch wrapped around both sides of the house. Seven full-length windows stood tall on the left, seven to the right, all in perfect Georgian symmetry. A similar balcony hugged the second story, yet instead of windows, doors graced the white bricks.

She crept forward. The Ferrari was parked in a large circular drive, partially hidden by discreetly placed shrubs. Mansfield was nowhere in sight. He must have disappeared through the enormous double doors, she realized, into the welcoming warmth inside.

Another chill raced through her. The grand house didn't belong here, anymore than Mansfield belonged inside it.

A friend's home. A contact. But as Cass neared the hedges bordering the veranda and the windows came into view, she saw the object of her investigation, pumping the hand of a man who looked shockingly like a butler. There was a woman, a stereotypical middle-aged woman in a gray dress, taking his coat and gloves. And then another woman, this one young but in a similar dress, handing him a tumbler filled with amber liquid.

Raindrops splattered around her, but Cass didn't move. She could do nothing but stare. For hours. While Mansfield was seated at a gleaming dining room table, alone. While he ate a full-course meal fit for a king, alone. While he paced the length of the parlor, alone.

While he went upstairs into one of the bedrooms, alone.

Cass hurried over to a large maple tree, its branches offering her scant shelter from the rain.

The French doors swung open, and the man who was becoming a troubling enigma strode onto the upper veranda. Glass tumbler in one hand, the other wrapped around the white railing, he stared out into the night. It was too dark to make out his features, but Cass didn't need light to see those restless eyes.

Or to feel them.

The wind whipped his hair about his shuttered face. He looked so alone standing there, so isolated.

Dangerous thoughts, Cass warned herself.

The rain picked up, cold shards pouring down in thick, unrelenting sheets. But Mansfield seemed oblivious. He simply stood there, staring.

Just as she stood there, staring.

A drenched eternity later, he hurled the tumbler over the balcony, against the nearest tree, then turned and stormed inside. The howling wind stole the sound of shattering glass.

Cass was left alone, except for the restlessness deep inside. It grew and festered, threatened to destroy.

"You shouldn't have followed him like that. Not alone."

Cass waved off Gray's concern. "I wanted to make sure he didn't circle back and catch you in the penthouse. Did you find anything?"

Gray frowned. "Other than a folder on you, not a damn thing."

Cass stiffened. She glanced around the immaculate hotel lobby, ensuring no one stood within hearing distance. "He doesn't suspect a thing," she said forcefully.

"No," Gray agreed. His tone was deceptively soft. "But he damn well wants."

A blast of heat went through her. "Well, looks like he's about to learn he can't always get what he wants, isn't he?"

"Careful, Cammy. He's a dangerous man."

"And I'm a dangerous woman," she countered. "I know my job, and I do it well. If I didn't," she reminded, "you might not be standing here today."

He scowled. "So where's Mansfield? Has he come back yet?"

Cass glanced toward the front doors, grateful this time she had a legitimate reason. "Haven't seen him yet, but then, Mansfield isn't exactly a creature of habit. The man comes and goes as he pleases."

He could return in five minutes, five hours, five days. Impossible to predict what he would do next. "I suspect he'll be here soon, though. He's been spending time with his nephew every afternoon," she said, spotting the child. He sat at the chess table, entertaining himself with magic tricks. "The kid seems to be the one exception to Mansfield's unpredictability."

She didn't want to think too much about that, either.

"You okay with the boy?" Gray asked too gently.

She glanced at Ryan, felt the answering ache deep inside. "Fine," she lied.

He eyed her skeptically, then let it drop. "Mansfield was still at the country house when you left?"

Grateful for something else to think about, she recalled the sight of him silhouetted in the window. "Snug as a bug."

"And what time was that?"

She was almost embarrassed to admit how long she'd stood in the rain. "Just before sunrise."

Frowning, Gray reached out and tucked a stray hair behind her ear. "You really want him, don't you?"

She flinched, stepped back from his touch. "What?"

"Mansfield," Gray said. "Behind bars. I can't imagine what else would prompt you to spend the night in the cold rain."

Cass didn't want to imagine, either. The mere memory sent a shiver through her. "We've waited a long time to nail him. I'm enjoying having some action for a change." She handed him a slip of paper. "Now get on up to room 223. I told Mr. and Mrs. Olsen someone would be up to help them with their luggage."

Gray's expression softened. "We'll talk more later. You sure you're okay?"

His concern warmed as much as it grated. "I will be unless Mr. Olsen calls down here looking for his bell-hop."

Gray mumbled something unintelligible, grabbed the luggage cart, then headed for the elevator.

Cass watched him go, tried not to laugh. Really, she did. But the sight of her macho, over-protective partner poured into his prissy little bellman uniform tickled her funny bone. "Don't forget your hat," she called to him, then laughed when he crammed it down on his head and stormed into the elevator.

"What's so funny, doll?"

Cass pivoted to find Derek lounging there, those sizzling blue eyes concentrated on her. Laughing. Knowing.

Chapter 6

A moment of pure male appreciation snagged Derek when he caught sight of her. She looked as provocatively beautiful as ever, with her dark hair secured in its sleek braid and her body poured into that tight little suit. The sound of her throaty laughter had lightened his mood the second he walked in the door.

Until he saw the bellman striding away, the fondness on her face as she watched him.

Only yesterday she'd kissed Derek with enough fire and passion to brand a man for life. Now the sparkle in her eyes was for another man, like a fickle butterfly flitting from wildflower to wildflower.

Something inside him went very cold.

"I didn't realize you were back," she said mildly, as though she didn't care, either.

Derek didn't like the stab of possessiveness low in his groin. "How could you, when you were busy carrying on with that bellman?"

A slow smile curved her lips, those lips he'd feasted

on the day before. "I find a man in uniform sinfully sexy," she answered glibly. "Airmen, firemen. Cops."

She was teasing him, Derek realized, and just like that, his anger turned to something far different. He didn't know how she did it, made him want to laugh, when only minutes before he'd wanted to give the too-pretty bellman a lesson with his fists.

"Uniforms, huh? Is that all I have to do?"

"I bet that little tassel hat would look dazzling on you. Or, maybe a snow-white sailor suit. You were a marine, right?"

"Merchant marine, not the same thing. And it's the navy that wears white." He grinned. "How about my birthday suit?" he couldn't resist asking. "It's a bit battered, but it's custom-made to fit, and I've never had a complaint."

The twinkle in her eyes intensified. "I was thinking more along the lines of a straitjacket," she said, deadpan.

He let out a shout of laughter. "Smart lady."

But she wasn't smiling anymore, didn't look lighthearted. "Look, I'd hoped we could just leave it alone, but apparently we can't. About yesterday—"

He stepped closer, killing her words by streaking his index finger along the side of her face. "I know, fearless. I hate unfinished business, too."

Her eyes widened, and an affirming rush of color suffused her flawless complexion. "Derek," she said, stepping back from his touch. "Please."

"Please what?" Countless possibilities surged, all erotic as hell.

"Don't touch me."

That wasn't one of them. "Why not? You liked having my hands all over you in the massage room."

She glared at him. "We've already discussed this—it's not a good idea to mix business with pleasure."

"Pleasure?" he repeated with a deliberately wicked smile. "No, I believe you mumbled something about socializing with your employer. The word *pleasure* never crossed your lips." To illustrate his point, he slid his finger along her slightly open mouth. "Until now."

He almost saw the tremor race through her.

"You know what I meant," she protested.

"Yes, I do," he said, leaning closer. "Just like I know what you want."

Rather than flinching the way he expected, she lifted her chin. "So you're aware of the fact I'd like nothing more than to use that overly inflated male ego of yours as a kickball, but you're standing here with me, anyway?"

A shout of surprised laughter tore loose from him. He'd never met a woman with her bravado, never found mere conversation so stimulating. He started to volley right back, but then noticed his nephew seated across the lobby. Ryan had quite an audience gathered to view his magic tricks.

"He's a cute kid," Cass commented, and her voice suddenly sounded softer, almost faraway.

Derek looked back toward her, surprised by how pale she'd become. "Yes, he is. I'd do anything for him."

If he didn't know better, he would have sworn she winced. "Kids have that effect," she said. "It's their innocence, I suppose."

Uneasiness speared through him. She'd gone from fiery to withdrawn in world record time.

He wanted to know why.

Even more, he wanted the fire back, the spark.

"Look," he said, reaching over her shoulder and taking her braid in his hands. Usually a touch brought her back to life. "Your shift's almost over. What do you say we take in a movie and pizza? I'm sure Ryan—"

"No." She said the word with absolute finality. "That's not possible."

"Sure it is," he pressed. "I haven't mentioned it to Ryan, but I'm sure he'll be up for it."

"No." She backed away from him, as though he held

a weapon pointed at her heart. Her braid slipped through his fingers. "I-I'm not good with kids. I have plans."

"Plans can be changed," he pointed out. She was willing to go out with Brent, laugh with the bellman, but not have dinner with him? "I've seen the way you look at Ryan, so it can't be him you're scared of."

"The way I look at him?" Her eyes took on a glassy sheen. "And just how is that?"

Derek thought for a moment before answering. "Like you want to put your arms around him and never let go."

She went sheet white. "No," she said again. "I—I have to go."

She pivoted and started for the door, but he caught her after only three steps. He didn't know what kind of game she was playing, but he didn't like it.

Hot and cold hardly seemed her style, and his nephew was an innocent target.

"What's the matter, fearless? You barge in on a room of drunks, but an eight-year-old boy is too much for you? I thought all women had that maternal knack."

A raw cry tore from her throat, one of pain and anguish. "Damn you," she hissed, then yanked free of his grip and ran for the front door.

Derek started to charge after her, but stopped abruptly. This is what he'd been working toward, he reminded himself. His in-your-face demeanor had finally triumphed. At last he'd pushed her away.

Somewhere amidst the innuendo and stolen kisses, the game had shifted. Shadows shouldn't befall someone who was as bold as sunshine. Dark clouds shouldn't mute the mercurial light of the moon.

But with lethal accuracy, he'd achieved both.

He should be relieved, he told himself. He could focus now. He could conduct business, then get the hell out of town.

Instead he couldn't shake the feeling he'd just smeared black paint all over a rainbow.

* * *

Like every other afternoon, Grant Park bustled with life. Not even the bitter cold sent the hardy Chicagoans inside, nor did it wipe the smiles from the children's faces. They were there, toddlers to teenagers, smiling and laughing, having a good time. Everything seemed simple, innocent, hopeful.

But not for Cass.

Happiness was an illusion, she knew. A carrot dangled then withdrawn.

She swiped hard at the tears falling down her face. She hated the thoughts ripping through her, hated the bitterness she couldn't squash. She'd not always been so cynical. Once, she'd believed in rainbows and white picket fences.

Once, she'd believed in happily ever after.

That had all changed in a devastating heartbeat, five years before. Christmas. A time of hope and renewal, when a blanket of snow covered the land like innocence. Despite the chill outside, warmth had seeped through Cass as she meandered through her house, a four-month-old Barney bounding at her heels. A thousand dreams had drifted before her that night, been trampled by a sharp knock at her door.

Cass wrapped her arms around her shivering body, but the gesture did nothing to fend off the chill. Nothing could. Not a coat, a furnace, not even a sudden heat wave. The wound was too deep, festering with grief and guilt, pain and longing. Familiar with the routine, she hugged herself tighter and began to rock. But she couldn't hold it in this time. Not the pain, the rage. The grief. They overflowed in the form of hot tears and slid down her cheeks.

Around her, life seemed so vital. New mothers pushed baby buggies while veteran mothers proudly watched their kids play soccer and football. She closed her eyes against the scorching reminders, yet that only gave way to memories. Of smiles and laughter and scraped knees, wet sloppy kisses, shouted I-love-yous.

The vortex spiraled closer, deeper, more inescapable and more inviting than ever. She could lose herself there, she knew, as she had before. There was peace there, peace and comfort and blessed numbness. All she had to do was—

"Good God, you're freezing cold." The harsh voice blasted through her, simultaneous with heavy fabric descending around her shoulders.

Run, came a warning from some far corner of her mind. The cop.

Let go, came a shaky, dormant whisper from deep inside. The woman.

Numb, Cass drew a deep breath. The cold air stung her lungs, but she found comfort in that, comfort in feeling something other than grief. Other sensations slowly dawned, the warmth seeping through her, the reassuring hands running along her arms, the heat of the breath playing against the side of her face. The rock-solid body behind her.

Mansfield.

Instinctively she relaxed against him, knowing she could lose herself there in his arms, too.

The hands ceased caressing her arms and slid around her, pulling her tautly against a solid male body. He held her there, infusing her with his heat. Not until she began to thaw did she realize how the wind had been biting into her. She hadn't felt a thing. The grief had been too strong.

She felt it all now, the sharp wind, the sheltering embrace. She noticed other things, too, like the texture of the wool coat draped around her body, the lingering warmth, the way it dwarfed her body, the way it smelled soothingly of sandalwood and smoke.

She started trembling, harder than before. And that was all it took. The arms loosened enough for him to turn her toward him, tilt her face to his.

Whatever he saw there, it had him swearing under his breath and crushing her against his chest.

She lost it then. All restraint, control, all pride. Tears became sobs. Unable, unwilling to stop, Cass wrapped her arms around him and buried her face against his chest, let the tide carry her away.

So long since she'd indulged in the grief, longer still since she'd let anyone see her crumble like shattered glass. Except Barney—he was always there, lapping at her tears, howling, desperate to ease her distress. But as much as he comforted, nothing compared with the security of Derek's embrace. In his arms she didn't feel so alone, so lost. She felt connected and right. She felt safe.

Which was the last thing she was.

An eternity later, when the tears ran dry, he pulled back and tilted her face toward his. "Tell me, fearless. Tell me what broke your heart."

The nickname helped her find some semblance of balance. No escaping the truth now, no walking away from it. What they'd just shared was too raw, too elemental. Too real. He would recognize a lie in a heartbeat.

Derek stood strong and steady, staring down at her with those devastating eyes of his. Yet they weren't telling her to go to hell, as they did most people, nor were they challenging her to an unspoken contest. They were simply focused on her, holding nothing but compassion and concern. Strength.

Cass squeezed her eyes shut and drew a deep breath, then released it and gazed up at him.

"I had a son," she rasped. The words scraped on their way out. "A beautiful little boy."

Surprise registered in Derek's eyes. Shock. Dread. Whatever else he'd found out about her, he hadn't found out about Jake. "Had?"

"Had." For five years Cass had held the pain inside, refusing to talk about it with anyone, not her family, not Gray. They hovered, ready to dash in if she tripped up and lost it. Which she never had. Until now. Until Derek's nephew had bounded across the Stirling Manor lobby and thrown himself into his uncle's arms.

"He would've been nine this year," she managed, her voice soft and pained. She didn't try to hide it, would not insult Jake by doing so. "Just like Ryan."

Derek lifted a hand to her cheek. He began a slow stroking motion, one that burned as much as it soothed.

"That's why you always stare at Ryan like he's an apparition," he murmured in a low, gravely voice. "And that's why you steer clear of him."

The bleak insight surprised her. "Every time Ryan smiles or laughs or just looks at me, I see Jake all over again." She could see him now, blue eyes glowing, as he'd said goodbye to her for the very last time. She could have stopped him. Just a word, a smile, any indication she'd only been teasing.

But she hadn't said a word. She'd stood there and waved goodbye, grinning like a hyena and laughing at her two boys.

Cass swallowed, needing to spew the rest of the truth. "Every time I remember Jake, the image of my sweet little boy is superimposed by—"

The horror of the truth blocked the words.

Derek's hand stilled against her cheek. "By what?"

"The coffin." The wind whipped sharper, in rebellion to the truth. "He was just lying there, so peaceful, in his Sunday best. I kept thinking he'd wake up at any minute, that I'd…that I'd see the mischief spark into his eyes one more time." The tears overflowed again, slipping down her cheeks and onto his hands. "But I didn't."

Derek swore under his breath and pulled Cass back against his chest. Her pain stabbed through him, as cutting and destructive as though she'd jabbed a screwdriver into his gut. Instinct had brought him to the park, the same instinct that led him to take her into his arms when he'd discovered her standing there. Never had he seen anyone

so desolate. It was worse than the first time he'd found
her here, the time he'd found the strength to walk away.

No power on earth could make him walk away this
time. Not now.

What remained of the sun quickly vanished behind a
swell of clouds. Without its warmth, a chill permeated the
park, rendering it too cold for habitation. Whereas minutes
before children had raced across the crisp brown grass,
now only a few stragglers remained.

Derek tightened his hold on Cass. No way in hell would
he let her slip away, not when she felt so soft and right
in his arms. Not when she needed him.

He eased back and tilted her face to his.

Tears still glistened in her amazing eyes, but he found
something else this time, something that tightened around
his heart like a straitjacket. Yearning. A yearning so pure,
so intense, it almost felled him then and there.

He smiled, not the wolfish one he'd perfected years
ago, but one of sincerity and compassion. It felt awkward
and rusty, but undeniably right.

"You shouldn't be alone tonight, Cass. I'm taking you
home."

It was the kind of neighborhood Norman Rockwell
would have loved, all manicured lawns and cozy little
houses. The grass was brown and the trees naked, but
Derek could easily imagine the vitality they exuded during
the spring and summer months.

Driveways snaked up between houses, some of them
cluttered with bicycles and skateboards, a few dotted by
stoic basketball hoops, most of them sporting family se-
dans, station wagons, and minivans. Smoke curled up
from almost every chimney, filling the bitterly cold night
with the enticing aroma of home. Derek recognized it immediately, and his heart constricted for the loss of something he'd never had.

Cass's house sat dark and lonely. No bicycles lay waiting in the driveway, no basketball hoop standing, no family sedan waiting in the driveway.

I had a son.

And this had been his home. Why Cass still lived there, by herself, in the midst of so many gut-wrenching memories, Derek couldn't imagine. He'd always found it smarter to pack up and walk away from pain, not leave himself smack in the middle of it. That's why he'd joined the merchant marines, why he'd spent the past six months in Scotland.

Obviously, Cass didn't share his philosophy. All at once he found himself dreading going inside, but Cass was already closing the passenger door and making her way to the back door. He followed, not wanting her to go inside alone.

"Cass, wait."

Her spine stiffened, but she continued toward the door, key in hand. So stoic. Most women he knew loved to wallow in their heartache, using it as a convenient tool for gaining sympathy. Not Cassandra LeBlanc.

He caught up with her just as she slid a key into the lock. As soon as it turned, he nudged his way in front of her.

Out of the darkness came a low growl, followed by a mammoth creature slamming into Derek's chest. He staggered backward, fell on his butt.

The furry beast straddled him.

"Barney!" Horror and laughter collided in Cass's voice. "No, boy. No! Down!"

The dog immediately ambled away from Derek. Darkness gave way to light, a tall lamp revealing a contrite looking St. Bernard sitting complacently on the floor, his tail swishing back and forth, eyes wide and beseeching.

"Well, then." Derek pulled himself to his feet. He'd long prided himself on his uncanny ability to sense danger, yet he'd had no clue about Barney until the dog was on top of him.

"Now you understand why I was trying to go inside first." Cass breezed by him and laid her hand against the dog's head. "That's a good boy, love, but Mommy's okay now."

Mommy. The word stabbed into Derek's erratically beating heart. "You could've said something," he pointed out. "A simple 'watch out for my killer dog' would've worked fine."

The chill remained in her eyes, the distant, polite smile on her lips. "You never gave me a chance."

The quiet reprimand stung more than it should have. He watched her standing there, his coat hanging limply from her shoulders, and wished like hell he could rekindle the fire in her.

He wanted the sunshine back, damn it.

"You're freezing in those clothes. Why don't you go change into something warmer? I don't want you to catch cold."

"Concerned about your employee's welfare?"

The retort lacked her usual panache. "I already told you—I look after those in my care."

"Look, Derek, I appreciate your concern, but it's really not necessary."

"Sure it is."

"I'm a grown woman. I can take care of myself."

He frowned. "That's why you were standing outside in freezing temperatures without even a coat. If I didn't know better," which he wasn't sure he did, "I would think you were purposefully trying to hurt yourself."

In another time, another place, with anyone else, the stricken look on her face would have delivered great satisfaction. He lived to outwit his opponents. But now, in Cass's cozy kitchen, the look only brought shame.

"You don't know anything," she said very calmly. "Nothing."

"Then tell me." Backing her into a corner didn't deliver pleasure, but like a snakebite, the past was poisoning her. Unless he could pull it out of her, she would continue to suffer.

And that was something Derek could not abide.

So he was left with no choice but to force the truth out into the open, even if that meant ruthlessly stripping away every shred of protection.

"I find you standing in the freezing cold park," he reminded, "crying for God's sake, without even a coat. You call that nothing?"

She looked past him. "I don't want to talk about it— my life is none of your concern."

He couldn't stand seeing her like this. In the short time he'd known her, he'd come to count on her for fire and honey, not ice and blandness. "As long as you work for me, it's my concern."

"Then perhaps it's time I resign."

Not quite fire, but at least a spark. "Is that what you want?"

"I…" The color in her cheeks heightened, glowing against the pale ivory of her skin. "I want to change clothes." With a flick of her eyes, she dismissed him. "Please, Derek. Just go. I'd like to be alone. Don't make this any more uncomfortable than it already is."

She vanished down the hall. Her exit would have been eloquent and scathing, had it not been for the devoted St. Bernard bounding after her.

Derek reveled in the small victory. Cassandra LeBlanc no more wanted him gone than he wanted to leave. If she had, she would have personally booted him out the door, not left him alone in her kitchen.

And what a kitchen it was. Most men would never notice the subtleties that provided insight into the home's owner, but Derek's years in the merchant marines had taught the importance of observation. Detail. Where the truth lay.

Cass's kitchen sprawled, spacious and functional, an array of white cabinets giving way to ample counter space, a handy island in the middle, a large bay window overflowing with a bushy ivy. The copper pots and pans on the wall gave the illusion of hanging haphazardly, but Derek suspected Cass had hung each one with precision, carefully creating just that illusion.

He turned to explore the rest of her house, then froze dead in his tracks. There, directly across from him, stood the refrigerator. A typical cream-colored refrigerator with ice and water in the door of the freezer, and like a typical refrigerator, it sported magnets. Pelicans and alligators, plantation homes and whimsical French Quarter scenes, each magnet clung tenaciously to pictures. Not photographs, but pictures drawn by hand.

Or in this case, scribbled.

The pictures of a child, made expressly for a mother. Cats and dogs. Hearts and flowers. A house with trails of smoke curling from its chimney. A stick figure child standing between a stick figure man and woman, hands clasped, smiles firmly in place.

I had a son.

Derek swore softly. From the look of the refrigerator and the kitchen and breakfast nook for that matter, Cass still had a child, and he could burst through the door at any moment.

Derek stalked from the kitchen and entered the adjoining room. A quick flick of a lamp revealed what looked to be a family room—an overstuffed sofa, two well-used recliners, several scatter tables, a large television next to a stereo.

A fireplace stood dark and empty.

Derek strode across the plush beige carpet and began building Cass a fire. He hadn't known what to expect from her, but certainly not this cozy home. Seated on the mahogany scatter tables, pictures stared back at him. Cass and a handsome brown-haired man standing in front of a street pole that simply said Bourbon. The same man stood by Cass in countless other pictures, some crowded with other smiling faces, others just the two of them. And several more with a child. As an infant. A toddler. A little boy.

Coal-black hair. Laughing eyes. A wide, inviting smile.

Cass's son. And by his side, her husband. The man she'd sworn to love and cherish for all the days of her life. Yet she'd never mentioned him.

None of it made sense. Where the hell was her husband, Derek couldn't help but wonder. She wore no ring. Had he died, as well? Or maybe he'd walked out following the death of their son. Had Cass loved him—

Cass's relationship with her husband didn't matter. It was in the past, and what Derek wanted had only to do with the here and now. With making sure she was safe and warm, making sure the past didn't steal her future. Odd, in using aggression to push her away, he'd only pulled himself in deeper.

He struck a match and shoved the flame against the kindling. Soon fire spread throughout the grate. But the heat didn't kill the chill in Derek's gut. He raked a hand through his hair. It was long again, hanging down to his shoulders. Marla hated it that way—unruly, she called it. Wild. He'd never let himself think that's why he preferred it that way, but a small smile touched his lips as he realized, then relished, the truth.

"What's the matter? Seen a ghost?"

Derek found Cass studying him from the doorway. An oversize New Orleans Saints sweatshirt hung down to her thighs, giving way to baggy black sweats covering her legs. Plush slippers adorned her feet. Her ebony hair clung to the remains of its French braid, leaving her eyes bare and exposed.

She'd gone from looking lost and vulnerable to looking completely at home. Yet still vulnerable.

But she did look warmer, he noted, all except for her eyes. There, the bleak chill remained. The contrast reached out and grabbed him, sinking its claws so deeply into his soul that he needed every scrap of willpower to stay where he was and not stride across the room and crush her in his arms.

"You look warmer," he commented.

Her eyes remained on him. "You don't."

How could he when he sat in a room surrounded by pictures of her husband and son? Judging him. Protecting her.

He was sorely tempted to give the man who'd once owned Cass's heart a show he'd never forget. "Show some compassion then. How about a drink to warm me up?"

A ghost of a smile tugged at her lips. "How about you leave?"

Still crouched on the hearth, he picked up the poker and stoked the fire. "Not until I'm sure you're all right."

"So gallant," she commented. "But I don't need a hero, Derek. I'm fine. Really."

He turned toward her. "Yeah, right, that's what you are. Guess you think I'm deaf, dumb and blind, too."

She stiffened. "I should be so lucky."

"You're scared," he challenged. "Scared of me, scared of what happens every time we're within a hundred feet of cach other."

She lifted her chin. "I'm not scared."

He stood. "Then prove it."

Chapter 7

A dangerous combination of excitement and caution twisted through Cass. Derek was right. She hadn't really wanted him gone, or she would have escorted him out the door herself. Thank goodness she was cautious enough to have nothing of her years of service with the Chicago P.D. visible. No pictures in uniform. No commendations. No files. They were all kept under lock and key.

"Prove it?" she asked.

A challenging light glinted in his eyes. "Prove you're not scared. Don't ask me to leave. Not yet."

That's exactly what she should do. But the words wouldn't form, not after the way he'd looked at her in the park. Held her. Made the chill go away.

"Scotch?" she asked, glancing toward him.

A slow, appreciative smile lit his face. "Perfect."

The way he muttered the word, with a little too much male appreciation, sent a rush through Cass. Instinct told her he wasn't speaking of the drink, but the fact she hadn't backed down from his challenge.

Drinks poured, she turned back toward the fire, only to find Derek sprawled out on her sofa. He leaned against the armrest, his legs stretched out before him. There was something intimate about seeing him lounging on her sofa, something entirely too seductive about the openness of his pose. It looked perfectly designed for her to sink into.

She strolled over and offered him a tumbler of Scotch. "Drink up, boss," she ordered with a ghost of a smile, "then you can be on your way."

He downed half the glass in one greedy gulp. "It's going to take more than your pretty smile to convince me you're okay, honey. You should know that by now."

"Can't blame a girl for hoping," she said with a wry laugh, then stepped toward one of the recliners.

His hand snaked out and nabbed her wrist. "Uh-uh," he said, shaking his head. Positioning his glass between his knees, he patted the sofa next to him. "Right here, doll. Next to me."

Cass took in the blatant challenge in his eyes, the same challenge that hardened his voice. A game, instinct warned, but at the moment she was too weary to compete. The tide of grief had subsided, but she knew how quickly it could return.

She sat next to him. "Happy?"

"Not especially."

She laughed. "You sure know how to shatter a girl's confidence, don't you?"

His eyes gentled. "That's not what I mean, and you know it. How can I be happy after what went down at the park?"

Again, she shivered. She didn't want to talk about what he'd seen, what he now knew about her, but she couldn't forget the feel of his arms encircling her, cradling, rocking and stroking, comforting.

Even more abominable, some place deep inside hungered for more. "Why were you there? Were you following me?"

He looked her dead in the eye. "I couldn't let you just walk away after what happened at the hotel, not when I knew something was wrong."

"Sure you could have."

A flash of naked emotion streaked through his eyes. "It was my fault you ran out the way you did—I had to make sure you were okay."

"Had to?" Annoyance flooded through Cass at how quickly he'd unraveled her that afternoon, caution at how skillfully he'd fitted the pieces back together. "Because I'm your employee?"

"Fearless." He used his index finger to turn her face toward his. "You know better than that."

"Do I?"

"You tell me."

His nearness squeezed every molecule of oxygen from the room. She could barely breathe, much less think coherently. "I don't know what you want me to say."

"Say whatever you want, just don't lie to me."

A blade of regret stabbed through Cass. His words sounded sincere, yet the entire foundation of their relationship rested on one colossal deception. Of course, the cop pointed out, if he realized that, he could be trying to draw the truth out of her, like the poison it was. But if he didn't...

That didn't warrant considering.

"You had no way of knowing." She steered the conversation to safer ground. "I shouldn't have reacted the way I did."

He dropped the empty tumbler and slid his hands behind her neck, where he fiddled with her braid. "Sure you should've. I had no right to say what I did."

Just when she thought she had him figured out, he veered off course. "What?"

"My little jab about Ryan unraveling you," he explained. "I was trying to get to you—"

"Don't worry about it." She didn't want to talk about it, think about it. She just wanted the scene behind her.

"Not an option," he answered smoothly. "Your son is part of you, a part you'll never lose, a part you'll never get back. What I said was cruel and uncalled for."

Cass fought the lure of compassion. "You didn't know."

"No, I didn't." Mansfield slid closer, his gaze on her, his hands working diligently at unweaving the braid, his words at her defenses. "But I'd like to."

Her hair slipped free. Longing nicked away at caution.

Abort! The warning reverberated through her, but other needs held her rooted in place. Slowly but surely his warmth was seeping inside and chasing away the chill. That, in and of itself, should have induced her to break away, but she'd forgotten how seductive warmth could be.

"It happened five years ago," she whispered. Those eyes. God, a woman could lose herself in their glittering intensity. They were dangerous enough when they were uncivilized, but now, all solemn and brimming with gentleness, they were devastating. "It was Christmas Eve."

Derek swore under his breath. One hand slid from her braid down her back. He began stroking in the same comforting, reassuring manner he'd used in the park.

What the hell was happening, some distant corner of her being demanded. This man was her prime suspect. He was jaded beyond repair, dangerous as hell. But his eyes brimmed with sincerity, and his touch held the promise of healing.

And she couldn't pull away had her life depended on it.

Which in many ways, it did.

"It was Christmas Eve," she said again, "and Randy— he was my husband—Jake and I were sitting around the tree drinking hot chocolate. Jake, being a four-year-old, was gleefully inventorying the presents. He had little stacks of them, one for him, one for Randy, one for me.''

The memory slashed in, sharp and jagged, debilitating, like an arrow through her soul.

She tried to smile, felt her heart break instead. ''When he finished, he pointed out my stack was smaller than his and his father's.'' And when she closed her eyes, she could still see his mischievous twinkle.

''It didn't matter to me. Truly, it didn't. But it was the spirit of the moment, and I thought Jake wanted me to share his distress. So I did. I went on and on about how he and his father hadn't done their fair share, how I'd been a good girl all year long and surely deserved as many gifts as he and Randy had.''

Derek didn't say a word, just sat listening. And watching. Stroking. Sharing his warmth, his strength.

''They were laughing so hard,'' Cass recalled. ''Randy swept Jake into his arms and told him they had a few hours left to catch up. Mommy, after all, deserved the best Christmas in the world.'' She could still see them, smiling and laughing, two indignant warriors going off in search of gifts. They'd each been wearing jeans and red-plaid flannel shirts, each donned a leather bomber jacket.

She swallowed hard. ''They hurried out of the house, and I just stood there, giddy and amused and laughing, watching my boys drive away.'' She sucked in a jagged breath, let it out slowly. ''That was the last time I saw them alive.''

The pain of her words shot into Derek's eyes. ''Jesus.''

''It was snowing outside,'' she murmured. ''A white Christmas.''

Derek pulled her into his lap and cradled her against his chest. His hands spanned the width of her back, one down low, one up high, tangled with her hair. She could hear the steady thrumming of his heart, feel the heat of his body.

"The roads were icy," she told him, speaking into his chest, needing to finish what she'd started. "Randy and Jake were only a few miles from the house when a drunk driver ran their car off the road and into a ditch."

The memory cut like a knife, slicing away the dam she'd constructed around the pain. "I was in the kitchen baking sugar cookies for Santa when the knock came on the front door." Cass pulled back and looked at him. She knew her eyes swam with grief. "I thought it was carolers."

Derek winced. "But it wasn't."

"No, it wasn't." It was Gray. And the second she'd seen the bleak lines of his face, she'd known. Instinctively, irrevocably.

"It was my fault," she admitted brokenly. Her husband and son's deaths hadn't been a careless drunk driving accident like the press reported. They'd been a message. A warning. *Don't mess with us,* it had meant, but the needless violence had backfired in the worst kind of way. "They died because of me."

"No." Derek slid a hand around to cup her cheek. He forced her to meet his steadfast gaze. "Not your fault."

"I could've stopped them," she insisted, but deep in her heart knew their fate had been sealed the moment she'd taken up the badge. "Do you have any idea what it feels like to live with the knowledge that you're responsible for the deaths of the two people you love most in this world?"

His gaze locked rock steady onto hers. *"It wasn't your fault, Cass."*

His voice was strong and steady, a lifeline she wanted to grab. The rough pads of his fingers slid across her face and into her hair. He soothed the strands down over her shoulders.

"You have such beautiful hair," he murmured. "Do you have any idea how badly I've wanted to know if it's as silky as it looks? To touch it like this, feel it slip through my fingers?''

Nowhere near as badly as she'd wanted him to. ''No.''

He leaned closer. ''Let me in, Cass. Let me help you. Let me make you feel better. I can, you know.''

The seductive invitation slipped past the pain and stole her breath. ''I bet you can,'' she sadly acknowledged, ''but it wouldn't last, Derek. It would only be fleeting and temporary, for the moment.''

A wicked heat kindled in his gaze. ''It would be longer than a moment, I promise you that.''

Her eyes drifted shut as she sank under his spell. Reality faded, all those nasty reasons she had to hold this man at arm's length. There was only need and heat, escape.

His mouth brushed over hers in the most seductive of hellos. ''Let me in,'' he urged, his lips lingering against hers. ''Let me help you forget.''

Temptation flowed through her like a heady nectar. She could lose herself in this man, his heat and strength, his promise. But the fire was too hot, instinct warned. All too easily it could reduce her to ashes.

You can't immunize against him, can't escape him. Can't survive him.

But Cass didn't care. The feel of Derek's arms around her, his hand stroking the hollow of her cheek, his body pressed to hers, left no room for memories, for ghosts, only for the here and now, the incredible way he brought her back to life. Her body. Her heart.

No. Not her heart. That was only loneliness speaking, need, the part of her that watched Gray and his wife and longed for that kind of unity. Derek wasn't here in the guise of her soul mate—

Derek.

The name splashed like cold water. Since when had she started thinking of him as Derek and not Mansfield?

This man was her lead suspect, she forcefully reminded

herself. He was a hot-blooded man who sensed a vulnerable female, who somehow knew she longed for a man's touch, his embrace, his possession.

Not his heart. Never that.

She couldn't let desire override sanity, fantasy blot out reality. She latched on to that pivotal truth and, like a drowning woman, used it to pull her from the murky waters.

Quickly the cop in her took control and rechanneled the passion from her body into her mind. Mansfield's guard was as low as hers. Any good cop would jump all over that.

Now was as good a chance as any to ferret out the man behind that killer smile. And his involvement with Santiago Vilas.

"Sometimes I just need something to ease the grief," she murmured, pulling back. She gazed into his eyes, deliberately filling hers with the hollowed out look she'd seen in one too many junkie. "That's when I turn to my friends. They never let me down. Just a few minutes, and it all goes away. The pain, the emptiness."

Derek went very still. "Friends?"

She smiled. "I call them that."

"Well, you don't need them anymore, Cass. You've got me."

She laughed. "There's nothing to be jealous of, Dare. These friends come in a bottle." To authenticate her act, she skimmed a finger down the side of his face. The dark stubble seduced her fingertips, making Cass wonder what it would feel like to lay her cheek there. "Four or five a night and I forget whatever's bothering me."

Surprise ignited in Derek's eyes. "With friends like that," he growled, but didn't finish the cliché. He swore softly and raised his hands to frame her face.

Cass sucked in a sharp breath. If a trace of regret lurked in his gaze, she chose to ignore that. And if a hint of redemption hid behind his grim smile, she ignored that, too.

He leaned closer, his hands holding her in place. ''You are a strong, beautiful, desirable woman, Cassandra LeBlanc. When I make you forget, it won't be with the aid of any so-called friends. Just you, and me. You'll never need anyone, anything else, again.''

The sensual vow triggered a torrent of need. For relief, fulfillment, but most of all, absolution. It burned through her like a raging forest fire, consuming everything in its path. Scorching, destroying, but leaving ashes that would one day nurture and replenish.

She couldn't go on like this. Couldn't let the past steal the future. But the pain wouldn't go away, nor the need. They fused into a passion more powerful than anything she'd ever known, and nothing she would ever be able to control.

He brushed his lips over hers. ''Me, doll. Let me in.''

With a low cry, Cass surrendered. Derek accepted her invitation and moved in, his lips slanting against hers, his hands cruising along her face, tracing the line of her cheeks, her jaw, then slipping down along her neck. Her skin burned where he touched, yearned where he did not.

''Derek,'' she murmured. ''Derek.''

''That's right,'' he rasped. ''Just me.''

She arched into his touch, loving the feel of his fingers toying with her collarbone then roaming down her sweatshirt to the swell of her breasts. He lightly caressed and circled, taunting, teasing. Heaven and hell at once, winter and summer, spring and fall, all combusting into a never-ending nirvana.

Her body turned molten, needy. The sensations crashed through her, forcing her to realize just how long had passed since she'd felt the need, the desire. Not just for a man, but to live. To really live. To enjoy.

She twisted in his arms, eager to lose herself there, pleased to feel him respond in kind. He pulled her down with him, until they lay on the sofa, arms and legs tangled, bodies pressing close.

The bulge in his jeans told her he was as lost as she.

A low moan tore from Cass's throat and ripped into Derek's gut. Sweet mercy, he'd wanted her like this, pliant and willing, since the second he laid eyes on the fearless New Orleans beauty. Yet nothing had prepared him for the intensity of her response. She was coming alive in his arms, her clever hands running over his body, caressing and demanding, arousing, torturing, yanking his shirt from his jeans and sliding up his bare flesh.

The fire in his blood flashed hotter. He wanted her with a single-mindedness that stunned him, one that warned he'd never be satisfied until he buried himself deep inside and made her his.

Awed, he slid his mouth down her neck, enjoying the way she arched into him. He wanted to taste her, all of her, every last delicious hill and valley. His hands led the way, fighting with the oversize sweatshirt until he found the bottom and was dragging it up toward her head. He stopped when he reached her breasts, stilled for a moment when he discovered them braless.

Then he indulged. Her breasts were full and perfect, and damn near sent him over the edge. But he restrained himself, determined to stoke her passion as high as his.

The breathless sighs tearing from her throat indicated he was doing a damn good job.

He toyed with the swell of her breasts, running his fingers enticingly close to her nipples, then backing off as she arched into him. He wasn't trying to tease her, just draw out her pleasure.

"Touch me..." Her legs fell open and wrapped around his. "P-l-e-a-s-e just touch me."

Derek advanced to her nipples, each forefinger dancing slow circles around the dark-mauve peaks. Moaning, she arched into his touch, causing him to abandon his deliberate movements and simply savor. His mouth joined his hands, greedily pulling one nipple inside and sucking thirstily.

Fire burned through him. He needed to bury himself inside her, right there, right then. She must have sensed it, too, because her fingers were fumbling with his jeans. One cool hand slipped inside and found him hard and ready for her.

Near the breaking point, Derek yanked at her sweatshirt, stilled when he recognized the crudity. No matter what passions ruled him, this was Cass, a woman who'd fallen apart in his arms scant hours before, a woman who'd suffered more pain than anyone should have to in ten lifetimes.

He couldn't just rip her clothes off and drive into her like a careless rutting animal, no matter what passions drove him. She deserved better. She deserved pleasure, a bed and sheets, not a wham-bam, oh-so-good-ma'am, on the sofa. And in front of a roaring fire, too. The cliché of it appalled him. He wouldn't do that to her. They didn't have long together—he would leave soon—but what they did have needed to be right. Special. Just like she was.

"Derek?" Her voice was soft, her tone uncertain.

He hated the confusion behind the question, in her eyes. She deserved certainty. "It's okay, honey," he whispered. "Everything's gonna be okay. I promise."

"Don't leave now...."

"Not even possible."

Breathing hard, fighting his own need, he rolled to his feet and lifted her into his arms. She felt right there, nestled up against his chest, her hair fanning out over his arm. Dangerously content, he carried her down the hall.

Cass wrapped her arms around his neck and urged his mouth down to hers. He kissed her as he walked, letting his lips and tongue make promises his body would soon keep.

Urgency veered him into the first room he found. He

crossed to the bed and laid her down gently, then stretched out alongside. He was tempted to just pull her close and hold her tight, but she was lifting her face to his, running her hands along his cheek. "Kiss me, Derek."

It was a frantic reunion, as though the separation had been years and not seconds. His hands returned to their earlier exploration, intent on finding the edge of her sweatshirt and freeing her from the cumbersome fleece. She pulled him closer, wrapping her legs around his. She practically purred when he pulled off her sweatshirt.

A sliver of moonlight made its way in through the window, just enough to illuminate the beautiful swell of her breasts. And her nipples. Sweet heaven, her nipples were all mauve and swollen, just begging to be kissed. And sucked. Worshipped.

He started to do so, lowering himself as Cass stretched out on the bed with catlike grace.

Then she froze. And moaned. Not in passion as before, but a low, keening cry, like a wounded animal.

And it sliced through Derek like a knife.

He fumbled for a bedside lamp, found one, flicked it on. Light poured through the room, turning his blood to ice. A Barney comforter covered the single twin bed, accompanied by an array of stuffed animals, including the infamous purple dinosaur. Cass lay dead center, still and stricken and half nude.

The sight shredded him. Her son's room. Good God, he'd brought her into her son's room. It was perfectly preserved, like the refrigerator art, as though the little boy could come bounding in at any moment, bright-eyed and smiling, ready to hear a good-night story. "Oh, Cass. Sweet Mary, have mercy."

The frozen look crumbled into anguish. She curled into a tight ball, wrapping her arms around her knees.

Helpless and appalled and desperate, Derek crawled over and pulled her against his chest. He cradled her when the sobs came, murmured soothing words when the shaking worsened.

A vicious string of curses roared through him. He should never have carried her into a darkened room. He should have indulged the fire between them and taken her right there on the couch, where it was safe.

Since when did he know a damn thing about being noble and doing the right thing?

But he'd had no way of knowing what minefield lurked in the darkness. No way of knowing Cass still had Jake's room ready and waiting. The reality of it ripped at his heart.

Living in a make-believe world wasn't healthy.

"I c-couldn't…" she sobbed into his chest. "I… c-couldn't…t-take it…apart."

The words, the hot tears that accompanied them, soaked through the fabric of his shirt, clear into his uncomfortably raw heart.

"I just c-couldn't," she cried. "It seemed so…s-so final. And I…j-just…c-couldn't let…my…my b-baby …go."

She started to tremble, violently. Her hands. Her shoulders. Her lips. Her entire body. No matter how frantically Derek ran his hands along her body, cocooned her with his own, she just slipped further into the fray.

"Oh, God," she sobbed brokenly, clinging to him like a buoy in a violent storm. "Oh, God, God, God, God, *God!*"

Derek had never witnessed such bottomless grief. The incoherent muttering and chanting, the shaking, the crying. They ripped and shredded, shattered and destroyed.

He'd never felt more helpless in his entire, godforsaken life.

He scooped her into his arms and left Jake's mausoleum behind, this time checking to be sure before entering another room. He found a king-size bed in this one—the bed she'd no doubt shared with her husband—and enough feminine accoutrements to give him confidence she belonged here.

Barney lay stretched out and snoring on a huge denim pillow in the corner.

"It's okay, honey," he whispered against her ear. "So help me, God, you're going to be okay." She was still naked from the chest up, and shivering, so when he laid her down in the bed, he slipped under the thick comforter with her.

He just wasn't ready to let go.

So he held her that way, stroking and soothing as her incoherent sobs subsided into the blessed escape of sleep.

Warmth. That was Cass's first sensation as she wove through the thick layers of numbness. It was a slow, groping process, one she wasn't sure she wanted to complete. But a vague surge of questions pushed her on.

Darkness. That was her second sensation, the one that came when she forced open her grainy eyes. She was nestled in her own bed, the thick comforter encasing her, the room dark but for a sliver of moonlight.

Derek. He'd been there. The memory was vague and nondescript, but intense in its own way, like the man himself. He'd carried her to bed, slipped in beside her, held her against him, stroking and caressing, murmuring nonsensical words as she'd cried for all she had lost, all she would never have again.

She shuddered in the darkness. The pain had been as sharp and debilitating as during those blinding days following the accident. Blessed years had crept by without a return of that level of anguish. That it resurfaced now made no sense.

I had no right to say what I did.

Derek held himself responsible. But there'd been cruel words before, spoken by others. They'd never hit Cass so hard. More than just Ryan's presence and Derek's taunts were responsible for her fall. Just what it was didn't bear considering.

Cass pulled herself to a sitting position and squinted into the darkness. The sound of breathing came to her, deep and peaceful.

Adrenaline surged. No wonder she'd felt warm upon waking, no wonder she'd been content to stay nestled in sleep's seductive cocoon.

A chill ran through her. *She'd spent the night in the arms of her chief suspect.*

But when she looked across the bed, she saw nothing but Barney, stretched out on the far side, big furry paws twitching, deep in doggy sleep.

Relief tangled with disappointment, frustration with sanity. Derek was gone. He'd left her, after all. Whatever else sizzled between them, she hadn't slept with him.

She slowly became aware of other things, like the flannel nightgown twisted around her legs. Funny, she didn't remember changing clothes, didn't remember anything beyond losing herself in Derek's arms.

Groggy and far too shaky, she rolled from the bed and stumbled into the bathroom, intent on a shower. She'd learned the trick long ago, that comfort came from a stream of hot water beating down on her. Slipping free of her nightgown, she stepped inside the glass stall, cranked up the water, and waited for the cleansing to begin.

Peace didn't come. The wounds were too raw. As she stood under the spray, a fresh wave of memories overtook her, this one as powerful as the night before.

Her marriage had been more like a comfortable old blanket than a fusing of souls, but Randy had been a good man, a wonderful father. They'd shared goals if not dreams and had planned a life for their son.

Losing them had left a brutal tear in the fabric of her life. She'd patched the pieces as best she could, but it had never been the same. Big black patches just never blended with anything else.

That was her cross to bear. She'd dutifully borne it, but nothing filled the emptiness. Nothing chased away the ghosts. They dwelled in the remnants of her heart, making their appearance during the quiet hours of the night, precisely why Cass relished any assignment that stole those hours from her.

But she was alone now, her defenses stripped away. The past rained down on her; the scalding water didn't wash it away. Both scorched. She gave herself over to emotion, and let the sobs begin anew.

It was a routine she knew too well. And she hated it. Growing weary, she slumped down against the cool ceramic tile and drew her knees to her chest.

"Sweet God."

The raspy words were part oath, part prayer, 100 percent heartfelt. Cass was vaguely aware of the shower door opening, the fully clothed man stepping inside, the strong arms closing around her. The pain in his raw voice remotely registered, the pain in his eyes. Go-to-hell eyes, she'd thought of them once, yet, at that moment, they said he was already in hell with her.

He pulled her to his body and held her against his chest, showing her what a powerful narcotic solace could be. And in that moment she'd never needed him, anyone, more.

She buried her face against his neck and wrapped her arms around his drenched shirt. Tepid water rained down on them. And her sobs subsided into shallow, ragged breaths.

And for that moment in time, it was enough. More than enough, it was what she needed, what she'd craved from the moment she'd peered through the darkness to find him gone.

That's why she'd gone to the shower, she vaguely realized, to wash away the dangerous, forbidden needs this man stoked. But the ploy hadn't worked, not as she'd intended, anyway. But in another way it had. Derek was there. He hadn't left her alone. He was holding her, giving her the most special gift she'd received in a very long time.

Himself.

Chapter 8

Cass took a drag of coffee, another, then another still. Not enough, though, not nearly enough to chase away the haze that surrounded her, to make her forget. She needed something stronger than French roast coffee to do that, like the so-called *friends* she'd told Derek about last night.

God have mercy, what had she let happen?

For months now everything had been black-and-white. Derek Mansfield masterminded a dangerous crime ring with tentacles throughout Chicago society. He possessed no scruples, no regard for anyone but himself.

Cassidy Blake, alias Cassandra LeBlanc, had been primed to bring him down. She knew his kind too well, ruthless, amoral scum who threatened the fabric of society. Only one thing mattered to his kind, and that was to get what they wanted, all else be damned.

But last night he'd held her in his arms while she sobbed against his chest. He'd refused to take advantage of her vulnerability, when all too easily he could have.

Because she would have let him.

Maybe even wanted him to.

The rules had changed. How could she view the man with the edgy eyes but tender hands as the enemy, when he, and he alone, had helped exorcise her grief? How could she crusade against him, when she craved the touch of his body, the mindless escape of his passion?

She knew better, damn it. Knew better than to get involved. Especially with a suspect. But not all the training in the world had been enough to prevent her two worlds from colliding once again.

Cass wrapped her thick terry cloth robe tighter, yet the chill remained. Two cups of coffee later, her body jittery from caffeine but still in a fog, she made a hasty decision and placed a phone call.

"Come on, Barn," she said. "We're going for a ride."

The big St. Bernard's eyes lit in anticipation.

After she threw on a sweater and old pair of jeans and opened the back door, she remembered Derek had driven her home from the park. But her car sat in the driveway, silently waiting for her use. Barney bounded over, ready for his favorite pastime besides eating and sleeping, and thumped his tail.

Anger marched in, mingling with the confusion. Through her years on the force, she'd been toyed with before, yet she'd always recognized the ploy. Never had it seemed real or sincere, heartfelt. Never had she entertained the ridiculous fantasy that it could be just that. Real.

And never, ever had it been seductive.

Until Derek Mansfield swashbuckled into her life.

She strode to her car and let Barney into the cold front seat. He happily settled into position, sitting as though he was a human ready to be belted in. That dignity wouldn't last. As soon as they headed down the road, the thankless mutt would press his wet nose to the frigid glass, eagerly waiting for her to roll down the window so he could hang his head out.

A sad smile touched her lips. The overgrown puppy represented all she had left of her little boy. She would never forget the day she brought Barney home, her valiant, doomed, attempt at securing him a more dignified name. Jake had loved the goofy purple dinosaur, and even though the clumsy puppy had been neither purple nor a dinosaur, Jake had been insistent.

So Barney it was.

And now he was hanging his head out the window, happily enjoying the rush of biting wind against his face. For thirty minutes he stayed like that, until Cass turned down the secluded road. She knew the route by now, had memorized her routine upon arrival. This was her first day trip, though, and she found herself unprepared for how much more splendid the old mansion looked against the backdrop of a clear, azure sky.

Cass didn't know why she'd been compelled to call in sick and drive over, without the shelter of darkness, and risk her cover. Maybe she'd hoped to do some more investigating. Or maybe she'd hoped to find Derek.

Maybe something altogether different drove her.

Standing amidst a copse of naked trees, Cass lost track of time. Only when she heard a vague, muffled barking did she realize how long she'd left Barney in the car. Her body ached, both from lack of movement and lack of sleep, and her stomach rumbled with relentless hunger.

More than twenty-four hours had passed since she'd eaten anything solid.

She returned to her car and headed home. Close to noon, she pulled into her driveway and opened the back door. Barney raced straight for the kitchen, heedless of the crumbled leaves in his wake, and began noisily lapping water from his bowl. Smiling at his predictability, Cass shut the door and leaned against it. Her hunger had faded, as it often did, leaving a restlessness in its place.

"You should be in bed."

The unexpected low voice should have had Cass reach-

ing for the Smith & Wesson strapped inside her leather
jacket. But it wasn't there now. And even if it had been,
the voice didn't surprise her. Nor frighten. Soothe, however...

"Here I was all worried about you," the low voice
continued, "yet you were only playing hooky." Derek
stepped out from the shadow of her baker's rack. His eyes
mirrored his derisive smile.

Not even Barney seemed to care. Done drinking, he
ambled off in search of his denim doggie bed.

Cass could only shake her head. "What—"

"I told you. I take care of what's mine."

She stood still, staring at the set of his shadowed jaw.
He looked tired, like a man who hadn't slept—

Jarred, Cass masked the reaction with nonchalance, a
practiced illusion, while her insides raced with excitement.

Suspicion, she corrected.

Her suspect had let himself into her house. He'd been
there alone. He could have seen anything, like the locked
study dedicated to the facts she'd accumulated about his
life, the damning pictures of him and Santiago Vilas.
"Like I've told you, big guy, I'm not yours."

"Ah, Cass," he drawled, moving toward her. Funny
that such a big man could walk so gracefully and with so
much authority. Yet he could. And did. He halted before
her, his body inches from hers, and tilted her face toward
his. "That was before."

"Before?"

His cobalt eyes darkened. "That was you and me last
night. Don't pretend you don't know what I mean."

"Derek—"

"I'm going to make you forget," he murmured, his lips
brushing over hers. "Remember?" he challenged with another well-executed caress. "And when I do, there'll be
no ghosts there with us. Just you and me."

Words failed her. He was right. She had been there last
night, and she'd practically begged this man to make love

to her. No, not make love. Have sex. Raw, mind numbing sex. His mouth had been on her breast. Her hand had been on his erection. He'd seen her cry. He knew about Randy and Jake. He'd held her naked, shivering body in his arms.

And he'd come to check on her.

The anomalies were outpacing the expected. Feminine instinct demanded she retreat before she waded in too deep, but the cop in her refused. Cassandra LeBlanc, sultry yet troubled hotel employee, had no reason to push Derek Mansfield away, no reason he would believe.

Not after last night.

Cassidy Blake, however, woman walking a line far too thin, knew she had to try. She raised her eyes to his, and tried like hell not to lose herself in the intensity blazing there.

"Derek," she began, her voice heavier than she liked, "let me explain."

A grim smile touched his lips, yet his hand didn't leave her face. It lingered, stroking. "Go right ahead."

He was crowding her, his big body sandwiching her against the wall. Impossible to breathe like that, much less think.

"I'm waiting."

With considerable effort she swallowed, then nudged past him. No safe harbor in the kitchen, so she headed for the warmth of the den, confident he would follow.

He did.

The sofa was her favorite spot, but also where they'd nearly made love the night before. Instead she sank down into a well-worn recliner. Randy's. "I don't know if you've ever lost someone you loved—"

"I have."

The two words were bitten out with such brutal finality, Cass had to look at him. He stood across the room, by the fireplace, vacant but for last night's ashes. His commanding presence was the same as always, the rugged appearance of the tan chamois shirt and snug black jeans. But his eyes were…different. Hard and bitter and…lost.

They looked right through her. "Derek?"

The question, a sincere one between a man and a woman, not a calculated one between a cop and a suspect, slipped out before she could stop it.

"My father."

"Oh, Derek." She rose to go to him, but he held out his arm, and his gaze hardened.

"Don't Cass."

Isolation. So easy to recognize, all the easier to ignore. She hurried over to him, her hands instantly finding his stubbled cheek. "There's no need to pretend with me, not after last night."

His hands raised to capture hers. "Weren't you the one just saying last night didn't change anything?"

Her hands stilled against his cheeks. "Don't throw my words back in my face."

"Why not?" he challenged. "They don't sound so good turned the other way around? Used to hurt, rather than to defend?"

Shock stabbed through her. In belittling what had passed between them, she'd hurt him, just as he'd somehow hurt her. "I'm sorry, Derek, I didn't mean—"

"I don't want your apologies."

A lump rose to her throat, a vague feeling of panic. "What do you want?"

His eyes gentled. "Your honesty."

Her legs almost went out from beneath her. "Derek—"

"And I'll give you the same," he said, leading her to the sofa. They sat, and he turned her to face him. His eyes were somber, honest. "I know about grief. I understand. When someone you love dies, part of you does, too."

The comment did cruel things to her heart, efficiently chipping away at the wall she'd tried to construct between them. She didn't want to hear this. Didn't want his trust.

But she sat there listening anyway, unable to turn away from the pain in his wounded blue eyes.

"I thought I must have done something wrong," he told her, "that if I'd been a better son, my father wouldn't have left me." He squeezed her hand. "I know what it feels like, Cass—that's why I couldn't leave you last night."

"Oh." Believable. Damn him, he sounded so believable. Sincere.

"That's why I came here as soon as I heard you called in sick. To make sure you were okay."

The wall around her heart crumbled even more. "Oh."

"I hated leaving you alone."

She knew she should say something, but too much emotion thickened her throat.

An oddly tender smile touched his lips. "Well, this is certainly a first."

Cass wished she could look away from him, at anything else. Couldn't. "What?"

"Rendering you speechless," he answered, stroking her hair. "I have to admit I've planned it for a while now, but I hadn't thought to do it quite this way."

Something deep inside slipped another notch. "Oh."

Damn it, where had her vocabulary gone?

Derek looked at her sitting there, at the unabashed confusion on her face, and felt an unfamiliar ache in his chest. She looked like a lost little girl, those deep, soulful eyes gazing up at him, her dark hair wild and tangled around her face. He wanted to haul her into his arms and make her forget.

But instinct warned that now was not the time.

"Come on." He pulled her to her feet and led her to the kitchen. "You need to eat."

She stopped and blinked up at him. "Eat?"

He laughed. When it came to answering statements

with a question, she was as ruthless as a cop. But much better to look at. And taste. And lo..."

"Soup," he said abruptly. "I brought chicken soup."

Her eyes shifted toward the stove, then grew even wider. "And champagne," she laughed.

"Between the two, one of them was bound to make you feel better."

She laughed. "You're impossible." Beaming a smile at him, she pressed a quick kiss to his cheek, then hurried over to the stove.

He watched her, drinking in the knowledge that she really was okay. He'd half expected to come over and find her in as many shattered pieces as last night.

He should have known better. Cassandra LeBlanc was a strong, courageous woman. If he'd learned anything since the moment he found her being harassed by those drunk bastards, he'd learned that. Her emotions ran deep, as still waters often did, but Derek realized she'd never let them rule her for long. At least not where anyone could see them.

Leaving her house during the dark hours of early morning, when the night was as cold and still as death, had been hard. But he knew better than to spend the night in her bed. He knew better than to start something he couldn't finish. But still. In the wake of all that sobbing and shaking, he expected her to be exhausted, to spend the day lost in sleep.

Yet here she was, dressed in a red sweatshirt and faded jeans, standing in her kitchen. She spun toward him, gazing at him with those sultry eyes he'd come to crave. They were rimmed in red now, circled by shadows. Something foreign lurked in them, something he knew better than to try to name.

"Smells wonderful," she said.

He shrugged off her praise. It felt too good. "It was nothing."

"Derek?" she asked, narrowing her eyes. "Something wrong?"

He didn't trust himself to speak. He saw too much in her beckoning eyes, her lush body, her broken h—

He had to get away from her, he realized, before the final die was cast. He was in too deep. He hadn't returned to Chicago to fall in lo— Bed, he corrected. He hadn't returned to Chicago to fall in bed with a woman.

He'd returned to settle a score.

He couldn't afford the distraction.

"Come on." He ignored the fledgling yearning in her eyes. With an effort, he ripped himself free of her spell and strode toward the kitchen. "You need to eat, and I have to get the hell ou—" He bit back the edge to his voice. "I have to leave."

And that, damn it, was that.

The shrill siren of an ambulance cut through the night.

"You surprise me, my friend," Santiago Vilas said. "Making contact close to the Stirling Manor is rather bold, is it not?"

He let the taunt slide. "Not at all."

Vilas looked down the dark alley. "You speak of rats and exterminations, yet here you stand, mere blocks from the family business. Where I come from, this is called tempting fate."

Overflowing trash bins cluttered the dark alley, their noxious odor mingling with the sharp wind blowing off Lake Michigan. "Ah-h-h-h," he drawled, elongating the word into a condescending rebuke. "Where I come from, rats hide in alleys. They often meet their demise there, as well."

But the rats were quiet tonight, as were the cats.

Vilas's lips curved into a sly smile. "Aren't you the clever one." He glanced around the alley, apparently seeing it in a new light. "Trying to sniff your rat out of cover, eh?"

Something like that. The files of the hotel workers had been scrutinized, yet he'd come up with nothing more suspicious than one particular bellman, John Dickens, whose past was littered with a police record a mile long, including several arrests for possession. The man should never have been hired—if he caught whiff of what was about to go down, as junkies often did, he could turn into a deadly wild card.

He would have to be watched.

"I grow impatient, my friend." The sly smile faded from Vilas's eyes, replaced by the cutting, ruthless one that rendered him one of the most feared men in his country. "Cat and mouse is one thing, but I am beginning to question your loyalty."

Loyalty had nothing to do with the game they were playing. "No need to worry, *Amigo*. Everything is unfolding according to plan."

"Then perhaps you should share this plan with me."

He enjoyed a slow smile. "What's the matter? Not sure how you'll keep your cover after the conference ends and your cronies fly the coop?"

Vilas laughed. "Ah, my friend. Who are you trying to fool? Not me, I hope. We both know I have no cover."

Vilas reached into the inside pocket of his black sports coat and withdrew a silver case, made an elaborate production of opening it and carefully selecting a long thin cigarette.

"So you're staying?" His gaze on Vilas, searching for the faintest flicker of a hidden agenda, or betrayal, he withdrew a lighter from his own pocket.

But he didn't offer the flame. He instead held the silver cylinder in his hand, just out of reach.

Vilas's eyes narrowed to tiny slits of coal. "I am an international businessman," he stated in an accented voice full of confidence and warning. "No one tells me where I can or cannot visit. If I decide to stay in Chicago a few extra days, then so be it."

A satisfied smile twitched at his lips, but he was careful to keep them a bland, thin line. Santiago Vilas was both feared and revered in his country. Sometimes it was easy to understand why; more often it wasn't. The man acted more like a spoiled three-year-old than the ruthless, vindictive front man for an international cartel of fortune, power and corruption.

"Now, if you will excuse me," Vilas clipped, "I have a party to attend."

More than ready to be free of the wiry man's company, he flicked the top of his lighter. A brilliant flame sprang free and Vilas leaned closer, but he held the lighter inches out of reach, for a carefully timed moment, letting the fire flare between them.

Vilas's eyes hardened. Only then did he offer the flame to the tip of his thin cigarette. "Be my guest."

A sardonic smile twisted the Latin man's lips. "I already am."

Minutes later, when Vilas had disappeared into the activity beyond the alley, a skinny black cat slunk by, a very dead mouse dangling from its mouth. And he laughed.

The cat continued his stealthy journey into darkness, pleased with the outcome of his hunt, eager to enjoy the fruits of his victory.

The heir to the Stirling Manor could relate.

Laughter and cheers blasted from the ballroom. A middle-aged man staggered out, a luscious redhead draped over him, and tottered toward the elevator. Their laughter was of the intimate variety, their intent obvious.

Cass headed toward the closed doors. The bankers appeared to be a conservative group, with their tailored suits and starched shirts, but give them alcohol and cigars, and inhibitions vanished. The casino party had been in full swing for hours, but Vilas had just arrived. She and Gray had been watching him all week, tossing his room on three occasions, yet the wily man had done nothing to raise suspicions. Until tonight.

For the first time in days, a sense of certainty settled over Cass. This was what she needed. A rededication to work. She was here to do a job, and as long as she focused on that, everything else would fall into place. No more contact with Mansfield outside the hotel, no more intimate scenes, no more sexual encounters.

No more dangerous longings.

The conference, their best chance at zeroing in on Vilas, was drawing to a close. She and Gray had been certain he would make contact with Mansfield, yet nothing had been confirmed. They'd been conspicuously absent from the hotel tonight, but Ruth had seen Derek leaving with Brooke. Vilas had strolled out shortly thereafter, only to return less than twenty minutes later.

The chief would not be happy. Not only had she and Gray failed to find hard evidence, but she was beginning to doubt Mansfield's involvement. There was no denying his littered past, yet that didn't make him the bastard responsible for piping cocaine and heroin into the upper-echelons of Chicago society. The Stirling Manor could merely have been a distribution point—or a setup.

Either way, Cass had no proof.

And soon the chief would pull the plug, and her involvement with Mansfield would come slamming to an end.

Inhaling deeply, she eased into her best Cassandra LeBlanc persona and sauntered into the ballroom.

The dichotomy almost had her laughing out loud. One minute she'd been standing in a nineteenth century manor house, in the next she was shoving her way through a crowded casino. Slot machines. Roulette tables. Card tables. Dealers in tuxedos. Waitresses in skimpy cocktail outfits.

Cigar smoke and drunken laughter filled the room. The lights were low, the crowd thick. She maneuvered around the tables and deeper into the room, past the cash bar, back toward the craps table. More men here, less light. The perfect hiding spot for Vilas. It was time for personal contact.

"Hey, little lady. Lemme buy you a drink."

She offered the balding man a smile, but shook her head in refusal. "Thanks all the same, but I'm on duty."

"Ah, that's okay, gal," boomed another man, this one taller than the first. His dark hair was slicked back, his eyes glassy with drink. "We won't tell anyone."

Cass smiled even brighter at him. She didn't have time to be detained, but as hotel management she had certain responsibilities. "I appreciate the offer, but I have several more hours ahead of me. No drinking on duty, you know."

The taller man grinned at the balding one. "You're a friend of Ashford's, aren't you, Len? You don't think he'd mind if we borrowed his gal here, do you?" He returned his leering gaze to Cass. "You *are* here to *serve* guests, aren't you?"

A nasty sense of déjà vu stole over her. Not quite two weeks had passed since Chet and his cohorts had pawed all over her. That night drugs had been responsible—she wasn't yet sure about tonight.

"If you'll excuse me, I really have to go." She moved away from the two, but the crowd pushed her back.

"Adam," the balding man slurred, "I think the little lady is shunning us." He raised a fat cigar to his mouth. "I distinctly remember old man Stirling bragging to my daddy that his staff provided any luxury a man could want."

"Well, well, well." Adam made a deliberate display of licking his lips, like a wolf moving in for the kill. "I definitely see a luxury I want."

Cass held herself rigid, but adrenaline raced. The bastards were talking about her as though she was a zoo animal up for auction. "Look, you're drunk and I'm—"

"A saucy one at that." Adam and Len closed in on her, trapping her against a back wall. All around her the party revved on, completely oblivious to her plight.

Plight. The word infuriated her. She was a cop, damn it. She'd graduated top of her class. She could take care of herself.

This helpless female role was for the birds.

Adam reached for her braid, what had been an erotic action when instigated by Derek was one that disgusted her now. He pulled it to his face, leaving her no choice but to follow close behind. The man reeked of whiskey and cigar smoke.

The woman in her disgusted, the cop incensed, Cass stomped her sharp heel down on his foot. His glassy eyes widened as he collapsed to the floor, cursing.

Len glanced at his friend, then turned furious eyes to her. "You little bitch," he swore, his beefy hands closing around her shoulders. The weight of his body crushed her against the wall. "I'll have your job for that."

"But not until I have *her*." Adam staggered to his feet. "You want it rough, then by God, rough it will be."

Diplomacy, firmness and martial arts down the toilet, Cass reached for the hidden pocket of her jacket.

"Oh, no you don't," Len chuckled, grabbing Cass's arm.

Adam took over, grabbing her other wrist and taking the one Len held to pin them above her head. His free hand closed around the collar of her jacket and yanked. Hard.

Black buttons popped free and clattered across the floor.

Fury tore through her. "Take your hands off me!" she growled. She again stomped her foot down on his, but he smiled more maliciously than before. "I don't really think you want to spend the night in jail," she warned.

"Finally, something we agree on." Leering, Adam

pawed at her. "The only place I'm spending tonight is in bed with you."

"Now that's where you're wrong."

The low, menacing voice surged through Cass. She had no time to think before Adam was wrenched away and thrown mercilessly to the ground. His body jerked once, then lay completely still. Out of the corner of her eye, she saw Len charge forward, then freeze dead in his tracks.

Derek. He stood there, dark eyes blazing with fury and challenge. "Cass," he said deliberately. "Come here."

She wanted to find relief in his appearance, but the dead calm of his voice triggered a surge of something far different. She went to him slowly, mechanically, gaze married to his. Her lungs worked frantically to process oxygen, but nothing could keep up with the frenetic beating of her heart.

The second she was within his reach, he pulled her to his side. Only then did he look away from her to where Adam lay unconscious on the ground.

"Call security," he barked to Gray in his bellman uniform, who had raced in behind him. "And get these bastards the hell out of here, before they end up spending the night at the bottom of the river."

Not a word was spoken as Derek dragged her from the deathly quiet ballroom. The card tables were vacant, slot machines still, roulette wheels deserted. Bankers and dealers and waitresses alike parted like the Red Sea to give them room.

Cass held her jacket together with one clenched fist. She stumbled after Derek, her straight, tight skirt no match for his long, furious strides.

"Derek—"

He glanced back at her, his eyes hotter and harder than before. Never had she witnessed such potent rage. The blue of his eyes, normally a seductive shade of cobalt, bordered on black. Every angle of his face looked sharper.

Never had Cass feared Derek Mansfield. Not in the way

a cop fears a suspect with a high-powered assault weapon, nor the way a woman might fear a man. But never had she seen him like this, like she had done the unthinkable and crossed an uncrossable line.

Her heart slammed against her lungs.

He held her hand clenched in his and led her down the spiraling staircase and across the hardwood floor, toward the elevator room. Not even when Cloyd said hello did Derek utter a word. With a curt nod he strode into the elevator and closed the door before the older man could join them.

He pressed the button for the penthouse and stared straight ahead but didn't say a word.

Instinct warned Cass the real danger had finally begun.

PLAY

Lucky 7

777

and you can get

FREE BOOKS AND A FREE GIFT!

PLAY LUCKY 7
and get
FREE Gifts!

Lucky 7

HOW TO PLAY:

1. With a coin, carefully scratch off the gold area at the right. Then check the claim chart to see what we have for you — **2 FREE BOOKS** and a **FREE GIFT** — **ALL YOURS FREE!**

2. Send back the card and you'll receive two brand-new Silhouette Intimate Moments® novels. These books have a cover price of $4.50 each in the U.S. and $5.25 each in Canada, but they are yours to keep absolutely free.

3. There's no catch. You're under no obligation to buy anything. We charge nothing — **ZERO** — for your first shipment. And you don't have to make any minimum number of purchases — not even one!

4. The fact is, thousands of readers enjoy receiving books by mail from the Silhouette Reader Service®. They enjoy the convenience of home delivery...they like getting the best new novels at discount prices, BEFORE they're available in stores...and they love their *Heart to Heart* subscriber newsletter featuring author news, horoscopes, recipes, book reviews and much more!

5. We hope that after receiving your free books you'll want to remain a subscriber. But the choice is yours — to continue or cancel, any time at all! So why not take us up on our invitation, with no risk of any kind. You'll be glad you did!

We can't tell you what it is...but we're sure you'll like it! A surprise **FREE GIFT** just for playing LUCKY 7!

visit us online at
www.eHarlequin.com

NO COST! NO OBLIGATION TO BUY!

NO PURCHASE NECESSARY!

**Scratch off the gold area with a coin.
Then check below to
see the gifts you get!**

YES! I have scratched off the gold area. Please send me the 2 Free books and gift for which I qualify. I understand I am under no obligation to purchase any books as explained on the back and on the opposite page.

345 SDL DNKT   245 SDL DNKN

FIRST NAME   LAST NAME

ADDRESS

APT.#   CITY

STATE/PROV.   ZIP/POSTAL CODE   (S-IMA-04/02)

Worth **2 FREE BOOKS** plus a **FREE GIFT!**

Worth **2 FREE BOOKS!**

Worth **1 FREE BOOK!**

Try Again!

Offer limited to one per household and not valid to current
Silhouette Intimate Moments® subscribers. All orders subject to approval.

DETACH AND MAIL CARD TODAY!

The Silhouette Reader Service® — Here's how it works:

Accepting your 2 free books and gift places you under no obligation to buy anything. You may keep the books and gift and return the shipping statement marked "cancel." If you do not cancel, about a month later we'll send you 6 additional books and bill you just $3.80 each in the U.S., or $4.21 each in Canada, plus 25¢ shipping & handling per book and applicable taxes if any.* That's the complete price and — compared to cover prices of $4.50 each in the U.S. and $5.25 each in Canada — it's quite a bargain! You may cancel at any time, but if you choose to continue, every month we'll send you 6 more books, which you may either purchase at the discount price or return to us and cancel your subscription.

*Terms and prices subject to change without notice. Sales tax applicable in N.Y. Canadian residents will be charged applicable provincial taxes and GST.

If offer card is missing write to: Silhouette Reader Service, 3010 Walden Ave., P.O. Box 1867, Buffalo NY 14240-1867

BUSINESS REPLY MAIL
FIRST-CLASS MAIL   PERMIT NO. 717-003   BUFFALO, NY

POSTAGE WILL BE PAID BY ADDRESSEE

SILHOUETTE READER SERVICE
3010 WALDEN AVE
PO BOX 1867
BUFFALO NY 14240-9952

NO POSTAGE
NECESSARY
IF MAILED
IN THE
UNITED STATES

Chapter 9

He stood with his back to her. In one hand he held a tumbler of whiskey, but other than that first hearty swig, he'd not brought it to his lips. He just stared out the window, feet shoulder width apart, body alert.

Cass had no way of knowing what he saw there, the darkness of the night or the darkness of something else.

Adrenaline surged through her, delivering a sickening sense of destiny. Events building toward this showdown had been put in place long ago. Month by month, week by week and, more recently, day by day, the dominoes were crashing down.

The tension in the room stretched strong and thick, almost drugging. And because of that, Cass couldn't believe her life was in danger. A man like Derek would never be satisfied with something as simple as life or death.

Betrayed, he would settle for nothing less than her soul.

"Are you going to say something," she asked, "or just stand there all night?"

"You don't want me to talk right now."

The timbre of his voice, deathly low though it was, soothed more than it should have. "Then perhaps I should leave."

"I'll pretend you didn't say that."

Her heart raced toward a destination she couldn't conceive. "I'm on duty. I should be down with the guests, not playing truth or dare with you."

"On duty," he repeated silkily, but wouldn't look at her. "I wonder why that thought didn't pop into your pretty little head before you pranced into the ballroom?"

Look at me, she silently seethed. "I was doing my job," she said through gritted teeth.

He still didn't turn around. "Your job is to man the reception desk. Your job is to be available to guests who need you. Your job is *not* to continually throw yourself into situations you are not equipped to handle."

Her throat tightened. "Are you talking to me as employer to employee? Or man to woman?"

The challenge slipped free before she could consider the consequences.

He stiffened. "What do you think?"

"What I think doesn't matter."

He threw back his whiskey, let the tumbler drop from his fingers. It thudded against the rug, didn't shatter.

Cass wanted to lay her hands against his stiff back, let her fingers ease the tension from his muscles. Only a few days had passed since she'd held him in her arms—since he'd held *her* in *his* arms. But it seemed like a lifetime.

She took a step toward him—

He pivoted toward her. "Do you get off on it, fearless?" he demanded, his voice hard and punishing.

She stilled, one hand holding her buttonless jacket together, the other pressed to her heart.

"Is that how you get your kicks now?" he went on, ruthlessly, "by playing superwoman? By playing damsel in distress, forcing someone to come rescue you?"

Temper sparked and sputtered. "No one forced you to *rescue* me."

"I'm going to pretend you didn't say that, too."

Cass bit back a startled gasp. When he looked at her like that, all concerned and protective and angry, she found herself struggling to think like a cop, longing to be just a woman falling in love. "Derek—"

"Don't Derek me!" He started toward her, his long legs destroying the space between them. When he reached her, he wrapped his hands around her upper arms and pulled her to him.

Her head snapped back. "Derek, stop it!"

"My, my, my," he drawled. "What a long way we've come, and in such a short time, too." He pulled her closer. "It seems like just yesterday you were standing in this very office, your head thrown back in a dare, smiling that seductive smile of yours, toying with me. Then you resisted saying my name. Now you can't stop repeating it. Have I grown on you that much, doll?"

A wicked thrill whirred through her. Warning. Anticipation.

"You..." She swallowed and tried again. "You give yourself far too much credit."

He looked down to where she held her ruined jacked clenched in her hand. "I don't want credit."

"What *do* you want?" she challenged. "My undying gratitude?"

His eyes glittered. "Not even close."

Her hand fell away. The crimson fabric parted, revealing her black lacy bra lapping neatly at her swelling breasts. They tingled beneath the flimsy fabric, even more beneath his languorous gaze.

"So beautiful," he murmured. One of his hands slid over her shoulder and down toward her breast. With his index finger, he gently skimmed her bra strap, teasing as much as taunting, threatening as much as promising.

Then the fury returned to his face. "Damn it, Cass," he swore, ripping himself free of her. He strode to the sidebar, poured another whiskey, downed it in one gulp. "I'm beginning to think you have some kind of twisted death wish."

Cass sucked in a sharp breath. Not the first time she'd been accused of such, but every time before, the accusation had come from someone who claimed to love her. Her mother and father. Her brothers. Gray.

"Don't be ridiculous," she snapped.

He scowled. "All I've done since we met is pull you out of one scrape or another."

"Nobody appointed you my guardian angel," she pointed out snidely. She didn't need him looking out for her, damn it. Didn't want it.

"You don't get it, do you?" His eyes took on a fevered glow. Funny. The angrier he became, the more dangerous he looked, the more she longed to feel his arms close around her.

"You think Chet and his buddies were just playing? They were high as a kite that night, Cass. If I hadn't shown up, they would've turned you into their personal play toy. Then there was the park. How many nights did you think you could stand in the freezing cold, without even a damn jacket, and not catch your death? If I hadn't gotten tired of watching—" He swore softly. "And what about tonight? You think those bastards were just shooting the breeze with you? If Ruth hadn't paged me—"

The ferocity of his words, his voice, his eyes, held her riveted. This was no mere employer-employee lecture, nor a simple exchange between a man and a woman. It was—

She didn't want to attach a name to what it was.

But deep inside, she knew.

God help her, she'd always known.

"Good God, Cass, one of these times I might not be able to get to you in time, then what?"

No way to answer the anger in that question, not with words. So she did the only thing she could, the only thing she wanted to. She walked straight up to him, raised up on tiptoes and pressed her lips to his.

And that was all it took. His arms closed around her with stunning force, pinned her to his body. His mouth slanted over hers, hungrily, almost desperately, demanding all she had to give.

The urgent kiss raced on. And on. Nothing gentle about it, nothing tame, nothing civilized. A wild mating of their mouths, a bold prophecy of what lay ahead. Cass vaguely remembered the sensation from before, but nothing prepared her for the homecoming she found in Derek's possession.

And that's what it was. Possession.

That should have stopped her cold. It didn't.

Derek tore his mouth from hers and glowered down at her. "Don't you learn? You keep playing with fire, darling Cassandra, and one of these days you're going to get burned."

She flicked her braid over her shoulder. "Maybe I like fire," she managed, her body and soul already consumed by it.

"I don't want to burn you, Cass."

"I'm not sure you'll have a choice."

His eyes, full of passion mere moments before, narrowed into cold slits of cobalt. He held her gaze a moment longer before striding across the room and jabbing the button to slide open the door.

"You should leave," he commanded, stepping back as she neared him. "Before I do something we'll both regret."

Regret. The prophecy of his words killed the rest of her passion. He was right. She had to go.

It took effort, but she pulled herself together and strode across that beautiful, damnable rug, walked out the door.

The panel slid shut behind her.

* * *

"Look, sir, there she is."

Derek swung toward the far monitor in time to see a pale Cass emerge from the restroom. She'd either donned a new jacket or repaired the one she'd worn earlier. With her hair still trapped in its trademark French braid, she looked tidy as a pin, spooked as a wild horse. She glanced around the foyer, found a smile, strolled toward the desk.

The transformation amazed Derek. Had he not witnessed it, he would never have believed she could be so chameleonlike. She was an operator, all right. Smooth as silk, strong as steel.

The front desk camera picked her up, but as Derek tracked her progress, the previous screen snagged his attention. A man emerged from the restroom. The bellman. He, too, tracked Cass's progress back to the reception area.

Fury lit through Derek. He'd heard the occasional rumor about hotel affairs, even a mention or two about Cass and John Dickens. But he'd never substantiated the claims, particularly not after she'd come apart in his arms.

The middle monitor granted an unencumbered view of Cass absently destroying one of the red roses he'd personally ordered for the front desk. For her.

Unfinished business smoldered between them. That one reality hit him blindside, and the inevitability of what lay ahead had him slamming his fist against the chief of security's desk.

"Problems, Mr. Mansfield?"

Derek gave him a curt smile, then stalked from the room.

Thirty minutes later he sat behind his mammoth desk, hands linked behind his head, watching John Dickens slowly enter his domain. The bellman walked haltingly, a lowly slave entering the lion's den. Dickens's palpable fear went a long way toward assuring Derek that Cass would never be attracted to such a weak man.

She was a strong woman. She needed a strong man.

"Mr. Mansfield." Dickens stopped a good five feet from the desk. "I was told you wanted to see me."

Eat him alive, more like it. "Do you like working here?"

"Yes, sir. Very much, sir."

"Do you value your job?"

Dickens's shoulders straightened. "Yes, sir. Stirling Manor has been good to me, sir."

Derek observed the man's every action, every response, every breath. "Do you believe in the sanctity of marriage?"

Dickens's eyes narrowed in confusion. "Of course."

Derek surged to his feet and leaned across the desk, splaying his palms against the rough wood surface. "Then stay the hell away from Cassandra LeBlanc, or you will not only find yourself without a job, but without a wife."

Something hot and volatile flicked through Dickens's eyes. Then it vanished. "I don't know what you're talking about."

"Then hell you don't," Derek growled. He tried to hold his anger in check, knew exposing it would reveal a vulnerability. "I saw you two tonight, how upset she was, the gleam in your eyes." He paused, dragging out the moment. "So help me God, you hurt one hair on her head, you're a dead man."

John Dickens squared his shoulders and advanced on his boss. "What's between me and Cass is my business and her business. I fail to see where it's hotel business."

"It's not hotel business. It's *my* business. And because I employ you both, I can make it hotel business if I choose. Cassandra LeBlanc is off-limits to you and every other member of this staff."

Dickens looked ready to chew nails. "She's my friend, damn it."

"She can be your *friend*," Derek ground out, "but rest assured. *Friendship* is not what I want from her. Do I make myself clear?"

Censure glittered in the other man's eyes. "Crystal."

* * *

Cass ventured down the semidarkened hall to the elevator room. Cloyd had retired for the night. Even the casino party had quieted down, most of the financiers having staggered to bed by the time the grandfather clock chimed the witching hour.

Technically, she was off duty and free to go home. Gray had done so a while before, but only after securing her word she would leave soon herself. He'd been tense, almost angry. She'd accused him of holding out on her, but he'd insisted there was nothing she needed to know.

She didn't quite believe him.

Time was running out. The chief was impatient, tensions around the manor at the boiling point. Gray and Derek were both watching her like hawks.

She couldn't go on like this, torn between woman and cop. It wasn't healthy, wasn't sane, sure as hell wasn't productive. One of them had to win, but not until she had proof. Either of Derek's innocence or his guilt.

Once in the elevator, she pressed the button for the penthouse. Derek had come downstairs hours before and vanished through the front doors, no doubt returning to the exquisite mansion north of the city. Cass couldn't blame him for preferring to spend his nights there, and she welcomed the opportunity to toss his office one more time.

As always, the watching, knowing eyes of his ancestors tracked her progress down the hall. And as always, she ordered herself to ignore them. They were dead—they could do her no harm. The only man who could harm her had vacated the building.

She made quick work of the lock on his door. The alarm sounded immediately, but because she'd studied him carefully when they entered together, she had no trouble silencing it.

Darkness filled the spacious office, but Cass could envision his tall form silhouetted against the window. He wasn't there, only the lingering smell of sandalwood and smoke. The potency gave her pause, sent her heart strumming through her chest. Never had a man unnerved her so. Not even Randy.

And that unnerved her even more.

Being in Derek's domain without him seemed a violation of some ridiculous trust she knew didn't exist. Nevertheless, uneasy, she went to work. His desk. His filing cabinets. The sidebar. The leather sofa. Under the thick Aubusson rug. She didn't know what she was looking for, a stash, notes, a plan, just knew she would know when she found it.

"You're a bold woman, Cassandra LeBlanc."

Cass jerked up to a crouch. Adrenaline surged. Her heart hammered. "De-rek."

A slow smile revealed his white teeth. "I love the way you say my name like that, all hot and breathy. My, my, we really have come a long way."

He stood in the shadows across the room, tall and still, watching her. A wicked light gleamed in his eyes, a panther who'd just cornered his prey.

She hadn't even heard him approach.

"What's the matter, fearless?" He moved stealthily across the carpet. "Cat got your tongue?"

She opened her mouth to speak, no words came out. No taunts, no denials, no excuses. She'd been reckless to slip up here without Gray to cover her. Even a rookie knew the folly of that, the danger of being caught redhanded.

She'd known it, too.

Perhaps that's why she'd been unable to stay away.

Derek stopped inches from where she remained crouched on the floor. He towered over her, his long legs shoulder width apart, hands shoved into the pockets of his trousers. His smoky-blue eyes simmered. "I warned you to leave before it was too late."

Somehow she managed to swallow. And breathe. Force words through her burning throat.

"It's already too late, Dare—we both know that."

He stared at her wide amber eyes, her tempting scarlet lips. She looked like a Greek goddess, poised for battle, eager for surrender. And he was more than ready to claim her.

But she was in his office. In the middle of night. When she obviously thought he had gone. That one fact doused the fire sizzling through him, at least temporarily. The sight of her on the security monitors, sneaking down the hall toward his office, had turned his blood to ice. The implications were heinous, didn't bear thinking. But he was a cautious man, in a dangerous game of cat and mouse. Not following up on his suspicion could only lead one place, a place he didn't want to go.

He'd learned that the hard way.

Cass shifted, sliding her long legs out from under her and curling them toward her side. The straight skirt slid farther up her thighs.

Derek suppressed a savage groan, then freed his hands from his pockets and rested them on his hips. The fierce stance had intimidated many a woman, many a man, but Cass merely gazed up at him with wide, beckoning eyes.

"That smile won't work this time, doll." He did a quick survey of his office, looking for anything out of place, finding nothing. "This room is off-limits. You know that."

She glanced down at the rug, back up at him. Then she held out her hand, where a ruby teardrop rested in her palm. "I lost an earring," she answered haltingly. "They're special to me, and—"

"And finding it couldn't wait until tomorrow?"

Her fingers closed back around the mateless earring. "There was no one here. I didn't think you would mind."

"I see." A blind man could have seen through her

story. "Having a passkey does not give you permission to access my office as you please and disarm my security system." He stepped closer, closed his hands around her upper arms and pulled her to her feet. She tilted her head to look at him, and when she did, the combination of fear and defiance in her eyes twisted his gut. "You don't expect me to buy that, do you?"

She didn't bat a lash. "Buy what?"

"Breaking and entering, hotel employee or not, is still a crime." He pulled her closer. "I gave you every chance I could, but you just don't listen. You know what happens now, don't you?"

Eyes wide, lips parted, braid draped over her shoulder, she nodded. Slowly. Provocatively.

Derek slid one hand along her shoulder, to the neckline of her crimson jacket. There, he lingered, traced her collarbone. "The truth, Cass. That's all I've ever wanted from you."

"All?"

"Everything." Inevitability burned through him. He'd tried. God, he'd tried. But the writing was on the wall, and rather than erase it, he could only heed it.

His fingers slid lower, to one of the ornamental buttons. A quick flick had it slipping through its restraint, baring the creamy skin of Cass's chest.

"You're a smart lady. We both know no one enters my office without my knowledge." He glanced toward the surveillance camera in the far corner of the room. "You had to know I would find you. Is that what you really wanted?"

Her eyes widened, revealing a flicker of uncertainty. Then it faded, replaced by languid fire. Licking her lips, she mouthed, "Yes."

More a rush of air than a word, but Derek's body responded, tightening, a warrior priming for the kill.

He was doing it again, he realized in some dimly lit corner of his brain. He was dragging someone down into his world. But staying away from Cass was no longer an option. He pulled her against his body, savoring the feel of her softness molding against his hardness. Their mouths met in a frenzied union, no time wasted for tender hellos, only the desperation of a reunion long denied. Their lips parted, giving way to searching tongues.

The mating of their mouths unleashed the full torrent of his need. He tore at the remaining buttons of her jacket, ruining the second of the night.

He couldn't have cared less.

His hands, followed by his mouth, sought out her breasts.

A black lace bra. There one second, gone the next. Two puckered nipples. Lonely one moment, adored the next. One with his fingertips. The other with his mouth.

Cass moaned and writhed in his arms. Head thrown back, body arched tight as a bow, her own hands fumbled with the fly of his jeans. It was happening too fast, too frantically. But as her fingers closed around his painfully hard shaft and began caressing its length, Derek knew they'd passed the point of no return. "Cass..."

Dazed amber eyes met his. "You," she breathed. "I was looking for you. That's all I want."

Her words wrapped around his heart. "You don't deserve—"

"This isn't about deserving." She returned her mouth to his. "This is about wanting...feeling."

And too strong for him to refuse. She looked so intoxicating standing there, nude from the waist up, breasts inviting him home. He was only a man, with a man's needs, a man's desires.

"I'll make you feel," he promised, reaching around and unfastening the back of her skirt. With guidance, it slid down and pooled at her feet, revealing two long legs and a pair of skimpy black panties, all encased by silk hose.

But not for long. Like a peasant paying homage, he

dropped to his knees and slid the restrictions from her shapely legs, freeing first one, then the other. All that remained between them was the black lace of her panties.

"I'll make you feel," he vowed again. Kneeling, he wrapped his arms around her waist and pressed his face to her hot skin.

She was trembling. His brave, fiery Cass was trembling.

He dipped lower, took the black lace between his teeth, continued the journey to the floor, urging her panties down with him, until she stood before him, naked and beautiful.

And trembling.

"Now," was all he said, all he needed to say. He lapped at the core of her femininity, kissing her in the most intimate way possible, tasting and loving. On a moan, she sank to her knees, fluidly rolling with him so that he lay sprawled above her.

"It's time to forget, Cass. Let me make you forget."

She answered not with words, but hands. They closed around him and guided him toward her slippery opening.

"Make me forget, Derek. Make me forget."

He wanted to draw it out longer than this. He wanted champagne and silk. He wanted them both gloriously naked, not half dressed on the floor, pawing at each other like rutting animals. But when her legs fell open and her body ushered him home, he forgot about wanting, and could think only of need. Basic, primal need. He pushed inside her.

"De-*rek*," she gasped. She was small and tight, almost virginal, not at all like a woman who'd given birth. Of course, that had been many years ago, another lifetime. In this lifetime the upward tilt of her hips welcomed him, urged him deeply inside. She shoved her hand through his unbound hair, dug the fingers of her other hand into his back. She was claiming him, consuming him, sucking him into her world.

No longer did he know who was taking whom, who

was making whom forget. He was only aware of Cass, the way her body sheathed his, the driving need that had him pumping into her as though their very lives depended upon it.

Because in a terribly real way, they did.

For Cass the feelings came so fast and furiously she could only savor. Heat and greed, need, regret. Salvation.

Two measly weeks before, that would have stopped her cold. And had her laughing out loud. Salvation in a criminal's arms. What a farce. But it wasn't a farce, because deep in her heart Cass didn't believe Derek Mansfield a criminal. He was a man. A fiercely gentle, savagely possessive, violently loyal man.

And for that one perfect moment in time, he was hers. When tomorrow came—''

Her body shuddered and jerked as they both tumbled over the jagged edge of release. Her legs closed around his, clenching him as tightly to her as she could.

When tomorrow came…

The thought didn't merit finishing.

Too often, tomorrow never did.

Chapter 10

She stood facing him, alone but for the eyes of God. Her whole life flashed before her, the triumphs, the tragedy. Her wedding to Randy. Jake's birth. The funeral. She'd loved them with all her heart but hadn't been able to keep them safe. They'd paid for her sins, her decision, her loyalty to the badge.

She'd paid, too, the most devastating price imaginable. Now someone else's life rested in her hands.

She'd heard salvation took on the most unexpected, unrecognizable of faces, but she'd never imagined this.

Mansfield stood before her, the beautiful day dancing behind him, an azure sky and glistening lake, sailboats. His fathomless eyes were concentrated solely on her. She'd thought them go-to-hell, but she'd never expected them to send her there as well.

And she'd never expected hell to be rooted in heaven.

Impossible not to look at him and feel the promise of life flood her. He had that way about him, of making her feel she was the only woman in the world. Yet when she moved beyond the hard eyes and grim mouth, beyond the long hair and flamboyant earring, when she moved beyond all that, she found more. Depth and intensity. Salvation and redemption. Eternity. And longing.

She damn well might be the only woman, the only one in this whole world, who could save him, not just from the law, but from himself. "Derek..."

His hard eyes softened. "I'm here, honey."

"Derek..."

"Shh." He cupped her cheek in the palm of his hand. "You're not alone anymore."

The timbre of his voice soothed as much as his caress. But another hand touched her body. It fell firmly against her shoulder, urged her back from Derek.

"It's time, Cass," came Gray's somber voice. "Time to choose."

The splendor of the sun-drenched afternoon gave way to a fierce wind.

"No," she cried. "I can't do it—*don't make me do it.*"

"You have to," Gray urged, pulling back.

The years of loyalty and trust between them told Cass she should go with Gray. But one night of passion held her rooted in place. Her gaze locked in a painful communion with Derek's. Confusion loitered there, the dawning of betrayal. "No-o-o-o."

"Cass..."

"Doll..."

"It's time to choose," Gray warned.

"I'll make you forget," Derek promised.

The tug-of-war stretched her to the breaking point.

"Cass," Gray said, "you have a job to do. Do it."

"Doll," Derek rasped, "you have a life to live. Live it."

They were ripping apart the carefully reconstructed threads of her life. "I can't do this," she screamed at them both. At herself. "I can't do this again! I won't. I—"

"Cass." His voice rang loud and true, the sanctuary

she'd been seeking. Another hand joined the first, gently shaking her. "Cass, doll, it's me. I'm here."

"No-o-o-o."

"Cass," he said again, sternly this time. "Wake up." Heat and safety, harbor. His arms encircled her, pressing her trembling body against the warmth of his chest.

It all came tumbling back, every glorious, damning detail.

She went to him, willingly, holding him as tightly as he held her.

"Cass." He tilted her chin toward his. "You okay?"

She looked at the concern in his eyes and wished she could say yes. That she could lose herself in his arms, that the truth wasn't hot on her heels. The dominoes were tumbling faster, racing toward the end. Everything would lay in ruins then, all the carefully prepared dominoes, all the compassion Derek had offered, the dreams he'd stoked.

Her life. His.

Yet the chief would be happy, and she would have done her job.

She wasn't okay. She wasn't sure she ever would be again. But she nodded, because she could do nothing else.

Dry humor tilted his lips. "Care to tell me about it?"

The wee hours of the morning came back to her, the urgency and need, the passion. Heaven and hell neatly combined and gift wrapped to boot. "It's not important," she hedged, surprised by the hoarseness of her own voice.

With one long finger he gently stroked the length of her cheekbone. "It made you cry—that makes it important."

Her heart vaulted to her throat. "Not now."

He studied her a moment, pulled her back into his arms. Rather than a return to the mindless passion of before, he simply held her, rocked her, blanketed her with his warmth.

Time stood still. And for a fleeting eternity, the world

lost meaning. There was only Derek, the way he made her feel.

Feel. When she got down to it, therein lay the heart of the matter. Derek brought her senses to life, her heart and soul beating in an urgent, insistent rhythm.

And for that one precious moment, feeling was all that mattered.

A sliver of sunlight slashed in through the partially open drapes and fell across Cass's nude body. Derek's bare chest rose and fell beneath her ear, yet instead of slipping from his arms and exploring the secret bedroom chamber, she nestled closer.

She was in way over her head. And God help her, she didn't want out.

It didn't make any sense. How could a man touch her so deeply, give her so much compassion and support, and yet have no scruples, no regard for right and wrong?

The question, its answer, taunted her.

She lay sprawled over Derek like a concubine adorning her master—her leg slung over his, head on his chest, arm draped over his abdomen. An odd intimacy had descended over them, a peaceful cloak of rightness. She refused to let reality intrude.

The first time had been fast and frenzied, an explosion of passion too long denied. She'd known it was going to happen the second he found her in his office. Someday, she supposed, she would come to terms with whether that was why she'd been there in the first place.

He'd carried her to the paneled wall at the far corner of his office. Groggy and dazed and not thinking at all, much less like a cop, she'd almost gasped when he fumbled with a gilded frame and sent a walnut panel sliding open. He'd stepped through the doorway and into a darkened room. A bedroom, she realized. One she'd never known existed, that could hold the key to her investigation.

But none of that mattered then, just as it didn't matter now.

Everything blurred after that. The lighting of the candles, the removal of their clothing, the long, sudsy bath in an enormous marble tub, the hours of thorough, deliberate, erotic lovemaking. Like an out-of-body experience, she'd hung on for the ride, the sensations too intense, too shattering for a mere dream. Everything they'd done had been real. Any doubt of that diminished when she opened her eyes and found herself sprawled over his body.

"Do you have any idea how good you feel?"

Derek's groggy voice surprised her. She glanced up into his eyes, felt warmth spread through her. "If it's half as good as you feel, we might never leave this bed."

He laughed. "Fine by me."

The warm honey of desire started all over again. "What we just did is illegal in several states—you know that, don't you?"

A wicked smile curved his mouth, lit his eyes. "Then arrest me."

The words hit Cass like brass knuckles. She stiffened, battled back a reality she didn't want to acknowledge.

Tensing, Derek slid from under her and lay on his side, facing her. Whiskers covered his jaw, sensuality glowed in his eyes. "What is it? Why the frown?"

"Nothing." The lie squeezed her heart.

His expression sharpened. "Like hell, nothing." He sat up abruptly and swore under his breath.

"What?" she asked, sitting as well. She clutched the sheet to her breasts.

"This." He gestured to the tangled sheets, the remnants of clothing strewn across the floor. "Deny it all you like, tell me nothing's wrong, but I can see it in your eyes. The doubt, the regret. The realization that you deserve better."

Shock speared through Cass. She couldn't believe how quickly he'd gone from sensuous lover to judge and jury. "Better?" she asked. "Than what?"

An unnerving intensity glittered in his eyes. "Me. Last night." He swore again. "I didn't want it to be like that. I didn't want to take you on the office floor. I wanted silk for you. I wanted champagne."

His words floored her. Simply knocked her flat.

"Funny," she whispered. "You gave perfection."

He winced.

"There were two of us in that room last night," she went on, before he could say anything else. "You, and me. And I'd have to say, we definitely took each other."

"Cass—"

She fought the memory, accepted the implication. She'd crossed the line, knowingly and willingly. "It was bound to happen, as inevitable as earthquakes along fault lines."

He lifted a hand to her face, gently stroked the hair back behind her ear. "Then why do you look like you want to cry?"

Because she did. She didn't know how he did it, how he saw beneath the surface to the truth inside. The fact that he did alarmed her. What else would he see, if he kept looking?

What would he discover?

What would he touch and caress?

What would he heal next?

That was easy. He wouldn't discover anything, touch anything, heal anything.

She wouldn't let him.

She couldn't.

"You're a good man," she told him. They had no future, but she couldn't let him doubt himself. Too many others had cast stones his way. "You're strong and caring, compassionate."

"I'm afraid you've got me confused with a Boy Scout," he said darkly.

She bit back a broken laugh. "You helped me face a

pain I've tried to wall away. I don't want you to regret what happened between us. It was inevitable.''

''But?''

''But I don't know where we go from here.''

''We can go anywhere we want to.''

''Last night was incredible,'' she said with a sad smile. ''Unbelievable. More than I ever dreamed possible. But it doesn't change the truth of who and what we are.''

He narrowed his eyes. ''You're a provocative woman, I'm a healthy man. What's the problem?''

''You and your brother own this hotel.''

Derek laughed. ''And?''

''Mixing business and pleasure isn't smart.'' The double edge of her words cut deeply. ''Lines exist for a reason. Crossing them only leads to trouble.''

The inevitability of her words ripped at her.

''Lines are temporary,'' Derek countered. He ran his hand down her side, from her rib cage to the valley of her waist, down the hill of her hips. ''Lines are for the weak, the cowardly. We can change them anytime.''

Everything inside Cass tightened. Melted. ''It's not that easy.''

''Why not? Weren't you the one who just said making love was inevitable?''

He'd done it again, twisted her words into weapons. The man didn't play fair. And because of that, neither could she. The cop in her knew she had to leave as soon as she could, or find a way to investigate the hidden room.

But the woman in her...the woman was beginning to think the cop was a fool.

She struggled to free herself from his arms, but the more she struggled, the more he domineered. ''You said you wanted it to be just you and me,'' she tried, ''no friends, no ghosts. I...I can't give you that.''

She could have sucker-punched him in the gut and not caused him to withdraw as viciously. ''Are you telling me we weren't alone last night? That Randy was with us?''

The allegation provided the perfect deterrent, but the betrayal in his tone, his eyes, kept her from grasping it. "That's not what I'm saying."

"Then—"

"Forget it." Guilt swamped her. She couldn't use Randy's death like that. It wasn't fair to Randy, wasn't fair to Derek. What kind of woman was she to sink that low? To throw the death of her husband into her lover's face?

There was only the truth now, as much of it as she could give without ruining everything. "I wanted this, yes. But this attraction between us, the intensity of it frightens me. Randy and I...we never had that," she admitted.

And it scared her to death. Her relationship with Randy had been comfortable and predictable, like an old terry cloth robe.

Derek was silk and fire.

His expression darkened. "What do you mean you never had that? You had a son together."

"We were friends more than lovers," she told him. Doing so seemed important. Vital. "He was a good solid man. We shared goals more than dreams, enjoyed our son together. But making love with him was kind of like brushing your teeth."

"Brushing your teeth?" Derek growled.

"Comfortable," she tried to explain. "Routine." Her heart was beating so fast she could barely speak. "He never..."

"Never what?"

"Looked at me like you do." The admission sounded devastatingly like a defeat.

Derek stilled, as though bracing himself for a punishing blow. "Looked at you like I do? And just how is that?"

Cass hesitated. She didn't know how to put it in words, didn't know if she should. Deepening the intimacy between them was dangerous.

But she could no more stop the pull than she could prevent the sun from rising.

"Like I'm the only woman in the world." The words tore out of her, shredding her heart along the way. "Like if you don't have me, you might just cease to exist."

Derek swore softly. He looked as though she'd gut punched him. "Looks are worth a thousand words, isn't that what they say?"

She bit back a sob. The truth, damn it. The truth was all she had. "I can't even think straight when you look at me like that, when you touch me." Couldn't focus on the case, the fact her job was to nail him to the wall. "I can't be that woman for you, Derek."

"Maybe you already are."

"Derek—"

He pulled her to him, cradled her against his chest. "I know you're scared, Cass." He tilted her head toward his. "I am, too. But I can promise you this. I'm not going to hurt you, not so long as I have a breath left in my body."

In his glittering eyes she saw an honesty and vulnerability that could easily destroy her. "Time, Derek. Please. I need time to figure out what's happening, how to deal with it."

To think, to breathe, to prepare herself for the brutal fallout from the lies she'd told, the truth she couldn't escape.

He frowned, looked as if she'd just asked him for the sun and moon and stars instead. "That's one thing I don't have to give."

"Derek—"

"Only now, Cass. Give me now."

His mouth claimed hers before she could protest. Instead she melted. Her body instinctively softened for him, his homecoming. No turning away, she realized.

Derek would never let her.

And when you got down to the inescapable truth, she

was exactly where she wanted to be. In his arms. In his bed.

In love.

Grandfather Stirling's house rose up against the winter day, creating the illusion of elegance despite the barren trees and gray sky. As a boy, Derek believed the house magical, fantasizing himself lord of the manor, that everything and everyone within its walls was within his control.

That one day he'd have it all.

Now those memories burned. After he finished his business in Chicago, he would never be back. It was one of those simple, inevitable facts, something he couldn't change even if he wanted to. His grandfather's house, the future he'd imagined, would never be his. He would never usher his wife through the doors and up the staircase, to the master chamber. He would never love her there, never hear the sound of his children's laughter ringing through the halls.

For the first time in too long, Derek found himself second-guessing what he'd never even questioned. Maybe it wasn't too late. Maybe he could make different choices from this point forward. Maybe he shouldn't be so hellbent on doing things his way, consequences be damned.

Maybe. Maybe, maybe, maybe.

Maybe he could bring Cass here. Maybe he could take her in his arms, carry her up the stairs, love her as thoroughly as he had the night before. Maybe it could be the sound of their children's laughter ringing through the halls. Maybe—

Maybe he was a fool.

His heart constricted, forcing him to shove the guessing game aside. Cass didn't belong here. He knew what would happen if he brought her for one day, one hour, one second. They'd make memories, unbearable memories that would haunt him long after their candle burned out.

Because it would burn out. It had to.

A sharp onslaught of wind cut through the trees, forcing their outstretched branches to shiver. Derek picked up a twig and rolled it through his fingers, just as memories and doubts rolled and tangled through his head.

"You bastard!"

Derek pivoted toward the angry voice. Brent stormed toward him, his sandy hair wild and tousled, his eyes hot.

"Well, good afternoon to you, too, baby brother."

"I always knew you had no scruples, but fool that I am, I thought *family* meant something to you."

The well-aimed jab hit below the belt. Derek held his face aloof, not wanting his brother to know how easily he could get to him. "What has you in such a dandy mood?" he asked blandly.

"It was pretty clever to turn off the video to your office, big bro, but apparently, in your blind lust, you made one critical mistake."

Derek had a bad feeling what came next. He didn't want to hurt his brother, but for once his own needs had come first.

"Oh?" he replied, twirling the twig between his fingers. "And what was that?"

"The hall camera. You left the hall camera on."

So he had, yet he hadn't known anybody else would be reviewing the tapes. He should have, though. Every time he labeled Brent harmless, his reckless brother proved him wrong. "Get to the point, bro. I don't have time for melodrama."

Brent charged him, something he hadn't made the mistake of doing since they were young boys.

He grabbed the collar of Derek's T-shirt. "I should've known the second I set eyes on her this morning, but I didn't think you would sink that low. Then I saw the video of her entering your office late last night, not leaving until almost noon this morning." He snorted. "Now I see you."

Derek placed his hands over his brother's and uncurled his fingers. "I see you, too, baby brother, but I really wish you would get to the point."

"I'll get to the point," Brent seethed. He let go of Derek's shirt and shoved his brother backward. "You dragged an innocent woman into your world. You threw her well-being to the wolves and just took her, because you wanted to." Brent sucked in a deep, ragged breath. "How could you do that to her? How could you not have even one trace of decency?"

Had the accusation come from anyone else, Derek would have leveled them with a swift kick to the gut. But this was Brent, the brother Derek had loved and protected his entire life, even if they butted heads every step of the way. And deep inside, Derek knew Brent was justified in his anger. He *had* dragged Cass into his world, something destined to bring her pain, more pain than anyone deserved.

Unless he could change events already set into motion.

But he wasn't about to let Brent waltz down this sanctimonious path. His brother had made mistakes, too. Dangerous mistakes that almost left Ryan to grow up without a father, just like Derek had.

"Don't pretend this is about protecting Cass, little brother. Don't pretend your world is any better than mine, because we both know you're no knight in shining armor. This is about want, little brother. The fact that you want her, but she wants me.

"I tried," Derek added, guilt getting the better of him. "I tried to stay away from her. Unfortunately, it didn't quite work that way."

"Like hell. You believe that, and you're going to find your sorry butt at the end of the line—or maybe the bottom of the river."

That said, he turned on his heel and stormed off toward his cherry-red convertible. The dry brown grass crunched beneath his angry steps, the wind whipped at his determination, but he never looked back. Amazing that such a pretty man could look so fierce. Without doubt, his brother was the angriest, edgiest, Derek had ever seen.

"Damn," he muttered under his breath, snapping the twig in two. He barely felt the sting of the wind as he watched his brother disappear down the gravelly drive and into the parade of naked trees.

"Oh, there you are!" Ruth exclaimed that afternoon. "I thought you'd *never* get here."

Cass removed her black felt hat and shook out her long hair. She didn't usually wear it loose, but with the bitter cold outside, she'd been reluctant to leave her throat and ears exposed. At least, that's what she told herself.

That Derek preferred her hair down had nothing to do with it. Nor did the red marks on her neck.

"What's up?" She slipped out of her wool coat and hung it on the rack inside the office door. "Something wrong?"

"Not something," Ruth teased. "Someone."

Cass stilled. Her first thought was Derek, that something had happened to him. Then the cop shoved aside the woman, and she thought of Gray, that his cover had been blown. "Someone?"

"Not just someone," Ruth supplied. She milked the silence for all its worth, a habit she'd picked up from Cass. "Him—Mr. Merry Sunshine. He's looking for you."

"Oh?" She posed the question innocently, trying to ignore the carnal melting deep inside. "I wonder what he wants."

"He's called down here every ten minutes, demanding to know why you're so late."

"Maybe I should go see him."

"Good idea. It's not smart to keep Mr. Mansfield waiting."

"Of course not." Cass moved around the desk and onto

the hardwood floor. She forced herself to walk slowly, when in truth she wanted to run. To Derek. Away from the truth. But she didn't. Nor did she glance into the mirror as she passed it. How she looked didn't matter. She was an employee going to see her employer, a cop going to see her suspect.

A woman going to see her lover.

That one truth burned. Somehow, some way, she had to find a way to erase the terrible lie she'd created. The second Derek discovered why she was really at the Stirling Manor, she could kiss their relationship goodbye.

Relationship. The word gnawed at her as she rode the elevator to the penthouse. *Relationship.* She didn't care for the rush the word created, the longing. Just because Derek had treated her to a night of incredible sex did not mean they were destined to share a great love affair.

Nor, for that matter, did it mean he was an innocent man.

But a place deep inside insisted that he was.

She took the long, ancestor-crowded corridor at a brisk pace. They were all staring at her, as usual, but this time they seemed to be assessing, judging, almost guarding Derek against mal intent.

Her.

The door to his office slid open. Before, she hadn't understood the perfect timing; now, she knew he tracked her by security monitors. Like last night. Thank God he'd accepted the earring story.

She needed to be more careful.

She needed to step back from the edge before she took a long, hard free fall.

"You're late." Derek was across the office before Cass could register what was happening, drawing her into his arms before she could put up a fight. His mouth swooped down on hers, claimed hers in a greedy hello. She responded instinctively, her whole body surging to life against the fire of his kiss. She pressed into him, tried not to moan when his hands sank into the loose locks of her hair.

He pulled back and glowered down at her. "Where were you?"

She tried to suck in a breath. Couldn't. "At home. Why are you looking at me like that? What's wrong?"

"No games. Your shift started over thirty minutes ago—where have you been?"

The suspicion in his voice struck a nerve. "Games?" She twisted free and stepped away. "I'm half an hour late, and you accuse me of playing games? Did it ever occur to you something could've happened? That I could've been ill? That I could've been in an accident? Could be hurt?"

The blood drained from his face. "Hurt?" He moved toward her, his eyes doing a slow survey of her body. "Who hurt you? What happened? Just tell me the name and I'll—"

Cass didn't know whether to laugh or cry. Or drop to her knees and beg for mercy. The abrupt switch from combat to concern caught her off guard and touched her deeply. Instead she launched herself into his arms and returned her lips to his.

"I'm fine," she murmured. "Just kiss me."

His hands were everywhere, sliding over her body, stoking fires that had been smoldering since earlier that day.

"Derek..." Pulling back, she stared up into his eyes and couldn't resist laying her hand against his cheek. "What's wrong? Why were you looking for me?"

A wicked smile curved his lips. "You have to ask?"

"Ruth said you sounded angry. Has something happened?"

"Yeah, something's happened, all right." He pulled her to him. "And it's going to happen again and again and again."

This time she did laugh. "Derek, I'm on duty."

"But I'm the boss."

"I—"

"More." He sprinkled kisses over her cheekbones, her eyes, her nose. "I told you, once would never be enough."

Infinity wouldn't be enough. In Derek she'd found something she'd never expected to find again, the will not just to move through life, but to dance, to sing and laugh, to savor each moment and look forward to those yet to come.

Her hands slid down his body to the bulge in his pants. Unable to suppress her answering moan, she began to rub, slowly, deliberately. "Not here," she murmured. "Not here."

A masculine groan tore from his throat as he lifted her into his arms and crossed the office. "I'm sorry," he ground out. His eyes blazed down at her, two sapphires on fire and in pain. "You deserve better than to be mauled every time I see you."

Her heart slammed against her chest. "It's not that—"

"You deserve candles and music, silk sheets and flowers." They slipped through the panel and into the adjoining bedroom suite. The orderly room bore little resemblance to the rumpled love nest she'd left earlier that day. Either Derek let a maid into the room, which meant he had nothing to hide, or he'd straightened the room himself.

"I don't need any of that," she told him. "Just you." Then she added truthfully, "But being with you like this here, at the hotel, makes me uncomfortable."

He looked down at her in confusion.

"This is where I work," she explained. "Everyone knows I just came up here. I can't start doing this. I can't disappear into you office for hours on end and—"

"You're worried about your reputation?"

The surprise in his voice cut like a knife. "Not my reputation. My life. My pride. My dignity. I don't want to be a casual roll in the hay, Derek.'' She wasn't sure where the words came from, but once they started, they took on a life of their own and refused to be quelled. ''I want it to be special, more than just sneaking off to your room for a quickie.''

For a moment he said nothing, just looked down at her. Then he closed his eyes, but not before she saw the self-loathing lurking there. ''Is that what you think this is? A quickie?''

She drew in a deep, jagged breath. ''Not for me.''

He opened his eyes, but they remained guarded. ''And for me?''

''I don't know.''

''You don't know?'' he growled. ''You—don't—know? What the hell kind of answer is that?''

The ache in her heart intensified. ''An honest one.''

He shoved a hand through his hair. Like hers, it was unbound and loose around his face.

An idea occurred, a measure to kill two birds with one stone.

''Let's get out of here, Derek. You're right. You're the boss—you can give me the night off, if you want.'' She cast the line and prayed he would bite. The need to prove his innocence drove her forward. ''Let's not waste it here at the hotel. Let's go somewhere special, wherever you vanish to most nights.''

Derek shook his head. ''What are you talking about?''

The estate, she wanted to scream. His domain. His lair. The magnificent house that protected his secrets.

''I've seen you leaving late at night, and you don't come back.'' When he began to retreat even further, physically and mentally, she rushed to finish. ''I'm on duty a lot of nights, and I've always been aware of you. I've seen you leave, and I've spent hours watching the door, waiting for you to come back. But you never do.''

He was across the room now, staring out the window. His lack of reaction chilled her to the core. The plan had seemed so brilliantly simple. Nothing unusual had been found anywhere within the hotel; he'd not been seen with Vilas. The house in the woods was the only other likely place for evidence. If Derek took her there, his lover, he had nothing to hide.

If he refused...she would have to rethink everything.

Something deep inside warned of touching it, yet she toppled a pivotal domino.

"Where do you go, Derek? And why don't you come back?"

Chapter 11

Derek stared out over the city. Around him lights twinkled and glared, laughing, taunting. Who had he been trying to kid? What kind of selfish jerk was he, thinking he could have Cass and keep her separate from his life? Of course she would want in. After the intimacy they'd shared, it was only natural to ask the questions she was asking and expect answers.

But he couldn't give them to her, not all of them. Not yet.

Maybe not ever.

"My grandfather has a house north of the city," he told her innocuously. "I spent a lot of time there as a kid." Still spent time there, when he wanted to forget the dangerous game he was playing and be just a man.

"It sounds lovely." Her hand rested against his shoulder, followed by her body to his back. "I'd like to see it."

And he could see her there, too. Too well. "Maybe sometime."

Cass slipped in front of him, eyes wide. "Tonight," she prompted. "Just the two of us. We're lovers now. We shouldn't keep secrets from each other."

He took in her upturned face, the gorgeous hair cascading around it, the hope radiating in her eyes. It would be easy to spirit her away to his grandfather's house, far from this world, this life. They could pretend there, hold destiny at bay.

But he knew the truth would be waiting around the corner, primed to shatter any idyllic spell he could create.

No one ever wanted him for who he was. Not his parents, not Marla, certainly not a class act like Cass. He wasn't sure what she wanted, maybe just the healing power of mindless sex, but he sensed the danger of indulging the heat between them.

"One night of mind-blowing sex," he forced himself to say, "doesn't mean I'm ready to take you to the family home, doll."

She staggered back. "We made love, Derek. We shared. We communicated. I thought—"

"That we'd be a couple now? An item?" Because he couldn't take much more, he parried even more viciously. "That we'd hold hands in the park and share hot cocoa? That we'd—"

Hurt registered in her eyes. Betrayal. And a devastating shimmer of tears. "Go to hell, Derek."

He held himself very still, when in truth he wanted to crush her to him and never let go. Instead he pushed even harder. "Ah, Cass. I'd rather not take you *there,* either, though I do seem to have a knack for the place."

She looked as if he'd just confessed to being Lucifer. "Just forget it," she rasped, then turned and strode from the room.

He didn't follow.

Three days crawled by. Three long, agonizing days, but not one word passed between Derek and Cass. Just looks.

Long, hot, soulful looks, those of brooding and hurt. Of anger.

And Cass withstood them all.

Then, that third night, while she stood at the front desk—picking at a new arrangement of white roses, everything changed. The front door swung open, and a woman breezed in. Cass recognized her instantly. She'd studied so many pictures, the woman's image was etched into her mind.

Marla Fairchild. The woman Derek had asked to be his wife. The mother he'd wanted for his children.

"Well, well, well," Ruth commented. "If it's not Lady Godiva herself."

Cass tried to laugh at the blatant sarcasm, but she was too preoccupied by the woman strolling toward her. Long, blond hair. Flawless skin. High cheekbones. Wide eyes. Full lips. Diamonds dripped from her ears, her neck, her fingers. A plush leopard-print swing coat danced around her long legs.

"Bet she's not wearing anything under that coat," Ruth snickered.

The same thought had already occurred to Cass, and with it rushed a primal surge of disgust. "And here I thought tonight was going to be business as usual."

"Just wait till the boss gets a load of her. Trust me, any hope you had of a dull evening will be long gone."

That's what she was afraid of. Derek was upstairs, she knew. The last time she'd seen him he'd been striding toward the elevator, sparing nothing but curt looks for those who dared to call his name. He'd been dressed to kill, his dark hair queued back, accenting his deep-set, go-to-hell eyes. A double-breasted, black Italian suit had completed the image.

"Tell Derey I'm on my way," she purred.

Cass pulled herself back from the fog and came face-to-face with the infamous Marla Fairchild. The woman stood boldly across the reception desk, looking down her elegant nose at her.

"I'm sorry," Cass replied coolly, "but Mr. Mansfield has asked not to be disturbed."

Ruth, who knew darn well Derek had said no such thing, shot her a puzzled look.

"Not to worry," Marla purred. "I'm not going to disturb him. Bother him, probably. Disturb him, never."

Cass stiffened, rejecting the punishing thoughts that swam forward. Derek had known this woman intimately. "Sorry," she returned, not missing a beat. Composure was something she'd never had problems maintaining; she wouldn't start now. "He specifically said he wanted to be alone."

The bold words were a gamble, but Cass needed to know if Derek had invited Marla to the hotel.

"He'll want to see me." Marla laughed, low and throaty. "Well, maybe not see," she conceded. "That's far too passive for my Derek. But the rest will hold true— trust me."

The innuendo slashed at Cass's heart. Take away the "see," and that left only the "want."

Of course Derek would want Marla. Cass knew firsthand what a voracious sexual appetite he had. She also knew she had turned her back on him. What had she been thinking? That he would come begging to heel? That he would haul her into his arms and tell her he was wrong, that he would take her to his grandfather's house and prove he was an innocent man?

That's what it came down to. She'd been so convinced that once she set foot in the estate, she would have proof of his innocence. But he'd foiled her plans, her dreams. He'd refused, without the courtesy of a viable reason. He'd simply refused.

That's why she was staying away. The last thing she needed was to fall back into his bed, if in only a matter of days she would be slapping cuffs around his wrists.

But now Marla was smirking at her, primed and ready to take Cass's place. "There's nothing I can do. Once Mr. Mansfield gives an order—"

"Marla." The husky voice resounded through the now-silent foyer. He strode toward them, still dressed like a mob hit man in his Italian suit, his hair still queued back.

The cameras—he'd foiled her again. She'd hoped to get rid of Marla before Derek could lay eyes on her, but he'd obviously caught sight of his fiancée on the surveillance cameras—the same cameras that had brought Cass into his arms, then his bed.

And now he was ignoring Cass, focusing on the dazzling blonde posing for him. Marla had turned toward him, left hip tilted forward, a perfectly elegant, diamond-clad hand resting there. Not just any diamond, either, but an engagement ring. And unless Marla had already gotten over him, which Cass doubted, the sparkling ring was the one Derek had given her.

But he didn't go to her, as Cass expected. He halted ten feet away, and merely stood there, a single brow arched in challenge. He was testing Marla, Cass recognized, refusing to go to her, making her go to him instead.

"Oh, Derey…" She rushed across the hardwood floor and flung herself into his arms. "It's been a long time."

"It certainly has."

Cass watched in an agonizing fog as Derek and Marla strolled toward the elevator. Their shoes clicked against the hardwood floor, taking them farther away from Cass and twisting the knife deeper into her heart.

The pain of it almost sent her to her knees.

Marla lay sprawled on the sofa. Her plush leopard print coat was bunched up around her thighs, revealing her long legs. She was just as icily beautiful as Derek remembered.

No wonder he'd never seen beyond the next tumble in the sack.

"I see six months haven't changed anything," he commented, curious to discover the reason for her visit.

Her pouty lips slumped into a frown. "How can you say that, Derey?" She shifted, her coat riding higher on her legs. "Six months have changed everything. We should be celebrating our half year wedding anniversary," she reminded. "Instead I can hardly get you to look at me."

Derek paused by the window. "And which stings worse, Marla? That we're not married, or that I'm not eating out of your hand?"

"You're being cruel."

"I'm being honest. Can you say the same?"

"Oh, Derey. Do we have to drag that up again?" she pouted. "How many times do I have to tell you I'm sorry?"

That was easy. "You don't."

Marla bolted to her feet and rushed to him, throwing her arms around his neck. "Do you mean it, Derey?" she gushed, glowing. "Are you finally ready to let go of the past?"

He stood ramrod stiff. "Sweetheart, I let go of the past the second I walked out that door."

She pulled back. "What are you trying to say?"

"I'm not trying to say anything," he told her bluntly. He stepped free of her clinging arms and moved out of her reach. "I *am* saying there is nothing you can say, nothing you can do, to erase what you've already done." That was the way it was with him: no second chances. Ever. "You used me. I was never anything more than a nifty little toy to help you win your dear daddy's respect."

Her bottom lip began to quiver. "That's not true."

"My God, Marla, do you think I'm an idiot?" The memories were whipping back now, slapping him all over again. "I was there. I saw the plans."

"They were just some stupid drawings, Derek." She

raised her hands, dropped them to her side. "Ideas and fantasies. Dreams."

Betrayals. "You can lie to yourself, but don't lie to me. We both know the truth. They were extensive, elaborate plans for the Edinburgh resort, drawn up and ready to roll."

Marla stepped toward him, paused when he cut his eyes. "My father owns an architectural firm. You knew that. Why was it so shocking we would want to bid on the Stirling resorts?"

Derek just stood there and stared at her. He'd thought himself in love with this woman, that he'd wanted her to bear his children.

"You know the damnedest part, Mar? If only you hadn't counted your chickens before they hatched, it would have all been yours. That was going to be my wedding gift to you, exclusive rights to every Stirling Manor from that point forward." He'd already had the paperwork prepared. "But you couldn't wait, could you? After so many months of whoring yourself for your father's company, you got sloppy when the end was so close you could taste it."

"That's not true!" she protested. "Maybe at first," she conceded, "but later, after I got to know you, I fell in love with you. How can you doubt that?"

He'd heard enough. They'd already had a scene like this once, the night before their wedding, when he'd confronted her with the drawings. He'd found them at the house he'd built for her, while he'd been filling her closet with the trousseau he'd commissioned for their European honeymoon. He still remembered the disbelief, the cutting sense of betrayal.

Marla wasn't marrying *him*—she was marrying the heir to the Stirling Manor. The truth had been a bitter pill to swallow, one he should have seen all along but had been too blinded by lust to consider. Days later, when he'd found himself alone in the rugged highlands of Scotland,

his anger had receded, replaced by numb indifference—
the same thing he felt now.

"Nothing has changed, Marla, and nothing will. Quit
wasting my time and get out of my hotel. This time for
good."

Well-timed moisture filled her beautiful eyes. "I was a
fool to come here," she sobbed brilliantly, "thinking you
might have actually changed. What is it my daddy said?
'Once an unforgiving bastard, always an unforgiving bastard'?"

Derek took the description as a compliment. "It's
called survival, I would think you, of all people, would
know that."

"I loved you," she whispered.

"You know what?" Derek shot back. "I think you believe that, I honestly do. And for that I feel sorry for you,
Marla. You only love one person—and that's your precious daddy."

"That's not true." She rallied. With a flick of her wrist,
her coat fell open, confirming Derek's suspicions and revealing nothing but her perfect body, and a black garter
belt.

"I know you still want me," she purred. "Let me show
you how sorry I am, Derey. Let me remind you how good
we are together." She cupped her full breasts, raising
them, squeezing them until nothing but her nipples remained between her fingertips. "One night, Derey. No
strings attached. One night, then we'll both know if you
can just walk away."

Cass refused to let herself think about Derek and Marla,
what they were doing upstairs. She would not let herself
go there. Instead she stood in the lounge and studied Santiago Vilas. He sat not ten feet away, smoking a thin cigarette, a nearly empty glass of Scotch by his side. She
hadn't seen him for a few days; in fact, if she didn't have

access to registration records, she would have thought he'd checked out.

Call Gray. That was her first thought, the result of training, but she cast it aside when she remembered Gray was off site tonight. She could call him, anyway, wait for him to arrive, but the moment could be gone by then.

The fog lifted, and the cop in her took over. She was here to do a job, a job that had seen her through the past five years, a job that would be there long after Derek left her life.

Reckless energy surged, and she sauntered over to Vilas. "Good evening, Mr. Vilas. I trust all is well?"

An intrigued smile curled the thin lips beneath his mustache. Very openly, very deliberately, he took her measure.

"Other than the fact I've been stood up by my comrade," he answered in his heavily accented voice, "I'd say things are getting better all the time."

After a few moments she owned Santiago's undivided attention. First about nothing in particular, then about the city of Chicago, then how he was spending his time.

"You've been with us almost two weeks. How much longer will we have the pleasure?"

"Ah-h-h-h." He drew the word out like a caress. "A pretty lady like you, I imagine you can have the pleasure as long as you'd like."

His words slithered through her. "The hotel, Mr. Vilas. Will you be staying much longer? I trust you're finding everything up to your standards?"

His eyes darkened. "Funny you should mention that, *querida.* Just this morning I discovered something wrong with my room." He paused, surveyed the length of her body. "Perhaps you'd like to see for yourself."

Maybe she'd been barking up the wrong tree. Maybe Vilas himself would produce the evidence she needed to clear Derek's name. "Perhaps I would."

He kept his hand at the small of her back as he guided

her from the smoky bar. He walked confidently, head high, stride brisk, a man with a purpose. Cass matched him step for step. Each click of her heels against the hard-wood floor echoed like an ominous battle cry.

"Hang on a sec," she said as they passed the reception desk. Smiling, she glanced toward Ruth. "Have I missed anything?"

"Not a thing," Ruth answered with a sympathetic smile. "Not a peep from upstairs."

Dejection tore at Cass, but she used it to make her strong, not weak. "Mr. Vilas is having a problem with his room. Since everything's quiet here, I'm going to go have a look."

"Perhaps we should call one of the maintenance men instead."

Vilas pressed his hand more firmly against Cass's back. "That won't be necessary."

Apprehension swirled with adrenaline, recklessness with caution. For years Cass had laid her life on the line, never giving a damn about consequences. She'd already lost all she had to lose. Yet after one night in Derek's bed, she found herself dreading what came next. She could find something, she realized. She could find the ev-idence she needed to link her lover to the front man of a renowned crime ring.

Her heart rebelled at the thought, but the cop in her realized there was only one way to find out.

"One of the bellman said he needed to speak with me," she told Ruth, hoping Ruth could decode the message in time to get Gray to the hotel. "But…" she drawled, smil-ing at Vilas, "I may be a while. Be a doll, Ruth. Let John Dickens know."

Realize he's not here, she added silently to herself. *Re-alize I'm asking you to call my friend and get him down here before it's too late.*

"Be a sweetie and hand me my purse, will you, Ruth?" Still smiling, she accepted the small black leather bag, grateful for the emergency supplies she always kept in-side. "Never know what a girl might need."

"Here we are, *querida*." Santiago Vilas halted outside his door and turned toward her. "I'm so fortunate you decided to give me personal attention, yes?"

"That's my job," she returned smoothly. "Yes?"

He slid his key into the door and ushered her inside. Years of training coupled with her familiarity with the hotel gave her the courage to walk into the darkened suite. Just to the right would be a Tiffany lamp, so she reached for it immediately, before Vilas could close the door and eliminate the lighting from the corridor.

But when she flicked the switch, no light shone forth.

Vilas closed the door, casting them into darkness. "Ah-h-h. This is much better."

"Is this the problem?" She felt rather than heard him move toward her. "You have a burned-out lightbulb?"

"Little one." A scratching sound followed his voice, giving way to the flicker of a match. "Let's not waste time with games. We both know why you're here, yes?"

She forced herself to swallow. "Of course."

"Very good." The light of the match glowed in his eyes. "It will be very good indeed." He gave her a slow appraisal, then went about lighting candles, putting on music, pouring wine.

All the while Cass scanned the room, looking for any-thing of use.

"Here, little one." He handed her a goblet. "Drink."

She raised her glass. "To a fruitful encounter."

He clinked his glass to hers.

Keep him drinking, Cass thought to herself, slow his senses and reaction time. In her pocket she had her gun. In her purse she had enough amphetamines to knock him on his ass.

"You are very beautiful," he cooed, drawing her into his arms.

Her skin crawled at his touch. Only one man had the right to touch her like that, hold her, make her his. And he was upstairs with his fiancée.

"So beautiful," Vilas said again, leaning toward her.

Cass stiffened. "Mr. Vilas…" She stepped from his embrace. "I'm afraid there's been some kind of mistake."

His eyes hardened, as did his hold on her arms. "No mistake, *querida*. I invited you to my room, you accepted. We both know what happens now."

"You said you were having a problem," she reminded. "As assistant manager, I came to check it out."

He smiled. "And I'm sure you will be very thorough indeed."

Chapter 12

Derek looked at Marla standing there, offering him free use of her beautiful body. She would do anything, he knew, anything to wheedle her way back into his bed, including whoring herself once again. It would be the ultimate payback to spend the night ransacking her body, only to send her packing in the morning.

Yet Derek could think of no one but Cass. He had lost himself with her, for the first time since—since when? Years had passed since he'd stopped plotting and planning and calculating, and simply let himself feel.

Feel. Is that what being lost was about?

He couldn't let that happen, knew feeling led to loss and disappointment, to pain.

"Derey…" Marla's hands abandoned her breasts and traveled down the curve of her waist. "Don't keep me waiting—I can see the fire in your eyes."

He stepped so close he could feel heat radiating from her body. Those pouting lips of hers parted in anticipation as he bent toward her, closer…closer…

"I'll tell you one more time," he ground out, his hands clenching her coat together and brusquely tying her sash. The phone began to ring. "Then I'm calling security. You are not welcome in my hotel—you are not welcome in my life."

Recoiling, Cass retrieved her hand. "I'm afraid there's been a mistake. When you mentioned a problem, I thought—"

The ringing of the telephone interrupted her words. Instinct had her reaching for the receiver; Vilas's icy voice stopped her cold. "My room," he clipped. "My call."

"Just trying to help," she answered sweetly.

Heat flashed in his eyes. "I'll let you help, *querida,* after I take care of business." He edged her hand off the receiver and pulled it to his ear. "You are late, my friend. I'm now otherwise engaged."

Cass thought about bolting for the door, but Vilas's mysterious conversation held her rooted in place. He was doing his best to cloak his words, but she realized this conversation had something to do with a meeting.

Behind a veil of nonchalance, she watched, straining to hear the voice coming through the phone line. Male, that's all she could tell.

"You've kept me waiting long enough," Vilas snarled. "Now I ask you to wait one night. Sounds fair, yes?"

Another moment of silence, this one punctuated by Vilas's victorious smile. "That is what I thought."

He replaced the receiver, then returned his attention to Cass. A low light gleamed in his eyes, not quite a fire, but every bit a pyre. "Ah, *querida*...do not look somber. There is no need."

"I'm on duty," she reminded, "I can't stay."

He pulled her to him, swaying with the music. "Your job is to serve the guests. I'm sure the boss would want you to serve me, as well."

"You're quite right," she said sweetly. "Customer service is a top priority, but every second I spend with you, is a second I'm not tending to other guests." In a well-practiced move, she twisted free from the cage of his arms. "Truly, I must return to my duties at the front desk. If I don't, we'd be rudely interrupted any moment."

He stepped toward her. "I'll take my chances."

"But I won't." She backed toward the door. "I don't want ten or fifteen minutes with you," she told him, her voice purposefully dejected. She wanted all of him. Behind bars. "But if I stay, that's all we'll have." Though it sickened her, she gave him a once-over. "Our time is coming. Rest assured, our time is coming."

And it was. So help her God, it was.

Disappointment dragged at his features. "Go if you must, *querida*. I do not want you by force." He strode toward her, stopping close enough to drag a finger down the side of her face. "Remember one thing—you started something here tonight. We will finish it."

Warning hardened his voice, his eyes. She smiled anyway, languidly, then turned the knob behind her and slipped through the door. It took every ounce of willpower and training not to run down the hall, away from that vile little man. But she didn't. Shoulders square, spine straight, chin high, she turned and walked serenely down the hall, surprised, in fact, the staccato rhythm of her heart could not be heard echoing through the corridor.

The wall of aristocrats heard it, though. The scorn in their eyes revealed they knew what game she was playing, knew and didn't approve.

Neither did she. Not anymore.

"John Dickens wasn't here, so I figured whatever he wanted to see you about could wait until tomorrow."

Cass offered Ruth a strained smile. "That's okay. I'll get with him later."

Ruth's eyes narrowed. "You okay?"

"Never better." She stared at the dying embers in the

fireplace. Only hours before it had raged magnificently. Now, like her master plan, it was nothing but smoldering ashes.

"Right." If her tone hadn't driven home her disbelief, Ruth's snort did. "That's why you're as pale as a ghost and have hardly said a word since you came down from Mr. Vilas's room. He do something to you, honey? Just because he's a guest doesn't give him the right to paw at you. Mr. Mansfield—"

"No." Heart drumming, Cass swung toward Ruth. "Not a word of this to anyone." Twice already Derek had intervened when her investigation tempted her to go too far. Thus far she'd had the luxury of hiding behind hotel responsibility, but sooner or later that excuse would wear thin.

"Everything is fine," she added, smiling to back up her words. "I'm just tired."

Ruth eyed her a moment longer. "It *has* been a wild night," she admitted. "Who would've thought Marla Fairchild would have the audacity to waltz back into this hotel like she owned the place?"

The memory of it still turned Cass's stomach, bruised her heart. "She almost did, didn't she?"

"Own it?" Ruth shrugged. "Well, I suppose if Mr. Mansfield had married her she might have, but the hotel isn't what she wanted from him. Not really."

"Oh?" She'd unearthed precious little about Derek and Marla's aborted engagement. They'd been the toast of Chicago, then the day of their wedding Derek vanished.

Ironically, all traces of drug trafficking vanished at the same time.

Ironic, like hell. It didn't take a genius to link the two, nor to link Derek's return with the appearance of Santiago Vilas.

But sometimes things weren't what they seemed, Cass knew. Sometimes the more obvious a situation appeared, the more likely it wasn't. "From what I've heard, Derek and Marla didn't—''

Cass's words broke off when Ruth began clearing her throat. Puzzled, she glanced at her friend, followed her gaze toward the foyer. Derek stood there, still clad in his black suit, inky hair unbound, making his cheekbones look more pronounced, his eyes more deeply set.

Cass's breath stalled in her throat.

And her heart took a long, slow free fall.

He strode toward them, toward her, his eyes hot and demanding. Every instinct Cass possessed surged to full alert, but she just stood there, watching him advance.

Run, some part of her commanded. The woman? The cop? She didn't know. Not anymore. Had the entire world depended on it, she couldn't have moved, any more than she could look away.

"G-good eve-ening, Mr. M-Mansf-field," Ruth stammered.

He didn't spare her a glance. His eyes were on Cass, Cass alone. She'd never seen him look this fierce, like an avenging warrior swooping down on the enemy.

He halted in front of the desk and just stared at her. Not a word was spoken. Not a word was needed.

Derek had come for her.

The world around her faded. Time slowed. As though he were willing her to do it, Cass moved around the desk, toward him. Her steps were slow and deliberate, her gaze locked upon his. When she neared him, he snatched her wrist, then pivoted and strode toward the elevator, dragging her behind him.

But he wasn't dragging. She was right there with him.

Every detail flashed excruciatingly clear. The echo of her heels across the hardwood floor. The woodsy scent of his cologne. The gentle power of his grip upon her wrist. The certainty that she must follow him, that at long last she'd reached the turning point she'd been seeking for months. Maybe years.

Cloyd ushered them inside the elevator. He chattered amiably as they rode up, but his voice barely registered. Cass's heart thundered too loudly, in warning and anticipation, in joy.

Love and lies, she wondered maniacally. How could the two flourish side by side?

Derek said nothing as they stepped off the elevator, nor as they entered his darkened office. Rather than jabbing the button to close the door, as she expected, he pressed it gently, then strode across the plush carpet and poured a drink. One drink. For himself. Water. He threw it back, poured another. Threw it back, turned to face her.

"Come here."

Not a request, but a command.

He knew. God help her, he knew.

The cameras. He'd warned her that he knew every move she made, but she'd thought he would be too occupied with Marla to give a damn about her whereabouts.

She'd been wrong. He knew exactly where'd she'd been, no doubt had his own suspicions about what she'd done.

And he wasn't just angry about it. He was coldly furious.

She stopped before him, refusing to reveal the unease swirling through her. "Contrary to what you may have been told, this silent brooding act isn't the least bit appealing."

The blue of his eyes hardened into blazing shards of cobalt. "Don't you ever, *ever* do something so foolish again." His voice was low, lethal. "Don't you know what kind of man Vilas is? Don't you know what could happen to you, alone in his room?"

Impossible to tell whether his attack came from concern or possession, but it ruptured Cass's composure all the same.

"Nothing happened to me," she defended. "What do

you care, anyway?'' she added, her tone deliberately snide. "You haven't said one word to me in days."

His sudden smile was somewhere between blinding and devastating. "So that is what this is about? Revenge?" He pulled her up to her tiptoes, so close she had to tilt her head back to see his eyes. "You saw me with Marla—"

"No." It couldn't be. Just couldn't. "Vilas said there was a problem with his room."

Her words, honest though they were, didn't cool the fire in his eyes. They fanned it.

"And you," he mocked, "fearless champion against all that is wrong in this world, believed him?"

She angled her chin and narrowed her eyes. Said nothing.

"So that's the way it's going to be." He flicked his gaze down her body, returned to her face. "Fine." In one fluid move, he tracked her back against the paneled wall of his office, held her there.

She wanted to push him away from her, to slap his arrogant face and walk out on him. But even more she wanted to give over to him, to match his fire with her own, to lose herself in a mindless reunion with his body.

Which she did.

She opened to him, mouth, body and soul. Heated kisses gave way to desperate moans. Sliding hands to possessive caresses. He pushed her skirt up her hips, pulled down her hose. She unfastened his pants, yanked down his briefs, freed his erection.

Her body cried out for him. Her heart. She felt like a junkie who'd been deprived of the very substance she couldn't live without. Derek. Only Derek. He was what she needed, she realized, despite everything. The past three days without the healing power of his touch had been torture. The past several hours, imagining him with Marla, hell of the worst kind.

"Now," she panted. "Oh, God, please. Now."

"Look at me," he commanded hoarsely.

Desperate to feel him inside her, she looked into his passion-glazed eyes and felt her heart swell.

"Mine," he ground out, then pushed inside. "From this day forward."

"Yes," she answered, though she wasn't sure the word made it past her raw moans. He was pumping into her, filling her. Completion and possession, pure and simple. No less blatant than if he'd branded her with a hot iron. No less permanent, either.

"You," he growled. "Only you."

"You," she promised. "Only you."

Their reunion spiraled on, building, deepening, desperate. If the wall hadn't been there to support her back, she would have collapsed beneath the power of his passion. But she clung to him, welcoming each deep thrust with an arch of her hips. Her body strained for release, but even more, it strained for him. She welcomed his mouth to hers, loving the feel of body to body, heart to heart.

They came together in a firestorm of passion and fulfillment. Limp, rattled to her core, Cass wrapped her arms around his now damp suit and held him as tightly as she could.

Derek pulled free of her arms. He looked down at her, his eyes fevered and confused. Maybe even lost, like a warrior stunned at the atrocities he'd just witnessed. Committed. Without a word, he jerked up his pants and strode to the door.

Then he was gone.

Shocked, confused, devastated, Cass slid down the wall and sat on the floor, staring at the closed door. His sweat still clung to her body, his scent, his seed. But he'd left her.

She tried to make sense of what had happened between them, of how anger could combust into...into...

She wasn't sure what it combusted into. She would have called it possession, but it hadn't been dirty or one-sided. Desperate and needy, certainly. Mindless. Undeniable. The fusion of two souls who couldn't stand to be apart.

Tears welled. She fought them, knowing they didn't change a damn thing. They hadn't brought back her husband and son; they sure as hell wouldn't change the way she'd come to feel about the one man who had the power to help her heal, the same man whose imminent hatred might just topple her once and for all.

Love couldn't grow from lies, she knew. Love healed. Lies destroyed.

But reality didn't stop the low keening sounds, the deep, gut-wrenching sobs that tore through her body. She was in too deep. Despite everything, she'd responded to him on a primitive level that propelled her to throw caution to the wind and simply feel.

Feel. There it was again, the damning truth she couldn't escape. It would all end soon enough, though. The last domino would crash, the truth would spill out, and Derek would never touch her again. Not in anger. Not in possession. Certainly not in passion.

"It won't be much longer now." Derek dragged a silver letter opener along the glossy page of a magazine, watching in grim fascination as it desecrated the manor's most recent rave review. "I know, I know," he agreed impatiently. "Just a little longer. A few more days and everything will fall into place."

Moments later he replaced the receiver and leaned back in his chair, bracing his crossed ankles atop his desk. Soon he would free himself from the shackles of this place. Soon all the watching eyes would be turned elsewhere. Soon it wouldn't matter what Cass did or said, who she saw.

But not soon enough.

He'd had everything under control, unfolding according to plan, when he discovered Cass's indiscretion. At first he'd thought Ruth's frantic call a mistake, some kind of warped joke, a trick of his paranoid imagination. Cass and Vilas. As if. No way in hell. But the proof had been irrefutable, and it had shattered his hard-won resolve to stay away from her.

Sex. That's all he wanted their relationship to be, the safest avenue of all. Just sex he could handle. Just sex and it wouldn't matter if she got tarnished by the game he was playing.

Just sex and it wouldn't matter when she walked away.

But it *did* matter, all of it. Because it wasn't just sex, none of it. It was more, so much more. Any doubts had been eradicated the second he discovered her trip to Vilas's room. His blood had boiled, his heart thundered. A long-dormant battle cry had risen to his throat, turning him into a madman until he'd found her—reclaimed her.

She was his, damn it. His. His heart, his soul. The first person who'd made him want to be a better man.

And he didn't share.

But he didn't keep, either, at least never before.

"Hi-ya, Uncle Dare!" Ryan raced around the desk and skidded to a halt by Derek's side. "Why do you look so mad?"

Normally his nephew's innocent smile melted away the demons, but not today. "I'm not mad, son, just thinking."

Ryan scrunched up his face. "Must be about something bad, then." His expression grew solemn, as though debating a monumental decision. Then his smile returned, brighter than before. "Tell y'what," he began, eyes shining. "Dad said we could go to grandpa's house today. Wanna come?"

The invitation appealed, as much for the peace the house provided, as for the escape it would furnish. Escape from the manor, from Cass, but most especially, from himself.

"You sure about this?"

Cass looked up from the teddy bear in her hands. "It's

time," she told Gray's wife, Dawn, and meant it more deeply than she'd once thought possible. For years she'd lived in a numb fantasyland where she didn't have to face all she'd lost. Now she knew the time had come to rejoin the land of the living.

They sat amidst the sanctuary of Jake's room, surrounded by toys and balls and stuffed animals, stacks of shirts and shorts, scattered pairs of shoes, anything and everything a four-year-old boy would need.

Barney was there, too, sitting back from the chaos, watching the scene with big, sad, doggy eyes. It was as though he sensed what was happening, and was no more ready to say goodbye than Cass was.

But the time had come.

Dawn picked up a small leather jacket and brought it to her face. "Maybe we should wait—"

"No." Dawn's support warmed Cass. She'd known this day would come, yet if someone had told her the trigger would be an affair with her suspect, she would have laughed in their face.

She wasn't laughing now.

"I can't dwell in the past," she told her friend, absently stroking a stuffed purple dinosaur. "Jake will always be here," she said, rubbing the ache in her chest, "in my heart, but I can't keep pretending I'll find him here in this room."

"Oh, Cass..." Dawn leaned forward and pulled her friend into a hug. "I'm so sorry."

"I know. Trust me, I know. But I'm okay." Despite the chaos of overflowing boxes, the room already looked barren.

"Just think..." Cass sniffed against the painful lump in her throat. "You can turn this room into that plantation drawing room we've always talked about." A highly talented artist, Dawn had been hounding Cass to let her paint a mural in the house. Something southern, Cass always

said. A little slice of heaven way up north. "I can already
see it…. Tapestried sofa and wing chairs. A fire in the
hearth. French doors thrown open to the outside, revealing
the thick white columns of the verandah…"

Cass stilled, though in some far corner of her mind, she
realized Dawn continued the illusion.

"…sprawling oak trees in the distance…"

Whose house was she describing? The lush splendor of
Oak Alley, one of the great Southern plantations?

"…a gravel road winding away from the house…"

Or the startling beauty of Derek's grandfather's house,
as out of place in the northern woods of Illinois as Derek
was in the confining high-rises of downtown Chicago.

Derek. God, what had she let happen? She'd hardly
slept the night before. Every time she'd dropped off, he
came to her, eyes blazing, touch branding. She should be
mortified and offended at the way he'd taken her, not
stimulated and alive. There'd been so much more to his
touch than mere possession. It was the desperation, she
knew, the need, that tore at her heart and had her craving
more.

"Cass?"

Dawn's voice came to her through a tunnel, pulling her
away from Derek's arms and into Jake's room.

"Cass," her friend said again, this time accompanied
by a tug on her arm. "Cass."

"What?" She blinked, confused by the panic in her
friend's voice.

Dawn's eyes widened, then motioned toward the doorway.

Cass followed the direction of Dawn's gaze, then went
completely still. The purple dinosaur slipped from her fingers.

Derek lounged in the doorway, shoulder propped
against the frame. His hair was loose around his face,
much as it had been the night before, emphasizing the
sharp lines of his cheekbones, the deep recesses of his go-

to-hell eyes. Only they weren't condemning her now, they were blazing, overflowing with…with *what* she didn't know. But it pulled at her as potently as his passion had last night.

"Derek."

He scanned the room, no doubt taking in the stripped bed, the emptied drawers and shelves, the boxes overflowing with her child's life. No doubt remembering the night he'd almost made love to her here, the same night he'd rocked her in his arms while she'd cried out her grief.

His eyes met hers. "We need to talk."

They did. Desperately so. But the thought of it, the possibility of what might be said, or left unsaid, had her stomach clenching. "We've said all there is to say."

"I haven't."

"Derek—"

"All I'm asking is for you to listen."

Her heart thundered in her chest, making breathing painful. "Make it fast."

He glanced at Dawn, back at Cass. "Alone."

Cass swallowed. Part of her yearned for Dawn to stay, insurance that nothing would spiral away from her. What a joke. Things had already spiraled hideously out of control.

She looked at the frozen, fascinated expression on her partner's wife's face. "It's *okay,*" she told her. "He's right. We need to talk."

Dawn didn't look convinced. "I don't know, Cass." She glanced around Jake's room. "This might not be the best time."

"It's the only time." No way to prevent the sun from setting. She stood, reached down and helped Dawn to her feet. "Don't worry—it'll be okay."

Dawn frowned, but relented. "Okay, but call if you need to. You have my cell phone number." She twisted toward Derek, gave him a sharp, scathing look, then glanced back at Cass. "If I don't hear from you, I'm calling."

Derek took her measure, slowly and deliberately. "You look familiar," he said at last. "Do I know you?"

The hotel. Dawn had been at the hotel to see Gray. Cass's heart stumbled at the realization, but with a bright smile, she covered. "I highly doubt you know her, Derek, unless you've taken to hanging around the local PTA in your spare time."

His eyes narrowed in question.

Dawn shot him another loaded glare, but left. Drawing a breath, Cass closed the door and turned to face Derek.

"This is a surprise," she began, needing to start somewhere. "After last night—"

"I'm sorry." He stood directly before her, not close enough to touch. But close enough to feel. "I was crazy," he admitted. Regret roughened his voice. "When Ruth called—"

"Ruth called?"

"She told me she was worried about you, that you were alone with Vilas. I could barely think straight, see straight. I only knew I had to get you away from him."

"I wasn't *with* Vilas. Not like that."

He lifted a hand to her cheek. "I know."

The certainty in his voice soothed as much as it surprised. "Do you now?" the cop in her asked. "How do you know that?"

"Because you couldn't have given yourself to me like you did, if you had been."

The bold statement was the last thing she'd expected to hear. And it floored her. "So that's what last night was?" Hurt welled. "A test? Your way of finding out—"

"No." He had her pressed against him in an instant, gently but firmly taking her upper arms in his hands and staring down at her. "Not a test, Cass. It was…" For the first time since she'd known him, uncertainty ravaged his eyes. "It was me being out of control, fighting for what I consider mine. It was—"

"Inevitable," she supplied. Any anger or uncertainty she'd harbored fled, just like that. She leaned into him, wrapping her arms around his waist and holding him, so tightly nothing could ever take him away from her. Not anybody. Not anything.

She began to shake, as much in fear as in relief.

"Easy," he murmured, pulling back to look at her. "You're right, it was inevitable. But that's no excuse for my behavior." The words tore out of him, fierce and raw. "Damn but we're in a hell of a mess. I don't know what to do with you, Cass, doll. I've never known anyone like you. So honest, so good."

The words stabbed into her, obliterating any trace of self-respect. Love shouldn't grow out of lies, but it had.

"There are things you don't know," she found herself saying. "I'm not who you think I am."

"And I'm not who you think I am." His thumb stroked the hollow of her cheek. "I'm not a good man. I've done things, things I'm not proud of. You deserve better—"

"Shh." She placed her hand on his. She knew what he'd done, and she loved him, anyway. "The past doesn't matter."

"Yes, it does." Three words. But he said them with the finality of a death knell. "It's never really past, Cass. Never fully gone. That's why I pushed you away, why I stayed away. I don't want who I've been to hurt you."

She brushed a kiss across his lips. "We can't let the past steal the present—it's all we really have."

His eyes glowed. "A man could go three lifetimes and never find a woman like you."

She'd never known words of promise could slice so sharply. "Derek—"

"I'll take today, but mark my words, I'll fight for tomorrow, and every day thereafter, if it's the last thing I do."

Chapter 13

"I haven't been honest with you."

Shock rocketed through Cass. They sat on the floor in front of the fading fire, Derek's back against the sofa. She sat between his legs, leaning back against his chest.

"We've both kept secrets, Derek. Sometimes they're all we have."

"But I want to share mine, Cass." He slowly unfastened her braid, as though unraveling the secrets between them could be as simple. "It's time to lay the truth of who I am on the line, and let you decide if you can live with it."

"Derek—"

"I'm not proud of some of the things I've done, but they've made me the man I am, the man who wants nothing more than to keep you safe."

"You do keep me safe. From myself, from my past."

"I want more than that. I want the future. But to have that, you need to know where I've been, what I've done." He was quiet a moment, his fingers stilling in Cass's hair.

"When I was in the merchant marines, I became involved with a woman. Her name was Sasha, and she conceived my child."

Cass twisted toward Derek. "I didn't know—"

"She got rid of it." The fire in his eyes turned ice-cold, giving her a heartbreaking clue as to the origin of his hallmark, go-to-hell expression. "Murdered my child."

"Oh, Derek." All she could say, yet nowhere near enough. "I'm so sorry."

He dragged his fingers through his hair, clenching them around the shoulder-length ends. "It was a long time ago," he said by way of dismissal, but pain strained his voice. "I was young, foolish, naive. I thought she loved me. I thought she wanted *me*. But all she wanted was a good time."

Cass closed her eyes against the horror of it.

"I would have married her, but she laughed when I asked her, said she'd gotten rid of the child, why complicate things with permanence?"

She opened her eyes and looked into his soul. "You wanted the child."

"My real father died when I was just a kid," he said. "I hardly remember him. But I remember what it felt like when he smiled at me, when he held me and swung me around the room. I remember his laugh, what it was like to be loved by him."

"And you wanted to share that with your own child."

"Yes."

Pain jackknifed through her heart. "Your mother?"

"Remarried." He uttered the word so matter-of-factly he could have been speaking of going to the dentist. "Brent was born less than a year later, their only child together."

He said no more, didn't need to. Cass could imagine it all too well; the truth underscored the men Brent and Derek had grown to be.

Brent, his polished, country-club exterior, his spoiled, self-centered interior.

Derek, his rough, rebellious exterior, his lonely, vulnerable interior.

"I'm sorry," she said again. "I can't imagine what it must have been like."

"I don't want you to even think about it."

His gallantry warmed and chilled at the same time. "I can handle it."

"But I don't want you to." He brushed a kiss against her lips. "You had a good childhood, didn't you? You were happy? Loved?"

"I was." The answer was simple and honest and straight from the heart. "Of course, four older brothers often made things difficult."

Derek's sudden laughter halted her words. So rare that she heard the deep rumble. When she did, she simply wanted to savor.

They stayed that way a long while. The heat of the fire warmed them as they held each other and traded stories of the past. He deftly turned the tables to her life and not his, as always, and she found herself reliving her childhood in New Orleans. The excitement and adventure of the French Quarter, the haunting allure of the swamps and deserted plantations.

Time lost meaning. One minute the sun shone through the windows, the next it was the moon. Cass lay in Derek's arms, completely content with the world. She was building memories, she knew, stockpiling them, devastating memories she could cherish when they were all she had left.

He told her about Marla, how she'd been using him to prove herself to her father. Design contracts for the Stirling Manor were all she'd been after, something Derek would have gladly given her, until he found out she'd been counting on them all along.

Maybe Marla had grown to love him, but it hadn't mattered to Derek. Same song as before, different verse. No one really wanted *him,* the man he was. Not his mother, not Sasha, not Marla. They'd all used him for one thing or another, demonstrating that love was just a fairy tale created to sell books and movies.

All the carefully woven threads of her life were coming apart, she realized. Soon they would lie in shreds, beyond repair, and her work would be done. Derek would discover the truth, and instead of adoration, his eyes would hold contempt.

The love and the lies had tangled like wild vines out of control. Sooner or later they would separate, and in doing so, one would destroy the other.

She had no idea how she would bear it. Deep in her heart she didn't believe he was behind the drug trafficking. She would prove that, yet the damage would be the same. The truth of her identity would come out, and he would know she'd been deceiving him. She could tell him she'd grown to love him, just as Marla had, but as with Marla, it wouldn't make a difference.

In the end the lies would destroy the love.

"Cass, honey?" He brushed his lips against her hair, his hands along her back. "Let me make love to you."

She turned in his arms and faced him. "*With* me, Derek." His body hardened beneath her, giving way to a provocative melting of everything she was, everything she ever hoped to be. "You're not doing anything to me. I'm right there with you."

The firelight shimmered on his deep-blue eyes. Dark shadows clung to his jaw, but his answering smile provided all the light she needed. He pulled her against his chest, just holding her, rocking her. Then he was stretching them out in front of the fire, gently ridding her of her clothing.

She did the same for him, taking pleasure in pulling his shirt over his chest, again discovering the dark coarse hair residing there. She traced it down his abdomen, farther still, until the waistband of his jeans halted her progress. Her fingers trembled as she fumbled with the button and zipper of his jeans. Anticipation taunted as she worked the denim down his long legs. She was already naked, wonderfully so, gloriously so, Derek's hand sliding over her skin.

Where before there had been urgency, now there was deliberation. Where before there had been greed, now there was patience.

And where before there had been desperation, now there was confidence.

She pulled the jeans free of his legs, stilled when she saw the silver-and-pearl coloration against the skin of his shin. A bruise, she thought at first, but as she slid down his sock, she realized the truth.

The discoloration of his skin was not a bruise, not a scar. It was a tattoo. She'd known he'd had one, yet she hadn't known where. Or what.

Now she knew. A dagger. The ivory-hilted weapon was emblazoned against his shin, as though strapped there long ago by a warrior preparing for battle. The sight of it hit her hard. The starkness of it, the symbolism of always being poised and ready to fight. To defend.

"Oh, Derek," she said on a sigh, sliding her parted lips down his muscular leg, to the dagger. She took it into her mouth, as she would take him in only a few moments, and let the truth slice through her heart.

"Oh, Derek," she moaned. "Derek."

"I know, Cass. I know about you and Mansfield."

Cass finished taping the last box and looked up. Gray stood across the room, his baggy sweats a stark contrast to his grim expression.

"What, Gray? What is it you think you know?"

Sunshine streamed through the window. The purple Barney curtains were packed now, along with the matching comforter. "I warned you not to cross the line."

She surged to her feet and marched across the room. "Look, big guy, if you have something to say, say it. If you don't—"

"You're sleeping with Mansfield."

She stilled. There it was, heaped out on the table between them. Cass knew she should feel a twinge of regret, maybe even shame, but she didn't. Couldn't. What she and Derek shared was too special to make her regret one second she spent with him, one decision she'd made. He'd stayed with her through the night, making love with her, tenderly sometimes, urgently others. With the first fragile light of dawn, they'd tackled Jake's room, packing boxes, he holding her when the memories grew too great and she dissolved into tears. Together they'd fended off her ghosts.

Mansfield was not the man they thought he was. Drunken and disorderly conduct, petty theft and DUI, all committed by a man under the age of twenty-one, didn't mark him a bad seed or a criminal. They equated rebellion, pure and simple.

"I sleep in my own bed," she said, "in the privacy of my own home." She knew the best defense was a potent offense. "How would you know what happens here, unless you've been following me?"

"Cammy." The harshness drained from his face, replaced by an empathy she hadn't expected. "Don't try to outinterrogate the interrogator who taught you everything you know."

"Who I sleep with is none of your business."

"It is when it's the man we're trying to bust."

Cass dragged a hand through her damp hair, evoking memories of the way Derek had washed it less than an hour before. Never had she known a routine task like sudsing shampoo could be erotic, that hands could feel so incredible as they massaged the pressure points along her head.

"He's innocent," she blurted. "I don't know what the

hell is really going on, but I do know Derek is not the front man. He's being set up, framed.... I just don't know by whom or why.''

''Don't think so, Cass.'' His eyes gentle, he reached out and cupped her cheek. ''If you were thinking clearly, you would see how irrational that is. Mansfield's our man, and we all know it. Coincidences don't just happen.''

Platonic affection had always marked her relationship with Gray, but now his touch reminded her too much of a parent trying to talk sense into a willful child. She stepped back and glared at him. ''I know what I'm doing. Can't we just leave it at that?''

''What you're doing is living a lie. You have to break it off.''

''Don't you remember what happened when you tried that with Dawn?''

''That was different. She wasn't a suspect. And at least I tried.''

''You think I haven't?'' The memory of Derek's devastating lovemaking burned through her. Not just the physical aspect, but the emotional bonding that punctuated it. ''It's too late for turning back. If I tried, Derek would never fall for it. All he'd have to do is touch me and I'd be lost.''

His expression hardened. ''Cass, this breaks every rule in the book. If you won't listen to reason, I have to turn—''

She shoved hard against his chest. ''You son of a bitch! Did I turn against you when you couldn't stay away from Dawn? You jeopardized everything, Gray. *Everything.* Your life, Dawn's. Mine. But I never turned my back on you.''

''That was different.''

''That's right. It was you and not me. But this is my life we're talking about. My *life*. Don't you dare take it away from me.''

"I'm not trying to take it away from you. I'm trying to help you, spare you more pain. With Mansfield in as deep as we think he is—"

"He's not. But even if he were, I'd deal with it." She hardened her voice, her eyes. "I've made my bed, Gray, and by God I'm going to lie in it. You can support me, or you can condemn me. The choice is yours."

He was flirting with danger. The Museum of Natural History was hardly a private place, hardly secluded, but he'd been drawn there forever. How fitting that it would be the stage for the beginning of the end.

Almost midnight, the sprawling concrete parking lot stood empty. Every now and then the vicious wind sent an empty can clattering across the pavement, high clouds shimmering across the crescent moon. Other than that, he detected no activity.

The jagged skyline sprawled before him, cold and sterile. Not far away, waves lapped against the edges of the lake, yet no beach greeted them. Only rocks shattering their eloquence and sending them crashing back toward the lake.

How fitting.

Footsteps fell against the pavement. He spun toward the sound, searching for the source. Twice before he thought he'd heard an approach, but he'd come up empty-handed. Now shadows snaked among the columns, making it hard to tell fact from fantasy. Some would call him a fool for conducting the meeting here, in plain view of Lakeshore Drive, but he quickened to the challenge.

Over the past few weeks he'd lost his edge. Tonight he was determined to get it back.

He saw him then, stepping from the shadow of a column. "Good evening, *amigo*."

Santiago Vilas stopped a good ten feet away. Dressed in all black, he blended perfectly with the shadows, the only giveaway the glowing tip of his cigarette. "And to you, my friend."

He'd waited so long for this test. Now he simply wanted to savor. Tonight the last piece of groundwork would be established, the beginning of the end.

Trust was a heady goal, one that would be secured with a simple exchange.

Under Vilas's trench coat a bulge could be seen, a package. "Nice evening, isn't it?" he said at last, his voice deceptively bland.

Vilas glanced around the deserted parking lot before answering. "It will be nicer once we seal the deal."

"So it will." He made a drawn-out display of glancing toward the jagged skyline. It was morbid and he knew it, but every time he saw stone and glass skyscrapers jutting toward the sky, he thought of ancient cemeteries, their weathered tombstones jutting up from the ground. "After tonight there's no turning back. Have you come prepared for that?"

"You insult me, my friend. You, after all, have kept me waiting for a very long time."

He slid his hand inside his coat pocket and withdrew a thick manila envelope. "Shall we trade, then?"

A feral smile twisted Vilas's lips. His gloved hand vanished behind his coat, and his eyes narrowed in anticipation. He withdrew the package. "This has been a long time coming."

"That it has." He held out the envelope and exchanged it for the package. While Vilas thumbed through the unmarked bills, he inspected the long-awaited samples. Small change compared to what lay ahead.

The sweet taste of success mingled with adrenaline. Finally. After months of planning and waiting, the game had begun.

He let his pleasure trickle into his eyes, his smile, his voice. "You've done right by me," Derek drawled. "Just as I knew you would."

* * *

Cass stood frozen, as stiff and unmoving as the massive column that supported her. The past blurred with the future, right with wrong, cop with woman. Two days. That's all Gray had given her to prove Derek's innocence. This morning forty-eight hours hadn't seemed like enough time, but in the end a few hours had been all she needed.

Disbelief and horror crashed down like an avalanche.

She'd followed him, expecting him to go to his grandfather's house. Answers lived there, she knew, she had only to find them. But he hadn't gone north as she'd expected, he'd ventured down to the lakefront. Now she knew why.

She watched Derek nod curtly at Santiago Vilas. The wiry Latin man smiled in return, then turned and slithered away. Derek stood there a moment longer, watching, waiting, obviously not trusting Santiago Vilas enough to turn his back on him. The moonlight shimmered against the coal black of Derek's hair, making him look as fierce and dangerous as she now knew him to be.

Her blood quickened, anyway.

Shock numbed her to the bite of the wind, but not the churning of her stomach. She'd let infatuation blind her to reality. She'd let herself forget everything she knew to be true about Derek Mansfield.

She'd convinced herself he was innocent.

She'd let love create the biggest lie of all.

Now the truth threatened to destroy her. Derek Mansfield was everything she'd ever thought him to be. A pusher, a user, a criminal.

Worst of all, he was also the man she loved.

"Everything went off without a hitch," Derek drawled into the phone. "Just like I knew it would. Tomorrow—"

Cass came into view, strolling down the hall to his penthouse. He'd sent for her an hour before, but he sensed no urgency to her pace, no excitement. Her eyes were eerily hollow.

"I'll call you back," he said curtly, hanging up the phone as he buzzed her into his office.

She entered, but didn't cross to him. Just stood there, shoulders back, chin angled, eyes cool and reserved.

"Afternoon, fearless." Caution and concern exploded through him. He'd never seen her like this, so distant, so aloof. He eliminated the space between them.

"You're a sight for sore eyes," he tried, drawing her stiff body into his arms and tracing his mouth along hers.

Under the gentle persuasion of his lips, she softened. Her mouth returned the hello, though it didn't invite him in.

"You okay?" he asked, alarmed by the difference. Everything had been fine the last time he'd seen her. They'd finally torn down their walls and invited each other in. Cassandra LeBlanc was a rare woman, not at all like his mother or Sasha or Marla. She wasn't using him for any ulterior motive. She wasn't going to walk away when she had no more purpose for him.

The realization opened up a whole new world, one where love could erase the lies he'd been forced to tell. "Cass, honey?"

A thin smile touched her lips. "I didn't get much sleep last night."

"You didn't get much sleep the night before, either." The memory of just how he'd kept her awake burned through him. "Why don't you slip into the other room and take a nap for a while."

"I'm on duty."

"I'm the boss," he reminded. "You do what I say, remember?"

She didn't laugh the way he wanted her to. "Really, Derek. I'm okay."

Like hell she was. Something was wrong. It wasn't like her to be reserved. She was his fiery angel, his brave, fearless vixen. He couldn't stand the thought of her backing down now, when victory lay so close at hand.

Derek took Cass's icy hands in his and drew them to his lips. "Come away with me."

She went very still. "What?"

"To Scotland. Let me show you the land, the life I've built there, away from all this."

His words, the ragged hope underlying them, destroyed what little willpower Cass had left. Her grand, foolish illusions lay shattered, but her heart didn't seem to give a damn. It beat anyway, defiantly, valiantly, commanding her not to forfeit what she felt for Derek.

Felt. That's what it kept coming down to.

Part of her wanted to yank her hands from his and run as fast and far as she could. But the other part, the part that knew no boundaries when it came to him, just wanted to fling herself into his arms and let his heat soak into her.

She couldn't seem to get rid of the chill deep inside.

"Cass? What is it? What's wrong?"

I love you. But the words wouldn't come. They couldn't. They were lodged behind the truth. "I've just got a lot on my mind," she hedged. "Why don't you—"

The ringing telephone interrupted her words. Once. Twice. Three times. But Derek made no move to answer. "Aren't you going to get that?"

"It's not important. You are."

The iron-clad cocoon the cop had built around the woman's heart started to crumble. "Derek, don't do this to me."

"Do what?"

Make me forget who I am and what I have to do. "Tempt me. I have a job to do. You have to let me do it."

Another truth, wrapped in another lie.

His somber look dissolved into an amused smile. "Here I stand, humbling myself at your feet, begging you to come away with me, and all you can think about is some two-cent hotel job?''

Before she could respond, the door slid open and Brent raced in. ''My God, big brother, I've been trying to call you! A bomb,'' he panted. ''At the manor.''

Derek grabbed Cass's hand. ''Slow down,'' he said levelly. ''What are you talking about?''

''San Francisco. Bomb threat—the whole building—going to blow.''

Derek turned toward her, his eyes deadly calm. ''We've got to get out there. You stay here. We'll finish when I'm back.''

Debilitating memories crashed around her, of another man she loved racing out the door, never to return.

Don't go, she wanted to cry, but knew she couldn't.

''We could lose everything,'' Brent panicked. ''Everything!''

''Let's go.'' Derek pressed a hard kiss to her lips. ''I'm coming back, Cass.''

Her heart shuttered. He knew what she was thinking. He remembered.

''Ryan,'' Brent rasped before he vanished into the corridor. ''Don't tell Ryan.''

Cass watched them go, questions racing through her. A bomb threat. It could mean a number of things, but the cop in her linked it to the transaction she'd witnessed last night. But why? A trick? A game? A contest for the upper hand?

When the phone began ringing, she ignored it. At first. Then she thought of Derek and his fierce command to stay put. Racing toward the phone, she grabbed the receiver.

''Derek Mansfield's office.''

''You have thirty minutes to evacuate the Chicago hotel,'' a maniacal voice intoned. ''Then you'll have nothing but a gutted heap of rubble.''

Chapter 14

Horror ripped through Cass like a wildfire out of control. A bomb. At the Chicago hotel. Years of training shoved aside debilitating emotions and sent her into high gear. A call to the station, to the bomb squad, to Gray. A call to security, the order to evacuate the hotel and all the other buildings within half a mile. Immediately.

The threat could be a prank, but that was not a risk she could take.

Her heart raced as she ran into the stairwell and took the steps two at a time. The elevator would have been quicker, but with the possibility of a bomb ripping through the building, she'd ordered them disabled.

The deserted stairwell didn't stay that way for long. The doors on each floor flew open, streams of panicked guests racing for safety. She helped them as much as she could, careful to keep her voice and demeanor calm.

"Easy does it," she instructed, encouraging everyone to focus on the evacuation and not their panic.

By the time she reached the ground floor, chaos had

taken over. Men and women and children ran toward the doors, struggling to exit while law enforcement officers worked to keep the evacuation orderly. No sign of Gray, but she recognized a few of the boys from the station, familiar faces from the bomb squad.

"It's been six minutes since the call," she told Bud Summers. Veteran narc, he had no reason to be there, no reason but Cass. He was the kind of man you could count on, rock solid in the face of crisis. "We've got twenty-four left."

"Where's Mansfield?" the silver-haired man wanted to know.

"On his way to San Fran. There's a threat there, too."

"How convenient."

Cass's mind sharpened. "You don't think—"

"No time for thinking now." Even in a crisis, Bud wore calm about him like a white boutonniere. "Let's get these good people out of here."

She wanted to leap to Derek's defense, but she knew Bud was right. The clock was ticking.

"Cass!" Ruth pushed her way through the crowd. "Thank God! I didn't know where you were. What's going—"

"Just get out!" Cass commanded. "Now!"

Ruth looked uncertain, but when Cass nudged her toward the door, she went without another word.

The cacophony of sirens blotted out all else. Fire trucks and cop cars, paramedics and the bomb squad. They converged on the manor, screeching to a halt and quickly going about their duty. A crowd gathered at a safe distance, drawn by the impending tragedy. Several officials shifted from manning the hotel to manning the streets.

Twenty-four minutes dwindled to twenty, fifteen, ten.

Cass refused to leave her post in the lobby. Duty kept her standing there, directing the evacuation.

"Everybody's out," Vince Fettici, chief of security,

told her. "We've checked every room—there's no one left."

"Thank God." Relief shot through Cass. The structure may not survive, but the people would. "Go on and get out of here."

Fettici started to leave, pivoted toward her. "Aren't you coming?"

"I need to check something. I'm right behind you."

He shot her one last look, then strode toward the door.

"Cass, get out of here." Bud stalked toward her. "There's not much time left."

Less than eight minutes. "Have you found it yet?"

"Not a trace."

"Could be a hoax." God, she thought, please let it be a hoax.

Bud frowned. "Or well hidden." His voice was as grim as his eyes. "We've got the dogs sniffing around, but we'll have to pull them, too, if we don't find it soon."

"Let me just—"

He took her arm. "Just nothin', Cass." They'd known each other for eight years. They'd trusted each other with their lives. "I don't want needless risks taken. Just get out and wait like the rest of us. There's nothing you can do now."

She glanced around the magnificent lobby, the massive fireplace, the towering shelves of leather-bound books, the comfortable leather sofas, the elegant hardwood floors. There was nothing she could do, she acknowledged, mourning the impending loss.

With a heavy heart she joined the throng of displaced guests outside, several hundred yards from the hotel. The shrill of sirens intensified the chaos, shoving onlookers, shouts of law enforcement officials.

"Cass!" Gray called, racing over. "Thank God you're safe."

"How could this be happening?" she asked. "How could we not have seen this coming?"

"There were no signs." He glanced at the chaos. "Don't blame yourself."

"I can't help it." Her mind raced to puzzle out the meaning of the threat.

"From what I hear," Gray said, tilting her chin toward him, "you're a real hero. Bud said you got everyone out of there in no time. Sorry I wasn't here to help."

A grim smile touched her lips. "We're a good team, you and me. Don't forget that."

He returned her smile, then vanished into the crowd, no doubt wanting to see what else he could do to help.

She stood there taking it all in, but a sense of surreality blanketed her. Only twenty-four hours before she'd been buoyed by the hope and conviction that Derek Mansfield was an innocent man, that soon she would prove that to the world.

She had failed. In doing so, she'd thrust all these innocent lives into danger. She took in the sea of horrified faces, men and women, guests and employees alike. The elderly couple from Wales, the honeymooners from Tulsa. The mother and daughter from Bloomington, the businessmen from Dallas. A cluster of maids stood crying.

Ryan. Don't tell him.

The forgotten words ripped through her as savagely as a bomb soon would the hotel.

Ryan. Derek's nephew had been at the hotel. Now he was nowhere in sight. "Ryan!" Cass shoved her way through the throngs of frenzied, displaced people. "Ryan, where are you?"

He would have been on the penthouse floor, in Brent's private chambers. Had anyone realized that floor was not deserted? Had anyone gone to get him?

"Ryan!" she screamed, fighting her way toward the hotel.

"Ruth!" She ran toward her friend. "I can't find Ryan! Have you seen him?"

Ruth's eyes filled with horror. "No. The last I knew he and Brooke were upstairs—"

Brooke. Another person she'd not seen. "Sweet God."

Cass shoved through the crowd and raced toward the hotel. "You can't go in there, miss," someone called to her.

She pulled a leather case from her inner pocket and flashed her badge. She ran, nudging her way through the crowd, around the hotel and toward the back entrance, where she knew the stairs would be deserted. Ryan. Derek's beloved nephew. *An innocent child.* She had to get to him, couldn't let another young life be snuffed out because she'd failed to see the writing on the wall.

Each breath she drew slashed more jaggedly than the one before, but she raced on, in the door and up the stairs. Two floors, three, four. The fifth. The sixth. Seventh. Eighth.

Her legs turned to jelly, her lungs struggled to work.

Memories of Jake's laughing face mingled with images of Ryan. Old wounds tore open. Pain pushed her forward, giving her strength when her body could find none.

The ninth flight of stairs took forever, but she raced toward the tenth, then the—

A fierce roar rocked the building. Everything swayed, rumbled. She groped for the railing, but her sweaty, trembling hands slid off the cool metal. A scream rose to her throat, but it never had a chance to escape. She thudded against the concrete wall, then crumpled, tumbling down the cold, hard stairs, where nothing but darkness awaited.

Spurts of smoke gave way to billowing clouds. They leaked up between skyscrapers and stained the azure sky. Derek wondered what was going on, but once he exited the I-90 and lost himself among the congested city streets, buildings obscured his view. The dark clouds came in snippets then. Smoke. Then nothing. Smoke. Then nothing. Trouble somewhere in the city, he knew, but didn't think much of it.

Too much else riddled his mind.

A bomb threat at the San Francisco manor. He'd raced off like a madman, but by the time he reached O'Hare, instinct had taken over. Now was not the time to leave Chicago. Questions could be raised, suspicions. His plan could damn well—

He turned a corner and his curiosity exploded into something far darker. He jerked his car around the taxi in front of him, ignoring the hostile honking and cursing, and bullied his way toward the manor.

The streets grew more congested, but Derek didn't let that slow his progress. He'd overlooked the obvious. He'd left her alone, unprotected, at Vilas's mercy.

An army of fire engines, police cars and ambulances greeted him, preventing him from driving within blocks of the manor. Everything clicked into brutal focus then, the reality of what he'd let happen.

Horror almost shredded him. He bolted out of his car and ran down the alley, freezing when he rounded the corner.

His grandfather's crowning glory. The source of the smoke. Broken glass. Firefighters in heavy black jackets running around. Cops barking out orders. Paramedics racing toward the entrance. Fierce, barking German shepherds.

And onlookers. Everywhere. Some pointing frantically, others wailing and crying, others just watching. Pedestrians and businessmen and…hotel employees.

He recognized them instantly, the concierge, the bellmen, the maids, all huddled together, staring at the manor.

It was like a scene out of some disaster movie, but worse. It was real.

Shock coiled in his gut. And he ran.

Swearing savagely, he muscled his way through the

gawking onlookers. A wall of cops came next, barking out orders and fighting to hold the swelling crowd at bay.

"Let me through!" His grip on reality blurred, reducing him from tycoon to warrior.

"Cass!" She hadn't been with the other hotel employees, the onlookers, the paramedics. "Cass!" he called again, hoping against hope she would hear him and run into his arms.

Nothing.

"Sorry, sir," said one of the cops, this one with a look of authority about him. "No one is allowed past this point—the situation is still unstable."

"This is my hotel. What the hell is going on here?"

A man approached him, a man he'd seen countless times at the manor. John Dickens, the bellman Cass referred to as Gray. "Good question, Mansfield. One we'd like to ask you."

Dread tightened. "Quit the word games and tell me what the hell happened here."

"A bomb went off," the bellman supplied. "Couple of minutes ago."

The words slammed into Derek's gut. "Jesus Christ. Where?"

"In the parking garage," the uniformed cop answered. "The dogs sniffed it out, but we didn't have time to disarm it. Damage is—"

"Where's Cass?" Derek roared, renewing his struggle to break through the police line.

"Cass?" the cop repeated.

Dickens grabbed the front of Derek's shirt. *"Cass?"*

In a fluid move he hadn't used since his merchant marine days, Derek broke free of the bellman's grasp. "Cassandra LeBlanc. Perhaps you'll remember her," he added, finding no pleasure in the hardening of the other man's eyes. "She was on duty."

The bellman swung around. "She was here a few minutes ago."

But she wasn't there now.

Derek took advantage of the distraction and broke through the line, bolting toward the manor. Dickens raced after him.

Four grim-faced firefighters stumbled out of the lobby. "Get the paramedics in here!" one of them yelled. "We've found someone in one of the stairwells." He drew in a ragged breath. "A woman."

Derek's lungs burned in rebellion. "Is she—"

"Oh, God," Ruth said, running up behind them. "Oh, sweet God, no!"

Dickens grabbed the hysterical older woman. "What?"

Horror sharpened her gaze. "Cass went back inside! To get Ryan."

Derek's heart slammed to a cruel halt—Ryan wasn't even there. He was at the house in the country with Brooke.

"Sweet God!" Dickens roared, and took off running.

Derek started after him, but a firm hand closed down on his shoulders. "Sorry, Mansfield. You can't go in there. It's a crime scene."

"It's my hotel."

"Exactly," said another voice. "And we've got some questions for you down at headquarters."

A clawing emptiness closed in on him. Cass. Her deep, sultry eyes. Teasing him, crying in his arms, loving him.

"Your questions'll have to wait," he growled.

Another pair of hands closed around his free arm and dragged him backwards. "Afraid that's not an option."

Cass. Inside the manor. When the bomb blew. "My lov—employee is in there."

"If anyone's in there, there's nothing you can do for them now."

Minutes twisted into hours. Two plainclothes cops hauled Derek to the station and left him in a small inter-rogation room. There he sat, for what seemed like forever, agonizing over the unknown. Cass. In the manor. When the bomb blew.

No one would tell him anything. Not about the bomb. Not about the manor. Not about the woman who owned his heart.

They wanted answers from him instead.

The bright light of the sterile room illuminated so much more than just the bare walls. He'd known better than to get involved with Cass, known better than to drag her into his world. But even the sure knowledge of what would happen to her hadn't prevented him from taking what he wanted.

And because of that, she could be dead.

Rage tore through him. Betrayal. A raw pain unlike any he'd ever known. He needed to ferret out the meaning of the bomb, but even more, he needed to know if the woman he loved still lived.

The door opened, and two belligerent cops strode through. "Okay, Mansfield. Maybe now you're ready to talk."

Derek surged to his feet and bolted across the room. "Cass. You have to tell me if she's all right."

"We don't have to tell you anything," the shorter one snarled. He shoved Derek back toward the isolated table. "That responsibility is all yours."

"You're a lucky woman," the doctors said, giving her a clean bill of health. "The bomb was small," Gray had explained, then lectured her thoroughly.

Minor cuts and bruises littered her body, but she was barely cognizant of them. They held her at the hospital for a seeming eternity. At the station they refused to let her see Derek. "It's out of your hands now," Gray had told her.

And she feared he was right.

Ryan was fine, she'd learned. He and Brooke had been at the house in the country all along.

She should go home now, she knew, but a need she didn't understand drew her to the badly damaged manor. It stood deserted, the guests transferred to other hotels, the staff sent home, a few weary cops on guard.

Sir Maximillian's grand dream was now a crime scene.

Still, she felt closer to Derek here. She could almost lull herself into believing tomorrow wouldn't come.

Long after the grandfather clock chimed two in the morning, a figure emerged from the darkness and stood before her. His face was shadowed, his eyes blazing.

Just the sight of him hurt. But the smell of his woodsy cologne, the jolt of his presence, they destroyed.

Cass did the only thing she could. She stood and walked into his arms. They closed around her, holding her against him as if she was the most precious thing in the world.

When he pulled back and looked her, she discovered more agony in his eyes than in her battered body.

He drew her hand to his mouth. Kissed her knuckles. Said nothing. Quietly, deliberately, he led her from the hotel into the cold of the night, into his waiting, heated car. They drove on, he not speaking, she having no idea what to say. His life was littered by people who had let him down. She didn't want to be one of them.

If one person, just one, had stood by him when times had gotten tough, he wouldn't be the man he was today.

Cass stifled a moan. The man he was today. It seemed morbid to be grateful he'd endured such a lousy life, but the man he'd become was the man she loved with all her heart.

They headed north along the lake, leaving the streets of Chicago behind. The cop in her warned her to be on guard, that a dangerous suspect was leading her away, no one aware of their destination.

But the woman in her abolished the thought.

The house rose up before her, as shimmering white in the darkness of night as it was in the light of day. His grandfather's house. The place where his truths hid, the place he'd never shared with Cass.

He stopped the car at the top of the drive, got out, strode to her side, lifted her into his arms. He cradled her to his chest and strode up the steps onto the verandah, toward the front door. It swung open, the butler standing in solemn greeting.

Derek nodded, said nothing as he carried her up the curving stairs. She tried to drink it all in, but he moved too swiftly. The next thing she knew they were in an upstairs bedroom. A king-size bed occupied the heart of the room, its massive cherry headboard a throwback to times gone by.

He placed her on the thick black comforter. Around her the room seemed to revolve, until she focused on the enormous hearth across from her, the fire licking in its grate as fiercely as it licked through her.

She endeavored to make sense of what was happening. He'd taken her to his grandfather's house, the part of himself he kept locked away. They were lovers, yet she hadn't been sure of his innocence. It hadn't mattered, though, because she was determined to stand by him. What she felt for him ran too deep to be cast aside because life tossed a nasty curve ball.

The love was stronger than the lies.

Too late she realized she was right. Derek *did* hide something in this house, just not the crucial link to Santiago Vilas she'd expected.

Something far more precious.

He hid his heart, that part of him that had been hurt, used and discarded too many times before. Here he could be himself. Here he could return to the innocence of childhood, when dreams still lit the future.

The truth unfurled before her, as bright and unshakable as the first shimmering light of morning. The insular man who drew his strength from this solitary home was not a monster. He'd merely locked away the most precious part of him, protected it, kept it far from anyone who could hurt it.

The ache in her heart intensified. Derek was opening to her, revealing his vulnerability and how much she meant to him. She had to tell him the truth, couldn't continue to keep it from him. Sooner or later the love and the lies would come crashing down. She would be dead to Derek then, just as his parents were, just as Marla was.

He came to her, eyes blazing. No words were spoken. No words were necessary. There was only hunger. And desperation. Need.

The dominoes were crashing down, swifter and more violently than she could have predicted. The lies and the truths, all that was lost somewhere between. The love.

It could only mean one thing: the end.

Derek fought sleep, unwilling to sacrifice even one moment with the woman he loved. She was alive. More than just alive, she lay naked and sprawled atop him, her head on his chest, leg slung over his. Her dark hair fanned out over his chest hairs, providing a playground for his fingers.

Contentment welled up inside him. Completeness. An overriding sense that this was what life was about, this peace and unity.

During the hours they'd held him at the station, grilling him with questions about who might want to bomb the hotel, his hunger for Cass had taken on a life of its own. Fear of the worst kind had gnawed at him, making him wild. When they'd released him, he'd driven to her house, only to find it empty, except for Barney barking at the window. Desperate, he'd driven around, but had not known where to go, until he'd found himself drawn to the manor. When he found her staring at the fireplace, everything had vanished except the need to spirit her away.

No words could convey the emotions tearing through him. Only actions. Wild, frenetic actions, followed by slow, savoring ones. He'd made love to her thoroughly, hungrily, tenderly. He feasted on all she so freely gave, yet rather than feeling fulfilled, he found himself famished.

She could have died. His fiery angel. Because of him.

Darkness gave way to pinkish rays of dawn. The sleepy sun peeked through the drapes, reminding him the coming day could not be avoided. Questions needed answers, answers explanations, explanations understanding. He would come clean with her and pray love outweighed lies.

He brushed a kiss across her hair. She sighed, nestled closer.

"Ah, God, Cass," he murmured. "Why now? Why now."

"Why now what?" She tilted her face toward his. Contentment shone in her eyes, her skin glowed.

All Derek could do was smile. "I didn't mean to wake you."

Her hand slid up his chest and cupped his cheek. "You didn't." Those fathomless eyes of hers studied his, a silent communion forging between them.

"Oh, Derek," she said at last. "We need to talk."

His gut clenched. The bubble of tranquility began to deflate, pierced by the knowledge that despite last night, she harbored her own doubts about the bombing.

"Cass," he began, dread pummeling him. "I didn't do it."

A moment of confusion clouded her face, followed by something strangely close to pain. "Derek—"

"No wait." He didn't want to hear questions or suspicions fall from her mouth. "I haven't been totally upfront with you. There are things you don't know, things—"

Her soft mouth closed over his, silencing his words. She kissed him wholly, longingly. Both her hands were on his face, her body fully over his. She held him there, her prisoner, kissing him as though her life depended on it.

"It's important," he ground out, sliding from beneath her. He sat and urged her up to face him. Tears swam in her eyes, sharpening the pain and dread. He'd never seen her look so desolate. Scared. She was his brave, fearless angel. That he'd reduced her to this ripped at him.

"The police think things," he offered, not ready for the possibility of her thinking the same things. "The press will say things. You need to be prepared."

Tears spilled over her lashes. "I've made my choice, Derek. I'm not going anywhere. You have to believe that."

The despair in her voice belied the courageous words. "I want to."

She pressed her lips to his. "Then do," she said. "No matter what happens, no matter how things may seem, believe it. Believe me."

It sounded as though she was the one begging for mercy.

"Ah, Cass," he soothed, threading his fingers through her hair. He couldn't take her pain, had to chase it away. "Cass…"

She smiled through her tears. "You are such a special man. You don't deserve this."

"What I don't deserve is you," he said roughly.

She flinched, as though he'd slapped her.

"But I thank God that you're here." He slid her down his body, positioning her. She took over, sliding down, encasing him to the hilt. The pleasure was so intense it was almost unbearable as she eased herself down, then back up.

Passion glazed her eyes, drowned out the fear and pain. He wanted to roll her over and thrust into her, but this was her show, her need. So, hands fondling her heavy breasts, he simply held on while she gave him the priceless gift of her body.

And her love.

* * *

Sometime later, as they lay spent in each other's arm, a knock sounded at the door.

"Mr. Mansfield, sir?" came the butler Montford's tentative voice.

Derek ignored him, not wanting to shatter the spell.

"Mr. Mansfield," Montford said more urgently. "There's a man downstairs, says if you don't come down, he'll come up."

A man. Waiting for him. It could only mean one thing. He swore savagely, looked down at Cass sleeping in his arms.

Her eyelids fluttered open. "What is it?"

He hesitated, hating that he'd walked into a trap of his own making. "Wait here. I'll be back in a second."

"What's wrong?"

He rolled from the bed and jerked on his jeans. "I'll handle it, honey. You just stay here."

She climbed from the bed, still naked. "Not on your life."

"Cass—"

"Didn't you say we're in this together?"

He took her hands. Regret shot through him. "There are things you don't know, things I don't want you to find out like this."

"Like how?"

Derek glanced toward the door, back at her. "There's a man downstairs. I'm betting he's a cop."

Her eyes widened. "The bomb?"

Derek had never imagined himself walking the green mile, but now he knew he had no choice. Not if he wanted to keep Cass in his life. "Among other things."

She paled. Glancing toward the door, she drew a hand to her heart. "Dear God, no. Not now."

Her words made no sense, but he had no time to question. "Just give me a few minutes," he said, crossing the room. "I'll explain when I get back."

"I'm going with you."

"Cass—"

"What's waiting for you downstairs affects us both," she rasped. "I'm not hiding up here like a coward." She quickly dressed, then crossed to him. Her hair was tangled, her face flushed. She looked exactly like what she was. A woman who'd spent the night in her lover's arms.

He took her hand and guided her downstairs. He wanted to spare her this, but knew he couldn't stop night from falling.

Downstairs a man waited. A man he recognized. A man he'd talked with, argued with. A man whose paycheck he'd cut.

John Dickens. The man Cass called Gray. He stood in wrinkled khakis and a sports coat, his face a grim mask. He stared straight ahead. Not at Derek, though. At the woman by his side. Derek glanced her way, only to discover she returned the man's stare, the same grim line marring her beautiful lips.

A damning suspicion twisted through him.

"Derek Mansfield," John Dickens said, stepping forward. He reached inside his jacket and withdrew a black wallet.

Before it flicked open, Derek knew what lay inside.

A badge stared back at him. "Mitch Grayson, Chicago PD."

Derek stepped off the last stair. "Son of a bitch." The light was coming on much too clearly. "Gray," he muttered, the nickname taking on a whole new meaning.

"That's right," Grayson confirmed. "Cass," he said, reaching a hand toward her. "It's time."

She tensed. More than just her fingers in Derek's hand, her whole body. But she said nothing.

"Cass..." Grayson took her free hand and pulled her toward him. "The gig is over."

But she just stood there, one frozen hand encased in

Derek's, the other in Grayson's. She barely even looked alive.

And Derek knew.

The truth stabbed through him like a deadly spear. He'd been torturing himself with guilt over entangling an innocent like Cass in his life, but now he knew that wasn't the case. Not even close. He hadn't entangled her—she'd entrapped him.

He looked at her standing there, at her pale, stricken face, and slowly uncurled his fingers from hers. He wasn't sure his heart still beat. Everything inside of him felt dead.

She pivoted toward him, looked up at him with wide, beseeching eyes. "Derek—I can explain."

Chapter 15

Horror ripped through Cass. Her heart beat frantically, desperately. "I—"

"Don't waste your breath." Derek held out his wrists to Gray. "Let's get on with it, then," he said flatly. "Let me guess, I have the right to remain silent."

"Stop it!" She batted down his outstretched arms and spun toward Gray. "You've got the wrong man, Gray. He had nothing to do with the bombing."

"This isn't about the bombing."

"Then what?" she demanded. Betrayal slapped at her.

Gray frowned. "Trafficking, just like we thought. We found the evidence in the wreckage."

"That's only circumstantial," she insisted. Derek would never forgive her betrayal, but she couldn't let him take the fall. "It's a setup, can't you see that?"

Gray remained calm. "What I see is a guilty man, Cass, the same one we've been closing in on for over six months."

Shame roared through her. She looked at her partner,

the man she loved as dearly as her own brothers, and at that moment detested him with every fiber of her being. "You son of a bitch," she snarled, her hand flying toward his face.

He caught her wrist. "You should be thanking me right now, Cammy. Not condemning me. Bud and the boys are less than ten minutes behind me."

"And I should thank you for that?"

"You're damn straight you should. If I hadn't gotten here first, they would have found what I found. You in bed with a criminal. And then your career would be over."

"I don't give a damn about my career!"

"Yes, you do, damn it. Mansfield has clouded your judgment, but not mine. I'm not going to let you throw away everything you've worked for because of one bad decision."

His censure burned. "Hypocrite," she accused, flicking her wrist from his confining hand. "How dare you judge me, when you yourself crossed the line with Dawn?"

"I'm not judging you. I'm judging Mansfield."

She twisted toward Derek. He stood stiff as a statue, eyes dead as stone, soul plain for her to see.

So much needed to be said, but deep inside, where the truth dwelled, she knew he would never believe her. Not now.

Not ever.

Derek Mansfield was not a man for forgiveness, not a man for second chances. She had only to look at the stern angles of his face, the savagery of his stance, like a warrior standing defiantly before the enemy. And she knew.

Derek Mansfield looked exactly like what he was. A man betrayed. *Badly,* betrayed.

She reached for him, but he sidestepped her touch. An insolent smile twisted the mouth that had worshipped her body only hours before. "I got to hand it to you, doll baby. You're one hell of an actress. I never once imagined you'd sell your body for the sake of the job.''

The comment almost knocked her flat. She began to bleed, not on the outside, but on the inside, from her heart. Yet she said nothing—because he was right. She was no better than a prostitute, trading her body for the good of the investigation.

"Derek Mansfield," Gray said, "you have the right to remain silent…''

"Cass, talk to me.''

She stood on the veranda, one hand curled around the railing. Bud and the boys had taken Derek away minutes before, Gray's cuffs securing his wrists behind his back. Only a faint uprising of dust could be seen where the car vanished down the road. An eerie stillness permeated the day. The naked trees just stood there, as though they, too, were paralyzed.

"Cass?''

She bit back a sob. Her fault, all of it. In trying to protect, she'd destroyed.

"Cass." Gray wiped at the tears sliding down her face. "I'm sorry."

The crushing reality of what she'd done closed in on her. "I can't…b-breathe," she panted, wrapping her arms around her waist and doubling over, gasping for air.

But it wouldn't come.

I never once imagined you'd sell your body for the sake of the job.

"He's r-right," she cried, straightening. "I'm no better than a whore."

"That's not true." Gray's hands closed around her arms. "You're a woman, Cass, a woman who fell for the wrong man."

"He's not the wrong man, Gray." Clear now, disgustingly clear. "We're the ones who are wrong. Dead wrong."

* * *

"I told you to never come here."

"Relax, my friend." Santiago Vilas set down a large box and pulled off a baseball cap. Outside, a truck sat waiting, the name of a national delivery company emblazoned across its side. "I was careful, which is more than I can say for you."

The caustic insult fueled the anger burning through Derek. Out on bail, he'd barely been home an hour, and even though he'd been working nonstop, there was still much to do. Close. He was so damn close. He'd be damned if he let it slip away now.

"I'm not going to do you a hell of a lot of good if I'm behind bars."

"The charges will never stick. We both know that."

"What the hell did you think you were doing?" Derek roared. He wanted to charge the slimeball, but somehow held himself back. "We never talked about a bomb."

Vilas laughed. "But we did talk about luring your rats out of hiding, and I did that quite nicely. You can rebuild the hotel. If the cops hadn't been found, the price would be much stiffer."

Derek didn't share Vilas's nonchalance. The man had set him up, used him as bait. And Derek could end up paying the ultimate price. His lawyer, the best money could buy, had grimly informed him of the evidence against him. It was damning, just as it had been intended to be.

Thank God his grandfather's connections were strong enough to secure bail. But being out from behind bars did not equal freedom. His every move would be monitored, making it difficult to complete what he'd started.

"The house is under surveillance," he reminded Vilas. "Unless you want to get dragged into this mess, I suggest you leave." He glanced at Vilas's crisp uniform and cut him a hard smile. "Deliverymen don't stay longer than a few minutes."

Vilas narrowed his eyes. "You should know by now who gives orders, who follows them."

Images came back to Derek, of the destruction at his grandfather's hotel. Images of Cass came, too, of her staring vacantly at the fireplace, sprawled out naked on his king-size bed, standing stone-faced among a circle of pig-headed cops.

"Oh, you don't need to worry about that," he told Vilas, his voice deceptively calm. "I know exactly where everyone stands."

And, most important, where they would fall.

"That is what I like to hear." Vilas pulled the cap back down on his head. "Quite frankly your lack of manners surprises me, my friend."

From the beady gleam in Vilas's black eyes, Derek knew the Latin man was baiting him. "I would invite you for tea, but the Feds outside might become suspicious." He narrowed his eyes. "If you're willing to risk it, however—"

"I sniffed out your rats, didn't I?" Vilas squared his narrow shoulders. He looked so damn proud of himself, so cocksure. "Now it's time for extermination."

Derek raised a hatchet and swung it toward the battered tree stump. Splintered wood chips exploded upon impact, flying up, then crashing onto the brown grass. He reared back and swung again and again and again. Brent had been by earlier, bemoaning the destruction at the hotel. The insurance company was refusing to pay, pending an investigation, believing the cops' accusations that Derek planted the bomb.

So much for innocent until proven guilty.

Sir Maximillian was on his way back to Chicago. It had been hell telling him what happened, especially his arrest. He hadn't been sure how his grandfather would react, but he sure as hell hadn't expected the wholehearted support the older man immediately threw his way, nor his insistence on returning to Chicago.

Derek's throat tightened at the memory.

He reared back and slammed the hatchet into the stump again. His body responded to the exertion, sweat pouring down his face, soaking his clothes.

"Thirsty?"

Hatchet high over his aching shoulders, Derek swung toward the low, throaty voice. Cass stood there, entreaty in her eyes, a glass of water in her hand. She looked oddly fragile, like a woman, not a cop.

The sight hit him hard. "Sorry, doll baby, but I only drink with friends."

The naive hope drained from her face. "We need to talk."

She stood there so benignly, a faded flower on a brutal winter day, as though all that stood between them was a trivial misunderstanding.

Rage careened through him. Regret. Betrayal. "You've got nerve showing up here."

"Nerve is about all I have left." She pulled her long wool coat tighter around her.

She was shivering, he noted, despite the knit cap snug on her head, the wool scarf around her neck, the gloves encasing her hands, the boots protecting her feet. For a change a snug French braid did not secure her hair. Tangled strands slipped from beneath her cap and dangled against her chest and shoulders.

The urge to hold her came hard and fast, the need to give her every molecule of his warmth. "You're wasting your time. And mine."

Her eyes filled, as they had that day in Grant Park, when he'd found her staring at other people's children. "Wait," she said, stepping toward him. "Let me explain."

He stood unmoving, towering over her, relying on his height and physical size to communicate words he didn't trust himself to say. Once started, he wasn't sure he'd be able to stop.

Never in his life had anyone cut him deeper. Not his mother, not Marla.

But it took every ounce of control he had to remember the lies and ignore the alleged pain in her eyes.

"I've got to hand it to you," he drawled with a casualness he didn't feel. "You're one hell of an actress."

The glass slipped from her fingers, crashed against the battered stump. Water sloshed against them, but she didn't glance down. "Derek, you have to listen to me."

"I don't have to do anything."

"I never meant for this to happen," she said, reaching for him.

He twisted away, his breathing heavier than while he'd been swinging the hatchet. "Never meant for what to happen? Never meant to use me? To get caught in your lies? Never meant to trade your body for evidence?"

Cass staggered back. Her skin went even paler, as though he'd hit her with his fists and not the plain and simple truth. "You've got it all wrong," she rasped. "The lies are all you see right now, but there's so much more. We can get through this," she said, the fervent wind dulling her words. "I'm sorry—"

"Don't be." He didn't want explanations, didn't want more lies to distort what he knew to be true. "It was a hell of a ploy. Get me addicted to you, to the way you make me fee—" He bit back the offending word. He didn't feel anything. "You thought you could get me addicted to that hot body of yours, turn me inside out so I forget to watch my ass."

The words sounded cold, even to his own ears.

Cass rallied, squaring her shoulders and narrowing her eyes like the fighter he knew her to be. "You think this is what I *wanted* to happen? You think I wanted to fall in love with a man I believed to be a criminal?"

The question, the passion in her voice, nicked at the

self-preservation that kept him alive. But he wouldn't fall for the lies again. Instead, he flicked his gaze over her body. "You forget, Cass. I know exactly what you wanted, and it had nothing to do with love."

She recoiled from the nasty words. "You're damn straight it had nothing to do with love. Not at first. It had to do with cracking a case I'd been working for months. I'm good at my job, Derek. I always get my man."

"You're saying I'm not the first to fall into your trap? Your bed?"

The thought of it turned his stomach.

Fire flashed in Cass's eyes, and her hand whipped toward his face.

He easily caught her wrist. "What's the matter? The truth hurts?"

She glared up at him, her breathing now labored. "You wouldn't know the truth if it stabbed you in the heart."

The accusation cut deeper than it should have. "Don't talk to me about truth and honesty, Detective." He looked at where his fingers curled around her slender wrist, hated how easily he could hurt her.

He abruptly released her and turned back to the stump, raising the hatchet and slamming it down one more time.

He didn't trust himself to speak.

"I tried to stay away from you," she said, her voice still strong but now angry, as well. "I tried to ignore the attraction, knew it couldn't lead anywhere but trouble. But you didn't exactly let me, did you?"

He didn't want to look at her anymore but couldn't let that remark slide. "You're saying this is my fault?"

"It's not about fault, Derek. It's about the lies we were forced to tell, the love that grew anyway."

The words scraped. "Don't talk to me about love and lies, *Cammy*. Don't pretend they're some pretty little package."

"You shouldn't have followed me, damn it! Not to the

park, my house, anywhere! You should have just left me alone.''

''How could I when you were everywhere? I'm a man, Cass. A man who thought he saw a woman in need and tried to help. If that's a crime, then fry me.'' He sucked in a sharp breath, enjoyed the sting all the way to his lungs. ''Tell me something, was it all a lie? Did you even have a husband and child, or was that just a story to worm your way under my skin?''

The blood drained from her face and she swayed. ''Damn you.''

He ignored the urge to steady her. ''You've already done that, doll.''

Moisture flooded her whiskey eyes, and all too quickly she looked like the woman he'd found at the park, the one who'd fallen apart in his arms. Not the cop who'd betrayed him.

''What happened to my family is as real as the way I feel about you,'' she whispered, a horrible quaver to her voice. She wrapped her arms around her body, but still she shook. ''You made me realize I couldn't hide behind a wall of pain. You made me feel things, Derek. You helped me let go of the past. You touched off the desire for a life I'd forbidden myself from even thinking about. And that's when I realized the truth, that you weren't the criminal I thought you to be, but a warm, generous man. That's what I've been fighting to prove.''

Unwanted emotion crashed through him, the desire to pull her into his arms and pretend she spoke the truth.

Instead he clapped. ''Keep it up, doll, and I'll nominate you for an Academy Award.''

''Damn it, Derek—''

''No, not damn it, Derek. Damn it, you!'' He couldn't believe what a fool he'd been. ''You're the one who said lovers shouldn't have secrets,'' he reminded.

She swiped the tears from beneath her cheeks. ''I had no choice.''

"We all have choices, Detective." He spoke as snidely as he could, hating himself, not her. "Some of us just make wiser ones than others."

Rather than retreating, as he'd hoped, Cass rushed toward him and grabbed his arm. "Derek—"

He went completely still. Poison coursed through his body. Betrayal. Desire. He looked down at his forearm, where her gloved fingers curled around flesh. "You don't want to touch me right now," he warned.

She looked up at him, defiantly, evocatively, much as she had that very first day. "Yes, I do," she said clearly and firmly. "Don't you understand? *I love you.*"

The words hit him like a punch to the gut, to the very core of who he was. Never had he wanted to believe something more.

"Love me?" he scoffed. "Well, you've got one hell of a way of showing it."

"We can get through this. I—"

"Save it, Cass." He yanked down his arm and broke her grip. "Save it for someone who gives a damn."

That said, he turned and strode toward his grandfather's house. He didn't want to hear anymore, see anymore.

He didn't want to be tempted anymore.

He never looked back. He wouldn't start now.

Derek raked a hand through his hair, shoving damp strands from his face. He'd been in the midst of a hot shower when Montford had banged on the door, apologizing profusely but announcing an urgent call on the secure line.

Now Derek stood by the small night table in his bedroom, water dripping down his naked body and puddling at his feet. If he'd been capable of feeling, he might have wrapped a robe around him to fend off the chill.

"We were so damn close," he ground out. "So close to that last nail in the coffin."

"It might not be as bad as you think."

"A cop, damn it." It sickened him to utter the word, much less accept the implication.

He swore, voicing his anguish aloud. There weren't many people he'd let hear it, less than a handful, in fact. Sir Maximillian, of course. Brooke. Sometimes Brent, yet not this time, not when he could blow everything sky high.

And Lucas Treese. They'd raised more than their fair share of hell together in their merchant marine days. Since then, life had taken them down radically different paths, but the friendship born in rowdy ports had survived the test of time.

They were in this together, as they'd been so often before.

"She's a cop," Derek told him, though of course Lucas, an FBI agent, already knew. "And there I was feeling guilty about dragging her into my world."

"From what I hear," Luc offered, "she's one of Chicago's finest—you couldn't have known."

"But I should have." The signs had been there, had he only been thinking with his head and not his hea—lower half. Hadn't he been the one to tell Vilas he smelled a rat? He'd not only let that rat flourish in his hotel, he'd let her demolish his penchant for sound thinking.

"How many times, Luc?" His gaze riveted on her crumpled panty hose abandoned by the foot of his bed. "How many times do I have to hit the same brick wall?"

"Quit raking yourself over the coals." Like other times, Luc was more than willing to help Derek pick up the pieces. He'd been there in the beginning, when Derek had joined the merchant marines to escape his stepfather's wrath, after Sasha, again after Marla. And Brent. He knew the whole truth, every last sliver of it, and accordingly, he'd been the one to help Derek past the sting of betrayal and exact a plan for retribution.

He'd been the one to rein in Derek's impatience six months before, the one to warn of FBI agents moving in for the kill. He was always harping about Derek's death wish, as though keeping his friend alive had become his own personal crusade.

"Put it behind you," he said. "Focus on what needs to be done."

Slowly Derek became aware of his surroundings, of the cool air slapping his wet skin. "It should have been over by now," he snapped, then pulled the spurt of anger in check.

Lucas let out a weary sigh. "It's not too late to abort. All you have to do is tell them. I'll back you up."

Like hell. That would be the easy way out, a cowardly move that would do nothing but jeopardize his plan and his life. Other lives hung in the balance now, other lives too precious to ever put at risk. Brent. And Ryan. The boy deserved to grow up with a father who loved him, a gift Derek never had.

"Don't worry," he told Lucas. "Just hang tight, man, and be ready for my call—I'll take care of everything else."

Cass watched the Salvation Army truck disappear down the street, the last of Jake's belongings on their way to brighten the lives of other little boys.

"Come on, Barn," she said, smiling despite the tears. "Let's get out of this cold."

Several minutes later she and Barney sat on the brick hearth. The big mutt lapped at the salty moisture on her face, then nestled his head in her lap and fell asleep. A pathetic fire crackled in the grate.

Restless, she reached behind her head and began braiding her tangled hair. Going to Derek's had been a mistake. Even though she deserved his animosity, she hadn't been prepared for the brick wall she'd hit.

Lost in thought, it took Cass a few minutes to hear the incessant knocking at the front door. A strange surge of hope shot through her, propelling her to scoot from underneath Barney and dash to the door. She pulled it open, not expecting, but hoping, to see Derek.

"Cassidy Blake?" a young man asked. The label on his uniform said his name was Paul and he worked for a local courier.

And he used her real name, not the one she'd been going by for months now.

Unease settled low in her belly. "Can I help you?"

"I have a delivery for Ms. Blake." He handed her a sealed envelope, then turned and hurried back to his car.

Cass looked at the envelope and knew beyond a shadow of a doubt the last domino had fallen. Closing the door, she sank down against the wood and sat crouched on the cool tile. She sat that way several minutes before tearing the seal and yanking out a single sheet of paper.

Ten words stared back at her.

"We need to talk. The Museum of Natural History. Midnight."

The deserted museum looked much as it had the night Derek and Vilas conducted their transaction. The parking lot stood empty, an abandoned sports car here, a broken-down minivan there. Sharp wind blew off the lake, pushing around crumpled fast-food bags and sending discarded cola cans rolling.

A full moon stood sentinel this night, its eerie glow occasionally waylaid by high, thin clouds. Shadows stretched across the concrete.

Cass stood shivering. No matter how tightly she hugged herself, the chill stayed in her bones. She'd been sure he would show up, tell her he believed her, that he knew she loved him, that he loved her, too.

She couldn't have been more wrong.

Derek Mansfield was not a man to forgive.

"Cass."

She spun toward the voice, heart leaping into a staccato

rhythm. She knew the voice, had heard it countless times before.

Clad in a long trench coat, a gentleman's hat hiding his blond hair, Brent moved toward her. He looked like a figure out of a fifties Hollywood flick, except no gallantry underscored his stance, only gravity.

Disappointment cut through her. "It was you."

"I know who you are," he said, stopping a few feet away. "I know what you did. I saw you at the house, saw Derek after you left." The tone of his voice said it hadn't been a pretty sight. "Leave him alone, Cass. Back off."

This was a first. Ever since she'd begun her association with the Stirling Manor—and the men who ran it—Derek had been the one to take charge, Brent the one to let him. This newfound strength, this sudden intervention, sent alarm bells clamoring. "Not on your life."

"He doesn't need you or your brand of help. He'll get through this, just like always. My brother's a fighter. If he's letting this happen, there's a reason."

Something more was going on, Cass realized, something more than one brother looking out for another. Brent suspected something. Either that or he was worried.

"There's a reason, all right," she ad-libbed.

I take care of what's mine, Derek had once said, but now those words took on a whole new meaning. There was no disputing the evidence gathered at the manor, only its interpretation.

Could Brent have been the guilty one all along? "He's trying to protect you," she realized aloud.

"Me?" he asked, his tone brilliantly befuddled. "There's nothing to protect. Not anymore."

Her patience wore thin. "This is your brother's life we're talking about. Riddles aren't going to cut it. Either you come clean with me, or—"

"Or what?"

"Or I'm taking you in."

He eyed her warily, suspiciously, then his shoulders

seemed to slump. "It was about a year and a half ago," he murmured. His eyes were glassy, his voice whisper soft. "Derek had been traveling. He came home late one night, unexpectedly. He found me…"

Cass swallowed. This U-turn wasn't what she'd been expecting. "Found you where?"

"At the hotel…in my office…unconscious."

"Unconscious?"

"My wife Susan had walked out on me—she told me she would make sure I never saw Ryan again. I was scared," he admitted, his voice trancelike. "So scared. And there was nobody there, nobody except the heroin."

Heroin. The facts of the case swirled through her mind. A series of high-profile drug busts, all connected to the manor. Several raids there, as well. Suspicion that the manor itself was linked to the trafficking. Not Brent, though. The other brother, the one who had a reputation for bucking authority.

The one who took care of what was his.

"Tell me what happened," Cass encouraged. Her throat was so tight, so dry, the mere act of breathing hurt.

Derek's baby brother stood before her, the flamboyant playboy extinguished, the remaining shell looking every bit as bombed-out as the manor.

"He went wild," Brent murmured. "Wild. I don't remember much, just snatches. Derek yelling, pounding my chest…the paramedics…the emergency room. Derek was there the whole time, telling me it would be okay, *willing* it to be okay. Making it be okay. But I was so far gone…"

"The drugs," Cass prompted, hiding her urgency. "Where did the drugs come from?"

"One of our guests," Brent mumbled. "It started out simple, just a little fun, a little relaxation. Things started getting tough with Susan, and Villy was there. He always had something to make me feel better."

Cass's pulse quickened.

"He wanted something from me," Brent went on. "I

didn't see it, not until it was too late, not until Dare came back and went ballistic. He saw everything so clearly—he always has. Villy used me as a puppet, a cover, a convenient front for his organization. By the time I realized it, I was in too deep. There was no way I could back out without losing everything, including my son, in the process.''

That last domino wobbled before her. ''What happened?''

''I don't know.'' His eyes cleared a little, yet they revealed nothing. ''When I got out from rehab, Villy was gone, and I had joint custody of Ryan.''

Courtesy of Derek, no doubt. *I take care of what's mine.*

''Villy was gone? Just like that?''

Brent nodded, said nothing.

I take care of what's mine.

The words taunted her, yet she couldn't pinpoint why. Brent had been Vilas's puppet. Brent had been the front man. Brent had been the one to drag the manor into drug trafficking. Not Derek. But since his return from Scotland, Derek had been the one sneaking around, the one to do business with Vilas, the one who'd stashed cocaine and heroin in his suite.

I take care of what's mine.

''Sweet God,'' she murmured, the truth slamming home.

Yes, Derek had done all those things, but not as a cold-blooded criminal, only a brother out for vengeance. He wasn't a man to sit back and wait for the slow wheels of justice to turn, her Derek was a man to *make* them turn.

''A setup,'' she said aloud, a setup more elaborate than the one she and Gray had staged. ''It all makes so much sense now. He was luring Vilas into a trap of his own making.''

But what then, she wondered. What had he planned to do next? He had no credibility with law enforcement.

Even with evidence to the contrary, the cops would never believe Derek Mansfield wasn't trying to cover his own tracks.

But more clearly than she'd ever known anything, Cass knew the truth.

"No wonder Villy backed off." Brent's eyes sharpened. "He replaced me with Derek. Dare must have convinced him that he had something better to offer." He closed his eyes. "I should have known it was too easy to be real."

An old-fashioned vigilante. The label sounded romantic, but Cass knew it for a reckless, dangerous act. Derek hadn't just put his future on the line, he'd slapped his life there, as well. And now, unless Cass could prove it, he could lose both.

"We have to find him," she told Brent, reaching out and grabbing his coat. Time to take charge, for the cop and the woman to work together.

"Well, well, well." A snide voice cut through the night.

Cass stilled, Brent stumbling into her.

"The lovely Cassandra LeBlanc—or should I say *Cassidy Blake?*" From behind one of the columns, a man stepped into a pool of moonlight, a pistol in his outstretched hands.

"We meet again."

Chapter 16

An eerie silence rang through the manor. Never in his life had Derek heard it that quiet, seen it that empty. Always, always, it had been the heart and soul of the Stirling Manor empire, the hub from which everything thrived.

Now it stood empty, a few sleepy cops wandering around, standing guard, sifting for clues. They'd tried to keep Derek out, no doubt suspecting he was going to tamper with evidence, but Derek would not be denied. A compromise had been struck: Derek would be admitted onto his property, but only under the watchful eye of one of the detectives.

No problem. He'd gone straight to the third-floor garage, the scene of the worst devastation. It wasn't as bad as he'd imagined, images of the bombed-out Federal building in Oklahoma City permanently etched in his mind. He considered himself, his family and the guests lucky as hell.

Minutes later he surveyed the lobby, where smoke and water had caused the majority of the damage. It could be restored to its original splendor, but he knew it would never be the same.

He needed to go upstairs, but detoured to the lounge instead. He grabbed a bottle of Scotch and poured a tumbler full. The liquid burned as it slid down his throat, prompting him to just stare at the half-empty glass.

He wanted no more burning.

Cass. The thought blasted out of nowhere, and all but leveled him with its force. No matter where he went or what he did, she was always there waiting. The desolation in her eyes haunted him. That she'd come to him didn't make sense, not after she'd gotten what she wanted. Unless...

No. He wouldn't poison himself with naive fantasies. Guilt had driven her to his house, nothing more. Absolution. That's what she wanted, something he couldn't give.

He'd loved her. Unabashedly. Irrevocably.

But no matter how hard he tried to banish them, images of her lingered. Cass standing on the edge of the park, crying. Cass throwing her head back in defiance. Cass coming apart in his arms. Her courage and pain, her strength, her vulnerability. Her passion. Her tenacity. All those traits that made Cass such an intriguing enigma twisted into a force he couldn't deny, wrapped around his heart with devastating tenacity.

At first the pull between them had simply puzzled him. Later, when it grew stronger every time he saw her, it had bothered him. That, too, had faded away, to the point where the foreign ache in his chest began to comfort.

Now it destroyed.

He wanted to throw back the immutable hands of time and recast the die. Have them meet another time, another place, under other circumstances. Just a man and a woman, not a cop and a vigilante.

Without the lies, the love might have been enough.

There was no such thing as love, he reminded himself. Only smoke and mirrors.

Derek threw back the remainder of his Scotch and

poured another. Sooner or later, the smoky alcohol was bound to numb.

"You son of a bitch!" Two hands slammed down on the back of his shoulders and hauled him out of his chair. Before he could react he was spun around, the front of his shirt grabbed and twisted by none other than Detective Mitch Grayson.

"What's the matter, bellboy?" Derek sneered. "The scam's over. Don't tell me you forgot?"

The cop's eyes hardened. "You've got a hell of a lot of nerve," he ground out, twisting Derek's shirt tighter. "Leave her alone, man. Just let it go."

Derek tried not to laugh. "Trust me, that's exactly what I plan to do."

"You've got a funny way of showing it." Grayson let go of Derek's shirt, but remained nose to nose. "She was so hopeful, so sure you'd come to your senses. I told her not to go. I warned her nothing good could come from it."

"I'd think anyone as close to Cass as you obviously are would know she does what she pleases, when she pleases."

Grayson frowned. "It's a habit I haven't been able to break her of."

And one of the traits Derek loved most about her. "Thank God for that."

"You really are heartless, you know that?" Grayson looked toward the empty tables scattered about the lounge. Some lay on their sides, untouched since the explosion. "She's been through hell," he muttered. "She deserves better than this."

Suspicion dawned, and Derek realized why Grayson was so protective of Cass. "You were there, weren't you?" he asked. He knew the beauty of partnership, something he and Luc had enjoyed for years. "You were there when she lost her husband and son."

"I was the one who told her. The one who saw the

light drain from her eyes. Who held her while she cried her heart out. Watched her fade away.''

Grayson's haunted eyes riveted on the bottle of Scotch. He reached behind the bar for a tumbler, poured two fingers and downed them. ''I always knew she would fall in love again, I just never thought it would be with a slime-ball like you.''

The words, the bitter tone, crashed into Derek. ''She doesn't love me.''

''I wish to hell she didn't.'' Gray slammed down the empty tumbler. ''But she does, with everything she is and then some. And because of that, one of Chicago's brightest cops won't accept what's right before her eyes. She insists you're innocent, that you were set up. That's why she went to meet your sorry ass at the museum tonight.''

''What are you talking about? What museum?''

''It's late, Mansfield, and I'm tired. I have neither the time or patience for games. I told her not to go, but when it comes to you, she won't listen. I better get down there, that's where I was headed when the boys out front beeped me. Knowing Cass, she's still standing there in the cold, waiting for a man who's never going to show.''

Derek's heart was slamming so fast now it hurt. ''I'll ask you one more time. *What* museum? And why would she be waiting for me?''

''The note, Mansfield, your twisted request to meet her at The Museum of Natural—''

''Sweet God.'' Hideous pieces slammed into place. ''I didn't send a note.''

''What do you mean?''

Derek didn't answer. He took off running through the darkened hotel.

''You look surprised, *querida*.'' A pleased smile tilted the corners of Santiago Vilas's thin lips. He moved closer, his gun trained on Cass. ''Don't tell me I've managed to catch one of Chicago's finest off guard?''

She scanned the area, trying to determine if she was

alone, or if he had backups in the wings. Because she didn't. Going against every scrap of training, she ventured down to the museum alone.

Because she'd thought love awaited her. Not deceit.

She pivoted toward Brent. "You set me up!" she seethed, but froze when she saw his eyes. Brent Ashford was a playboy and a businessman, not the cunning mercenary his brother was. Derek could hide his thoughts and feelings behind an inscrutable mask, but everything Brent felt marched across his face. Shock. Indecision. Fear.

"You give Ashford too much credit if you think he orchestrated this," Vilas chided. "He's not half the man his brother is. I would think you of all people would know that."

Slow and steady, Cass reminded herself. Lull the bastard into complacency, disarm him. "I know a lot of things, Mr. Vilas. Put down the gun and we can talk about them."

"I bet you would like that." His gaze raked over her. "Alas, you've already done enough talking for one evening. If you had kept that lush little mouth of yours closed, your lover would have lived to see another day. His ploy was clever. I never suspected."

Brent stepped closer to Cass. "Ploy? Give me a break. If my brother is crawling through gutters with slime like you, it's because that's where he wants to be." Disgust dripped impressively from his voice. "For him, rules and laws are made to be broken. All he cares about is humiliating the family."

"That's not the tune you were singing only moments ago." Vilas's smile widened. "Let's see, what was it the lovely Cassidy Blake said? Something about a trap of his own making?"

The words knifed through Cass. He'd heard. He knew everything.

"She's in love with him!" Brent sneered. He was by her side now, his body shielding her from the direct line of fire. ''She's desperate, grabbing at straws. She'd do anything to get him off the hook and back into her bed.''

Cass took Brent's lead. ''I convinced you, didn't I?'' she asked arrogantly, flipping her braid over her shoulder. Too often the line between acting and law enforcement stretched dangerously thin, the only difference between life and death.

''I'll convince everyone else, too—I won't let anyone take him from me,'' she vowed, meaning the words more deeply than Vilas could possibly know. ''Not the law, not his family, not you.''

''He needs help!'' Brent exploded, a new ferocity glittering in his eyes. He spun toward Vilas. ''That's why I asked her here tonight, to encourage her to stay away from my brother. She's poison, making him do things he wouldn't normally do. He needs help, not some misguided cop.''

A hollow little clap killed his words. ''Too bad the two of you never found Broadway,'' Vilas interrupted his voice smooth as silk. ''You make quite a pair, but I'm afraid you're wasting your breath. Derek Mansfield has been stringing me along for months, promising expansion into new markets, always finding one reason or another to delay. Caution, he said. Deliberation.''

If Cass had harbored any doubts, Vilas's revelations would have shattered them.

''...about making sure there were no rats in the manor.''

But she didn't doubt, not anymore. Because she loved.

''...I began to grow impatient.''

Derek had been trying to protect his brother, setting a trap for Vilas to make sure he never endangered his family again.

''...hence the bomb.''

Brent's body went rigid. ''It was you.''

''Who else?'' Vilas was clearly pleased with himself. ''I had to do something to sniff out our rats, since your brother was too busy sleeping with them. It worked, didn't it?''

''You set him up,'' Cass echoed. ''You set up everything.''

Vilas only snickered. ''That's what I love about cops. You're masters of the obvious, every one of you.''

''But why?'' Stall, Cass ordered herself. Keep him talking. ''He can't do you any good behind bars.''

''Circumstantial evidence never sticks, *querida,* you know that.''

''Then—''

''Like I said, I was growing impatient and wanted to sniff out whatever rats might be hiding in the manor. And I did.'' He stepped closer. ''You're here, aren't you? And we all know you for the traitorous little whore you are. We all know you slipped into Derek's bed merely to put the noose around his neck.''

The accusation stung.

''What now?'' Cass asked, grateful Brent wasn't doing anything stupid. This was her show, what she'd been trained to handle. ''Why did you follow me tonight?''

''I've been waiting for this moment since the night you got me worked up, then walked out on me. I didn't know what you were up to at the time,'' he sneered, ''but I do now.'' In one swift move, his free hand snaked out and grabbed her braid. He yanked her toward him, causing her to crash into his thin frame. ''Payback can be so much fun.''

''Let go of me,'' Cass demanded, twisting in his arms. ''I'm an officer of the—''

''Spare me.'' Vilas yanked her braid over her shoulder and jerked her head back. ''Nobody uses me and lives to tell—''

She slammed her foot down on his, rammed an elbow into his stomach. He gasped, staggered—

''Take your hands off her,'' Brent yelled, running toward them. All signs of the weak playboy vanished, in

their place radiated a valor and ferocity that would do
Derek proud. "She's—"

Cass didn't have time to intervene. Vilas simply raised
the gun. And shot. Brent's eyes went wide the second the
bullet slammed into him. His hands flew to his stomach,
blood gurgling around them. He looked dazed, confused…then crumpled to the ground.

Fury and alarm bubbled through Cass. She looked at
Vilas, at the insanity in his beady eyes. "Now, where
were we?" he asked eloquently.

She pulled free of him and ran to Derek's brother.
"Brent?" she asked, cradling his head in her lap. "Can
you hear me?"

His glassy eyes stared up at her, but no words came
forth. She pressed two fingers to the base of his clammy
throat, discovered a faint pulse.

Cass swallowed hard. She was no stranger to life-or-
death situations, but Vilas had caught her off guard.

She twisted toward him. "You won't get away with
this."

"But I already have." Smiling, he held the .45 at eye
level, then ran one gloved hand over its smooth barrel.
"By the time the curator opens up tomorrow morning,
what happened here will be nothing but a tragedy, one of
those senseless occurrences that makes everyone shake
their heads in dismay.

"It will be so sad," he went on, his voice mockingly
dramatic. "Prominent businessman and heroic cop found
slain, their bodies lying next to their killer, the man they
betrayed."

"Derek." Cass realized Vilas intended to frame him
for murder, then kill him and make it look like suicide. It
would be believed, too, by everyone, including Gray.
He'd warned her not to come. "It'll never work," she
said, stalling.

She had to do something, do it fast. Brent lay in a limp
heap, blood seeping through his trench coat and pooling
around him. His time was running out.

Her only chance was disarming Vilas. She'd done it hundreds of times in training, several in reality. But never had it been more critical. Her whole life flashed before her, the happiness and sorrow, the triumphs and tragedy. She wasn't ready for it to be over. She'd already lost a husband and son.

She owed it to them to triumph, to live life to the fullest.

Cautiously she stood. "You win," she said, raising her hands in the air and walking toward Vilas. Surprise registered in his eyes. He watched her approach, and slowly lowered the gun so that it was level with her chest. "I'm all yours."

"The hell you say!"

The fierce voice cut through the night. Cass glanced sharply toward the bank of columns, but before she could discern shadows from reality, Vilas grabbed her arm and jerked her in front of him. The nose of his .45 came next, jamming into her temple. Then he laughed, an animated sound that echoed insidiously through the quiet night.

"It's about time you got here, my friend. A few minutes later and you would have missed the main event."

Santiago Vilas stood stiff as a statue, eyes as black as night. Cass stood there, too, her body crammed to the front of Vilas's, a human shield. Her eyes, those beautiful eyes that never failed to seduce, were wide now, ominous.

Derek wanted to charge across the measly ten feet separating him from Vilas and destroy the bastard with his bare hands, but in the seconds it would take, Cass's life would be forfeited.

He wouldn't risk it.

Self-disgust flared, twisted with the fear and regret. She was in danger because of him, because he'd refused to listen when she tried to explain.

He held his own gun level, outstretched toward the bastard he'd been entrapping for months. This wasn't how he'd envisioned the final act. In his fantasies there had been plenty of time to savor the moment.

But in his fantasies the woman he loved wasn't caught in the middle. "Let her go, *amigo*. Now."

The violent wind sent the flaps of Vilas's coat whipping about his ankles. "Derek. How kind of you to join us."

"I mean it," he warned. "This is between you and me. Leave the lady out of it."

An evil smile twisted Vilas's lips. "You're the one who talked about exterminating rats. I merely grew impatient with your procrastination."

He stepped closer. "I'm the one she betrayed," he pointed out. He injected his voice with a contempt he no longer felt. "You would deny me the chance for retribution?"

Vilas's nasty snicker echoed among the columns. "It all started in the Garden of Eden," he snipped. "Did it not?" His free hand slid up along Cass's side, halting just beneath the swell of her breast. "Just as Eve handed Adam the apple of his downfall, the lovely Cassidy Blake handed the apple to you."

Her eyes narrowed, cut to her right. She wanted him to see something, Derek realized, following her gaze. The moon had ducked behind a swell of clouds, taking its light with it. Not much lay there for him to see, just a heap of—

Everything inside Derek grew brutally cold. His childhood flashed before his eyes, the disappointments, the loneliness, the one thing that had kept him going, given him purpose. His brother. The one he'd always looked out for.

Brent lay there, despite everything Derek had done to protect him, unmoving. A dark substance pooled around him.

Rage tore through Derek. But he couldn't let it show. He'd positioned himself with Vilas as a solo operator, not a man who would do anything to save his brother's hide.

"Time to say goodbye," Vilas announced. His hand

opened and grasped Cass's long braid. Then he yanked. Hard. "Drop the gun, Mansfield, or I blow her away. Right here, right now."

"Don't do it," Cass blurted. "He's going to kill me, anyway." She looked so brave standing there, defiant yet still vulnerable. "Don't let him manipulate you."

The fighter in him knew she was right, but the man who loved her more than life itself was willing to try anything to fend off the inevitable.

He looked at her standing there, his brave, fiery angel, and realized everything he'd ever done, everything he'd ever been, had propelled him to this moment in time. To give him the skills, the strength, the courage to see it through to the bitter end.

This was it, the turning point of his life.

"I grow impatient," Vilas warned.

"Fine." He looked at Vilas and crooked an insolent smile. "Have it your way, *amigo*. I've waited too long for this night to let anything get in the way."

"And just what is it you've been waiting for?"

The clouds scurried away, giving way to a bright pool of moonlight. Easier to see Vilas now, easier to see the madness in his eyes. "It's like I told you all along," Derek answered, careful to strip the disgust from his voice. "I have connections—you have merchandise. Together, there is nothing we can't have, nobody who can stop us."

Vilas only laughed. "I believed your lies once, my friend." He drew slow circles with the nose of the gun against Cass's forehead. "I won't make that mistake again."

Derek stepped closer. "She's a cop. You can't believe anything she has to say."

Vilas smiled broadly—triumphantly. "Prove it."

"Prove it?"

"Prove to me whose side you're on." Vilas inclined his head toward the gun in Derek's hands. "You lusted after the wrong lady, my friend. She betrayed you, and me. Now I ask you to prove whose side you're really on. Do the job for me. Kill your whore."

The little color left in Cass's face drained away. Fearless, that's what he'd always called her, yet he saw the fear now, hot and primal, blazing from her eyes.

"The choice is yours," Vilas taunted. "Tonight can be your last, or everything can go back to the way it was before. All you have to do—"

Caution dissolved into chaos. It all happened frantically fast, but for Derek the scene unfolded one excruciating petal at a time, steady and unstoppable.

Cass's gaze was riveted on Derek. Her body remained stiff. But her leg moved, raising enough to jam her heel down on the bridge of Vilas's foot. He let out a bark of pain. And she ducked as she plowed her elbow into his stomach.

His hand fell away from her head, and he doubled over.

She took advantage of his pain to twist and karate chop the gun from his hand.

It went clattering along the pavement, Cass lunging after it. Vilas pounced on her, Derek diving after him. He had his own gun, but it was worthless as long as Vilas had a weapon of his own.

"Get out of here, Cass! Run! Now."

"I'm not leaving you." Her gloved hands shoved beneath his and closed around the butt of the gun.

"You bitch!" Vilas roared. He lay on top of her, his body grinding hers into the ground. "You'll pay for this. You'll—"

"It's over, Vilas." A new voice. Gray's voice. "Give it up while you still can."

Vilas froze.

Breathing hard, Derek shoved Vilas off Cass. He rolled to his feet and pulled her with him, positioning her securely behind his back. Arms sliding around his waist, she handed him the gun, placing it securely in his hands, hers joining with his.

They pointed it at Vilas. "I've waited a long time for this night, you son of a bitch."

Vilas glared at him, hatred and defeat sharpening his eyes.

A semicircle of cops moved in, guns trained on Vilas.

"You okay?" Gray barked. He'd been waiting in the wings, waiting for Derek to get Cass away from Vilas. A surprise attack was always better, Derek knew. While Vilas had been focused on him, Gray had been moving in for the kill. It had been dangerous, but they were two highly trained men, fighting for a woman they both loved. One as a sister, the other as his life.

"You did good," Gray now said. "Real good."

Derek cut him a smile. "For Cass, I'd do anything."

He stood staring out the window. The glistening morning sun had long since chased away the lingering gray of the night. A brilliant ball of fire now hung low in the sky, sharing its light and warmth with everything in its path.

Except Cass. She was so cold, from the outside in, or maybe the inside out. Derek had yet to say a word to her. Not at the station, not at the hospital where they'd stayed with Brent until the doctor assured them he would be fine, not on the drive to his grandfather's house. He'd shot a few looks her way, heated, charged looks she couldn't begin to decipher.

But no words.

Cass was trying to give him his space, but she didn't understand why'd he'd taken her hand and all but dragged her to his car, then sped away. But wouldn't speak to her.

From looking at him, at his tense, rigid body, the hard set to his jaw, it was impossible to tell that his name had just been cleared, that the press was labeling him a hero.

She'd been in the room when he and his buddy, FBI agent Lucas Treese, had explained the sting, how they'd endeavored to bring Vilas down, when the chief had cleared Derek of wrongdoing.

A parade of emotions now marched through her. Happiness and relief, hope, but most of all, dread. Derek acted as if she wasn't even there, as if she didn't even exist.

And she couldn't take it. "Derek…" she started, moving tentatively toward him.

He pivoted toward her. He held a glass in his hand, one that contained a hearty shot of whiskey, a shot he hadn't touched. He stared at it a moment, then his features hardened and he flung it toward the fireplace. It crashed on impact, drawing Cass's attention away from the man, to the shards of glass raining down on the hardwood floor.

That's all it took for Derek to catch her off guard. He was on her in a heartbeat, having strode across the room.

And her heart revved to a staccato beat.

He looked fierce, like a man capable of great violence. But she wasn't scared. Not of Derek, nor the love she felt for him.

Not anymore.

He looked at her from those amazing eyes of his. Go-to-hell eyes, she'd called them. They'd shown her heaven and earth, yet now they showed her neither. They simply glittered with more emotion than anyone should ever experience at one moment.

Then he crushed her to him. Tight and comforting, protective. Arms like steel bands pressed her to the wall of his chest. His warmth soaked into her, chasing away the chill she'd lived with for too long.

The shaking started, from somewhere deep inside. She'd been stoically holding it together, yet now her fortitude crumbled, leaving her with nothing but the joy of Derek's arms around her.

He pulled back and stared down at her. His big hands found her face, framed her cheeks. "I love you," he ground out. "So damn much it scares me."

In his words she found hope and joy, yet in his eyes, those smoldering sapphire eyes, she found the haven she'd been seeking.

"It scares me, too," she whispered, shoving aside the shock and fear and taking a giant leap of faith. "Because it's bigger than I am, bigger than I ever imagined anything *could* be.''

The blunt tips of his thumbs stroked her cheekbones. ''I'm sorry,'' he shocked her by saying. ''So damn sorry for not listening to you yesterday, for turning you away. If I had—''

''Don't say it.'' His regret turned her inside out. ''Don't even think it. I'm the one who's sorry. I'm the one who almost cost you—''

''Don't say it.'' With a wicked grin, he tossed her words back at her. ''Don't even think it. You haven't cost me anything. You've given me everything.''

So many times she'd awakened at night, her body and soul crying out for him. And every time she'd simply lain there, stroking Barney's furry snout, mourning for something that could never be. But she had been wrong. It could be—it would be.

Happiness spilled into a trembling smile. ''God, I love you.''

His thumbs brushed away tears she hadn't even been aware of.

''It was an incredibly brave thing you did,'' she told him, still unable to believe it herself. ''You laid your life on the line for your brother. Sometimes I wasn't even sure you liked each other.''

A light glinted in his eyes. ''We like each other. We just don't always see eye-to-eye.'' His thumbs continued to stroke her cheeks in a feather-soft, rhythmic manner. ''Brent would never have survived a scumbag like Vilas. Ryan deserves to grow up with a father who loves him.''

Unlike Derek had. ''You risked *everything*....''

''I did what I had to do.'' He shoved his hair back from his face, but a few dark straggles remained against his cheekbones. They lent him an air of back-street danger. ''Luc made it easy for me. He was ready to step in and lock Vilas away the second I had enough proof.''

''You could have taken the fall in the process. Your sting could have backfired.'' Cass splayed her fingers against the warmth of his chest. His heart beat strongly against her palm.

"It was a risk I had to take."

"For your brother."

"Family is important, Cass. It's all we really have."

His words touched something deep inside her. She slid her hand up his neck and cupped the planes of his face. He looked hard and unforgiving, but she knew the rough exterior protected a heart of gold.

He frowned. "It must've been hell for you, fearless, thinking I was everything you despised—"

"Only at first. Only the cop. The second the woman met the man, everything changed."

"They're the same person, Cass. The woman and the cop. They're both you."

"And they both love you." That was the important part, the love that had grown from the lies. "I never knew how empty my life had become until you filled it, how much joy and hope I could have until you gave it to me. It tore me up—"

Derek silenced her words with a kiss, one of love and longing, desire and redemption.

Then he pulled back, and with a wicked, thrilling smile, lifted her into his arms and strode from the study. Into the sun-dappled foyer. Up the sprawling staircase. Into his room, where his king-size bed sat waiting.

He laid her down against the pillows and drew her hand to his chest. "Feel that?"

She smiled. "You got a thunderstorm going on in there?"

He smiled back at her, not the wicked one from before, but one of warmth and tenderness. "That's the way I feel about you."

Emotion swamped her. Tears rushed to her eyes, but she blinked them back, not wanting to blur the most thrilling moment of her life. "How do you feel, Derek? Tell me."

"With words or actions?"

She started to answer straight out, then surrendered to the naughty tickle somewhere near her heart. "Truth or dare?"

That irreverent light glinted back into his eyes. "Dare."

"I want it all," she said. "Words, actions, a future. Life. You."

"Careful," he warned, sliding down beside her on the bed. "It might take me a while to satisfy a request that... extensive."

"I'm in no hurry."

He drew her body flush against his, enabling her to feel every powerful inch of him. "We're talking years," he murmured against her eager mouth. "A lifetime."

Cass thrilled to his words, his touch.

"But let me start with this," he said, easing back to look at her. Lying face to face on the same pillow, he lifted a hand to trace her cheekbone. "I love you, Cass. That's the way I feel. Love."

Moisture flooded her eyes. The smoke and mirrors she'd once feared would drive them apart had brought them together instead. Defenses lowered, hearts stripped bare, love had found a way, a love strong enough to give them tomorrow, and every day thereafter.

"What was that you said about a lifetime?" she asked through her tears.

His gaze heated, his smile turned wicked. Very slowly, he slid his hand from her face down along her neck to her shoulder, where he gently urged her toward him. "Let me show you."

* * * * *

INTIMATE MOMENTS™

presents:

Romancing the Crown

With the help of their powerful allies, the royal family of Montebello is determined to find their missing heir. But the search for the beloved prince is not without danger—or passion!

Available in May 2002:
VIRGIN SEDUCTION
by Kathleen Creighton (IM #1148)

Cade Gallagher went to the royal palace of Tamir for a wedding—and came home with a bride of his own. The rugged oilman thought he'd married to gain a business merger, but his innocent bride made him long to claim his wife in every way....

This exciting series continues throughout the year with these fabulous titles:

Available only from Silhouette Intimate Moments at your favorite retail outlet.

Where love comes alive™

Visit Silhouette at www.eHarlequin.com

SIMRC5

INTIMATE MOMENTS™
and *USA TODAY* BESTSELLING AUTHOR
RUTH LANGAN
present her new miniseries

Lives—and hearts—are on the line when the Lassiters pledge to uphold the law at any cost.

Available March 2002
BANNING'S WOMAN (IM #1135)

When a stalker threatens Congresswoman Mary Brendan Lassiter, the only one who can help is a police captain who's falling for the feisty Lassiter lady!

Available May 2002
HIS FATHER'S SON (IM #1147)

Lawyer Cameron Lassiter discovers there's more to life than fun and games when he loses his heart to a beautiful social worker.

And if you missed them,
look for books one and two in the series

BY HONOR BOUND (IM #1111)
and
RETURN OF THE PRODIGAL SON (IM #1123)

Available at your favorite retail outlet.

Where love comes alive™

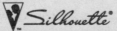

If you enjoyed what you just read,
then we've got an offer you can't resist!

Take 2 bestselling love stories FREE!

Plus get a FREE surprise gift!

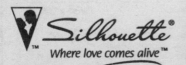